THE BATTLE FOR

THE *Isle* OF *Ree*

BOOK 2

THE BATTLE FOR

THE

OF

PJ THOMPSON

WESTBOW
PRESS®
A DIVISION OF THOMAS NELSON
& ZONDERVAN

WestBow Press books may be ordered through booksellers or by contacting:

WestBow Press
A Division of Thomas Nelson & Zondervan
1663 Liberty Drive
Bloomington, IN 47403
www.westbowpress.com
1 (866) 928-1240

ISBN: 978-1-9736-6608-0 (sc)
ISBN: 978-1-9736-6607-3 (e)

Print information available on the last page.

WestBow Press rev. date: 7/11/2019

I want to express my thanks to and appreciation
for my technical advisor, my husband Jim, without
whom there would have been no book!

Artist and Illustrator are titles spoken over me to describe what I do, but who I am is an image bearer of the Master Creator. I truly delight in bringing empty paper to life with truths written in the deeper places of my soul. As a child it looked like swirly lines, and silly characters of the familiar, but now, joy abounds as I sit with The Creator and surrender every word lettered, image drawn and color chosen to what He enlightens, which feels inadequate at best with my limited knowledge and skill.

Carla Autrey, *Artist and Illustrator*

CONTENTS

PROLOGUE

In Book I of <u>The Isle of Fire and Ice</u> Dare and Bardon are caught in a exciting adventure that sweeps them toward the fulfillment of an ancient prophecy.

Once, long ago, there lived a prophecy of hope in a land darkened with despair. The prophecy declares:

"In that time when wickedness holds full sway, two shall stand in evil's way.

Uriisis and wolf-marked, this Pair; shinning, like-marked swords will bear.

Their appearance will display, the Maker's mercy in that day."

Both Dare and Bardon worship the Maker and are the pair the prophecy reveals. The desperate young men flee their homes, on opposite sides of the island of Ree, to escape cruel treatment. The runaways meet in the middle of a rugged mountain range and join forces. Dare is an orphaned drudge and Bardon is the only child of the wicked King Bardock. They are captured and then rescued by a secret underground, which helps them escape the King's soldiers again and again. As they seek a safe refuge with the help of the underground, they meet allies from many hidden tribes. These tribes worship the Maker and are waiting for the prophecy to be fulfilled. They refuse to worship the King's wicked god, Choack, and must stay hidden or die. Along the way, Bar (short for Bardon) is marked by an enormous, awesome sea creature called an Uriisis and given important instructions. Dare is marked by a beautiful grey wolf named Starfire and becomes Bar's protector and healer. In the midst of a dangerous rescue, Bar and Dare find special swords to aid them in their battles against hideously deformed creatures created by an enemy ... a sere called Blalock. They also must deal with the tipeeke, an evil wolf-like creature and the braith, huge and very intelligent cats. These beasts were also created by Blalock.

As much as King Bardock would like to keep Bar and Dare's exploits a secret, it is impossible! The whole island of Ree is talking, in whispers of course, about the prophecy and the two young men that all the King's mighty forces can't capture. Meanwhile the underground realizes that they must fight the King in order to take back their island from the ever more evil ruler and his cohorts.

LOUKE

ERROR RAISED THE HAIR ON LOUKE'S SCALP
and kept his exhausted legs pumping. As he fled through dense
pine, he could hear the ragged sound of his own breathing. In the weak
predawn light, his eyes strained wildly to discern the faint game trail.
Thick undergrowth grasped at his clothing and tore his skin. Pine needles
and leaves flew up around him as he plowed through them. In his frantic
haste, he stumbled over a tree root and fell. Berating his clumsiness, Louke
desperately pushed himself to his feet and limped onward. He patted his
belt occasionally to assure himself that his few possessions were still there.
Without them, I cannot survive! His pack, water skin and knife remained
securely in place. *In truth, I may not survive with them.* In a flash of memory,
Louke saw again the horrible wolflike creature he was trying to leave far
behind, and he shuddered.

As a cautious runaway, he'd been jogging through Aaneleg Forest when
he'd heard the grunting and cracking sounds of an animal feeding. Before he
could change direction or react, he'd crashed into something soft and fallen.
He'd been appalled to find his hands buried in stiff, oily fur. His face had
been just inches from yellow teeth bared in a ferocious snarl, and his body
had been within striking distance of the animal's sharp claws. A horrible
stench had enveloped him like a fog and made him gag. He'd screamed in
disbelief and shock, revulsion coursing through his body. He did not know
which of them had been the most startled. With a choked cry, he'd raised

his walking stick and struck the animal's head with all his might. Then he'd bolted.

Louke was big for his age and very strong. For a time, he thought he might have killed the thing, but he kept running just in case. The creature must have been, at the least, stunned, because he heard no sounds of pursuit. Then a high-pitched howl of pure fury rent the tranquil spring night like a thunderclap. For a moment his heart and his body froze in numb fear. Quickly he jerked his trembling muscles into action and fled with all his strength from the creature now bent on terrible revenge. *What is the thing anyway, and why, why did this have to happen to me? After everything else I have been through, this just isn't fair!*

Behind him, he heard the beast's horrible cry—a high-pitched screech. Now he could also hear its feet tearing the forest floor as it ripped down the trail. *It's gaining! It's closer now, surely, than it was a few minutes ago!* Soon he must find help or climb a tree. He knew the latter was no solution and would only put off the inevitable. There were other creatures that were even now responding to the cries of the one chasing him.

Pain burned in his side, his legs, and his lungs. He knew he could not last much longer. *I must find help or a place to hide—soon!* Just ahead, he could see a dirt lane in the growing light of the new day. He burst out of the thick pine and stood gasping in the center of a country road. Trying to catch his breath, he searched first one direction, then the other for a wagon, a rider, anything!

As if in answer to his need, a farm wagon lumbered around the corner and traveled straight toward him. Louke was too breathless to speak, but he pointed wildly into the trees. The large farmer on the seat heard the howling, both close and distant. Evidently a man of decision, he sized up the situation quickly and pulled the old wagon up beside Louke. Reaching out a huge hand, he grabbed a handful of Louke's cloak and jerked him off his feet and into the wagon bed with one smooth motion. Louke landed with a bone-cracking thud on his back and lay sprawled in a daze. The man pulled a battered long knife from under his farmer's smock, just as the maddened tipeeke burst from the trees. The relentless beast leaped with fury at the wagon.

Perhaps the injury to its head had muddled its thinking, because the beast misjudged the distance and crashed with stunning force against the wagon seat. It bounced back onto the road with a painful screech. Howling furiously, it picked itself up and crouched for another leap, but before it could launch itself at the farmer, the wagon lurched away.

The man slapped the reins and shouted to his horse. The wagon jogged down the road at bone-jarring speed. However, the pace was not nearly as fast as a crazed tipeeke. The animal hurled itself after them. Louke managed to raise himself to his knees and cling to the seat, though he was being jolted severely. Looking over his shoulder, he saw the huge animal running powerfully. It would soon be in the wagon with them.

"It be catching up, sir!" he yelled as loud as he could to make himself heard over the deafening noise of the wagon, the horse's hooves, and the howling animal.

———————

The folk of Glidden had spent much of their creativity for the last few months leading the Blackrobes and the king's soldiers from one part of Ree to another. The frustrated soldiers continued to search for the elusive company of fugitives. They were always a few hours too late or in the wrong place.

In truth, the prince's company never left Glidden. Unfortunately, Tori and Lotu left a small troop at Tnasaelp, to keep careful watch over the area around Devon and Lavel's childhood village. The tipeeke with this troop terrorized livestock, forest animals, and travelers for miles around. No one who heard the reports of the animals' high-strung natures ever traveled alone or at night.

Citizens on the western side of the mountain range that split the island of Ree in two halves so hated their rulers and the king that many were willing to risk helping the underground spread wild rumors. The Blackrobes, sensing subterfuge, were furious but unable to intimidate any of those they questioned into telling them the truth. The king's power was much stronger on the eastern side of the island, where they certainly did not have problems getting information. Neither threats nor bribes gained them reliable information. The stupid yokels really didn't seem to know anything. The Blackrobes and soldiers had searched the area carefully and found nothing.

Finally, they decided to rethink their frantic activity and seek help, embarrassing as it was to admit that they needed it. They decided to seek aid from some of the rulers of the western fiefs instead of running from one place to another in frenzied haste. It was a very humiliating but a very wise decision. The first seat they resolved to visit was Ravensperch. Duke Roth had a wonderful reputation for keeping a tight hold on his lands and people; he was just the man they needed. They did not realize that their decision placed them within a few miles of their illusive prey, unfortunately for the prey.

———————

Devon, disguised as a farmer, had been on his way to visit his old village when Louke had barreled out of the trees. Now he was embroiled in a situation that was likely to get out of hand. He remembered with a grimace that Lavel had warned him not to leave their safe retreat. Devon was too unusual in size to go unnoticed. He knew this was true, but he wanted desperately to see for himself how his friends in the village were faring. So he'd left before dawn, in the hope that he could steal into his old hamlet and then out of it before anyone took notice of him. Now he needed a place to hide himself and the boy quickly. Where there were tipeeke, there were Blackrobes and the king's soldiers.

"Sir, it be getting ready to jump in the wagon!"

Devon pulled the horse up with one powerful hand and turned, knife flashing in the other, in time to see the tipeeke flying through the air. Because the wagon had slowed, the tipeeke's leap took it farther than the animal anticipated. It landed directly on top of Louke with a startled yelp and then a triumphant howl. Louke did his best to hold the snapping jaws away from his throat by grabbing the creature's neck fur with both his hands. With snapping teeth, wild yapping, and putrid breath just inches from his face, Louke screamed, "Do something!"

Devon succeeded in stopping the trembling, frightened horse, but he could not get at the tipeeke with his knife, for fear he would harm the boy. He could think of no plan other than the rough-and-ready one of pulling the animal off the lad by the ruff of its neck. It took all his great strength to lift the tipeeke free, and he received a slash from its sharp claws for his trouble. With a mighty heave he flung it to the ground. It lay there still.

Devon said, "Quickly, friend, get down from the wagon! This creature's companions are not far behind us."

Indeed, Louke could hear the once distant baying more clearly now. He noted his companion's air of command and large muscles, so he didn't argue. *He's right; they are closer—much closer. But why leave the wagon? The man is crazy! Crazy but strong, huge, and stern, so I'll do as he says—even though it makes no sense to me.*

Devon smacked the horse and yelled at it, hoping it would gallop down the road. After all it had been through—the howling and the terrible odor of *that* animal—the large plow horse gladly tore off. It had probably never in its staid life moved so quickly.

"Into the woods—hurry!" Devon pushed Louke toward the forest on the other side of the road.

The large monk hoped he could find an entrance to Glidden that Lock had shown him, while on the *inside* of the mountain. It would be difficult indeed to recognize it from the outside. Hopefully, the tipeeke would follow the wagon, not him and the boy. At least, that was his plan. It was a trick he had learned from a young Chi.

Devon became hopelessly lost in the thick density of the forest. He could not see the mountain or anything else in the tangle of huge tree trunks and verdant undergrowth. He could find no familiar landmark to determine their location. What he needed was some height. He looked the boy over to determine if he would be able to scramble up a likely tree. The boy's warm clothing had evidently protected his arms from the tipeeke's claws, and Devon saw no sign of injuries.

For the first time, Devon took a good look at his companion and realized, with shock, that he might be no better at tree climbing than Devon himself. The boy was as tall as Lavel—not nearly as heavy, but definitely as tall or perhaps even taller. His shoulders were massive, as if he had done some type of work that developed them. Rarely did Devon meet a man of his size, and this was just a stripling! The boy had ragged, shoulder-length brown hair, steady blue eyes, and tan skin, with a sprinkle of freckles that were barely visible under a thick layer of dirt.

Louke thought the large man foolish, but not because he was gaping at him; he was used to that. "There be water ahead, sir. You can see it glinting, if you look right through there." He pointed as if he were speaking to one who was slow.

It took Devon a moment, but he finally saw what the boy meant. "That has to be Gull's Pond! If so, I know where we are—too far north, by far, for the entrance I remember. We will have to cut south and quickly." Behind them, they could hear the howls of tipeeke on the scent.

Louke cleared his throat. "Uh, I used to live hereabouts, sir. If you like, I can lead us to the lake, where I've been many a time. There be a place there where we can hide. 'Course, if these animals have men with them who know the area, they might figure out where we are. It's up to you." His voice trembled slightly, the only sign of fear in him Devon could detect.

"Why didn't you speak up sooner?" Devon recalled all his floundering around in the unknown wood and wondered why the lad hadn't spoken up.

"Mostly I do what people say who can throw a hundred-and-twenty-or-so-pound animal out of a wagon with their off hand, to say nothing of pulling a hundred-and-sixty-pound boy into one with their right." Louke's face was solemn, but there was a twinkle in his eye. "Besides, you be doin' fine up to now without my help."

Devon warmed to this unruffled, burly young man who reminded him of a bear, a very large one. "A hiding place you can find easily versus one I will have to hunt for and may never find—that's an easy decision, lad. Lead the way and quickly. They're getting closer!"

They tore through the trees, making no attempt to be quiet, as the noisome howling reached a frantic, ecstatic peak. Their trail was easy to follow, and the enemy had evidently found it.

When they reached the shore, Devon said, "Only take time to pull off your boots, lad. Throw your bow and quiver high into the trees; perhaps they'll not find them." He tucked their boots into his belt, and they hit the beautiful but frigid waters of Gull's Pond running. "We cannot last long in water this temperature," Devon said anxiously as they began swimming.

Louke headed toward an avalanche of rock on the north side of the lake. Fortunately, it was not far.

When they were hidden behind jagged black rock but still in deep water, Louke whispered between chattering teeth, "You must swim underwater here." He removed his pack and attached a length of elong rope to it. "I won't fit through the opening with this on, so I'll drag it along behind me. It'll not take long. Just follow me."

At Devon's appalled look, he winked and disappeared into a very dark cave about five feet under the waterline. Wild thoughts flew through Devon's mind of drowning or swimming into a trap, but he shook his head and followed. Right now he had little choice. *Sure capture is definitely behind me—possible hope before me.*

After swimming down in the clear, sparkling water, he entered the dark cave. Its floor slanted up, and he could see wavering light at its end. He pulled himself along the rough rock to reach it. Suddenly, something grabbed his smock from above and jerked him hard around the neck. Devon turned and tried to feel his assailant. He realized quickly that there was no attacker; his hood had caught on a rough piece of jutting rock. He freed the tough cloth and then swam forward again with his lungs screaming and heart pounding. Two large hands and a pale face, framed by wildly waving hair, appeared at the opening. It was Louke, who had come to help tug him through. The opening was narrow, and Devon appreciated Louke's strength. Heaven knew his own was waning from cold and lack of oxygen.

After pulling Devon out of the tunnel, Louke quickly grabbed his waist and pushed him to the surface. Devon's head finally broke above the water, and he gratefully filled his lungs with crisp, clean air. He felt as if all the skin had been scraped from his upper arms. Louke surfaced beside him and shook his long hair out of his eyes.

"Thank you, lad. I'm not sure … I would have made it through there … without your help. It was a tight squeeze, and I was about out of air." Devon gave him a grateful smile that warmed his gray eyes. That smile and the kind words burned their way deep inside Louke and started to thaw a place that had long been cold. Kindness and appreciation had not been part of his life for many years. Unable to reply for the lump in his throat, Louke helped the large farmer to the shore. They both lay there gasping like two beached whales.

"Have you the strength to look, lad, and see what's happening?" Devon asked in a voice shaking with cold. "Is there any other way out of here?" he added as he searched the steep, rocky walls. They were at the bottom of a kind of cave formed by slabs of granite that leaned crazily against each other, far over their heads.

"Only the way we came in." Louke raised himself with an effort and crawled up the rocky slope to a crack between fallen boulders. It was a good place to view the lake's surface and the surrounding countryside.

Tipeeke raked the shore with their frantic paws as they dashed back and forth sniffing and howling, but they hesitated to enter the water. They ran up to the lake and then back again as if they could not quite bring themselves to take the plunge. Strange men in heavy black robes with deep hoods broke from the trees. They berated the animals fiercely for not going in the lake. It seemed plain to the men where their prey was hiding. They gestured at the rocks, but the animals sullenly growled and refused to enter the frigid water. One of the men took a stick from his belt and threatened them with it.

Louke didn't think much of such a simple weapon against the beasts, but to his surprise, they whimpered at the sight of it. The loathsome creatures flattened their bodies submissively to the ground. The man with the stick shouted and pointed at the water, and cowering, the creatures entered. The leader also ordered one of his men to follow them. The man unhesitatingly stripped off his robe and ran into the water in only his short breeches. It was difficult to see him clearly because of the sun's glare on the water.

The animals and man were swimming strongly right toward the avalanche of rock, yet Louke felt confident they would not find this hiding place unless a native of Tnasaelp was present. He and his friends had found this place only by accident. It had taken them a long time to gather the courage to explore the dark, sunken cave that led to the hidden grotto. Somehow, word had gotten out about their discovery, and they all had been scolded soundly. Their parents had warned them not to swim in Gull's Pond ever again. The water was too cold and the place far too dangerous. That was true, but they had often come here anyway in the heat of summer. He smiled for a moment at the pleasant memory. However, they had certainly not come in the spring, when ice was barely out of the water.

Louke was more worried about the cold making him and the farmer sick than he was about discovery. He scrambled quietly down. What would be would be. Right now, he needed to get out of his wet clothes and convince the farmer to do the same. The sun was rising hot in a clear sky and would soon pour into their hideaway. Perhaps its heat would be enough to warm them, in spite of the cool air.

Devon needed no convincing. They wrung the water out of their clothes and laid them on the rocks to dry. Devon found a warm place for himself in the sun, where he began to tear his undershirt into strips for bandages for himself and Louke. He'd discovered that Louke did have some minor scratches that would have to be treated.

Naked except for his short breeches, Louke scrambled back up to his spy hole. Soldiers lined the shoreline watching the man and tipeeke swimming in the frigid water. Both he and the tipeeke were searching among the boulders along the northeast shore and not near the underwater cave. Louke sighed in relief and climbed back down.

Devon gasped, appalled, as he caught sight of the young man's torso and legs in the bright sunshine. He was one massive bruise, with old bruises that were turning yellow and green and new ones that were black and blue. These had not come from some accident; Louke had been beaten—often. The young man stared at him calmly but with a hard glint in his eyes. "I don't want to talk about it."

"Agreed ... for now at least. Come here and let me tend to those scratches."

Louke hesitated but then came and sat on a rock. He allowed Devon to wash and bandage his wrists and hands. The young man gently returned the service and bound Devon's left forearm. "It really needs stitching, sir," he said, looking at his handiwork critically.

"Aye, well, we can take care of that later, when we're out of this mess."

Devon stared at Louke for long moments. A suspicion was growing in his mind. This young man appeared to have been living out-of-doors: His clothes were worn, dirty, and full of rents, and both leaves and twigs clung to them. His boots were battered, his hair had not seen a knife in a long time, and for all the bulk of his shoulders and hips, his ribs showed plainly through his skin. Louke knew he was being scrutinized, but he felt too tired to hold the big man's gaze and dropped his eyes. He hoped there would be no questions. The man had saved his life, but Louke wasn't going to tell him the truth, and he hated to lie to him.

"What is your name, lad?" They introduced themselves, but Devon asked no more questions. Then both lay back in the bright sunshine on warm rocks and baked the deep cold out of their bodies.

Later they would figure out their next step.

LAVEL LIBERATES

STOMACHS GROWLING WITH HUNGER, DEVON and Louke crouched in deep shadow near the pool's edge as the sun slowly set in the west. Difficult as it was to face diving into the frigid water again, they decided they needed to escape from their hiding place before dark. After basking in the sun all day, the waters of the lake and the two fugitives were as warm as they were going to get. Neither could face swimming through the tunnel in the dead of night, wise as that course might be, nor did they want to wait till the next morning, when they would only be hungrier and colder. From what Devon had learned about the Blackrobes' ways, he thought at least two tipeeke were undoubtedly stationed on the opposite shore. Though the Blackrobes and tipeeke had found nothing, the enemy was thorough.

They packed all their articles of clothing in Louke's pack in the hope that the lacing and elong seal would keep them dry. Their boots would not fit, and Devon carried these, as before, tucked into his belt along with his knife. Their footgear would be soaked, but both felt they needed to have their hands free.

Louke tried hard not to laugh at the sight of Devon with nothing on except his short breeches and the wide black belt that held their flopping boots and his long knife. Louke's attempt to cover his mirth with choking and coughing noises did not succeed. Devon reminded him, with asperity, that he also looked ridiculous with water skin, knife, and pack and rope attached to his belt and only short breeches on … and nothing else. "Aye, sir, we both would be embarrassed to have anyone see us like this, I'm sure," Louke responded ruefully. They both chuckled softly and felt their tension melt away.

The bright light changed to a soft golden glow as the sun sank below the mountains. The white clouds above became a beautiful, glowing rose, then a shimmering violet that gradually faded to gray. It was time.

Devon went first, in case he needed Louke's help shoving his bulk through the first entrance to the tunnel. The intense cold of the water shocked his whole body. His abused shoulders and upper arms cried out at being scraped again. Devon made it through without help and quickly swam to the tunnel exit, then up to the surface. The only sounds he heard on the other side were a night bird's mournful cry and the gentle lapping of water. After a few minutes, Louke quietly surfaced beside him. They looked at each other and nodded.

According to plan, Louke led the way. He slipped around the rock that hid them from view and then moved from shadow to shadow among the boulders along the north shore. Most of the time, they did not have to swim but could cling to the rocks and pull themselves along. In this way, they hoped to reach the eastern shore of the lake without being observed. Once they were on land, Devon would try to find the hidden entrance to Glidden. It would be difficult at night.

Residents of the lake and wood began their nighttime symphony: crickets chirped, frogs croaked, tree toads screeched, mosquitoes and gnats buzzed, and an occasional owl hooted. As they approached shore, the sharp fragrance of pine and the musty scent of decaying leaves reached them. They controlled a desire to rush into the protection of the trees and kept to their surge-to-a-shadow-then-rest pattern. They felt horribly exposed as they crawled onto the rocky shore and made their way across forty feet of open space to the dark forest.

Breathing hard and shivering, they crouched in the underbrush and listened intently for sounds of discovery or pursuit. They could hear nothing but their own ragged breathing and the normal murmuring of nature. Devon indicated with hand signals that he thought they should get deeper into the woods before they took the time to dress. Louke nodded in agreement and followed Devon as he trotted east.

When Devon felt they were far enough from the lake and possible watchers, he turned north. However, because of an outcropping of rock, which was probably part of the same avalanche that had filled in the north end of the lake, they were forced to turn south. This put them dangerously close to possible watchers, yet it was the direction they needed to go to find the elusive entrance.

At this point, they stopped to pull on their clothing, which had remained dry except for one corner of Devon's robe. They felt warmer immediately in spite of their soggy boots. Devon smeared his face and hands with mud that they found near a puddle, and Louke did the same.

Going north again they crept around the giant tumble of rocks, hoping they would soon be able to travel south. The shadows deepened around them; it grew harder and harder to see. Overhead the pine and spruce swayed in the breeze, and a few stars were appearing. Suddenly Devon halted; he and Louke looked at each other with a perplexed start. An awful odor of something both musky and rotten came to them on the night air and then passed away. Devon remembered that smell well from his captivity—tipeeke were close! They could smell the tipeeke only when the wind didn't blow. The fitful wind was coming from the north—it would blow his and Louke's scent right to the crafty animals. He crouched down in seething frustration. Now what?

Meanwhile, back at a small farm nestled in a valley at Glidden's feet, Lavel was anxiously pacing in a barn. Sher sat on a bale of hay, chewing a piece of grass and watching him in amusement. Twilight had turned to darkness, and Devon was still not back. Lavel was furious that his brother had left the safety of Glidden. Now, added to his anger was real anxiety. "Where can he be, and what can have possibly happened?"

Sher tried to reassure him. "The lad's more than able to take care of himself, Lavel." But memories of Devon's capture were still too fresh in Lavel's mind for him to be comforted.

The farm was used by Glidden folk as a rendezvous and a secret entrance to their tunnels. An old farmer lived there with his equally ancient housekeeper. When Sher, a skilled fisherman, had brought the farmer some trout, the farmer had told him that Devon had borrowed his wagon and some of his clothes before dawn. Devon had said he was going to get some supplies and would be back by midmorning. The farmer had grown worried when Devon hadn't returned, as much about his horse as about Devon, Sher suspected. The farmer had been relieved to see Sher, who he knew would tell those who needed to know.

"If he is still not back when the moon rises, I'll track him," Lavel said with finality.

Sher's merry face became suddenly serious. "Lavel, Lock will have your hide! You're known as part of the marked ones' party, and they've got a description of you down to the last hair. I know you're worried, but going yourself, without telling anyone, would be as bad as what Devon did!" Sher took a couple of steps backward when the big man glared at him. "I know it's not what you want to hear, but you know it's good sense," he protested as Lavel advanced toward him. Sher raised his hands to ward the man off and pled with a crooked grin, "Now don't get carried away."

Lavel grabbed him by the front of his vest and pulled him up to his eye level, leaving Sher's feet dangling many inches off the ground. Still, Sher met his large friend's gaze firmly. Silently he petitioned any god who might be listening for aid. Out loud he said sensibly, "We need to go tell Lock and let him help us plan what to do."

Lavel's blind anger faded as Sher's restrained and reasonable logic penetrated his seething mind. His sensible disposition and solid common sense reasserted themselves. He put Sher back on the ground and exclaimed, "I could shake him!"

Sher grinned and said, "Let's find him first."

Lavel managed a stiff grin. "Aye, you're right. Let's go find Lock." They both disappeared behind a stack of hay and lifted a cunningly hidden trapdoor. It opened into an innocent-looking storage room, but behind some barrels was an entrance that led to a labyrinth of dark tunnels. Heaven help the man who entered but did not know his way in the dark maze.

Devon knew the right thing to do: wait for a chance and be patient. What he wanted to do was flee, find that entrance, and end this ridiculous game. He and Louke crouched under a ledge that was part of the huge hill of rock they were trying to get around. When the wind was still, they could hear men's voices as they occasionally spoke to each other. They thought there were two of them. The tipeeke scratched, sniffed, and paced, sometimes dangerously close to them. The two fugitives broke weeds and grasses near their hiding place and then spread the juices on their clothes in an attempt to hide their scent.

The Blackrobes tried to feed the nervous tipeeke part of their own dinner to make them settle down. Though the tipeeke had not smelled the fugitives, they must have sensed something was not quite right, because their restlessness increased. They whined continuously and refused to eat. "They are the most irritating animals I've ever known!" one of the men cried with exasperation, throwing something to the ground.

"They do have one-track minds for sure," the other responded. "Here now, you two, sit and be still! Can't you watch quietly?" he remarked, irritated in spite of himself. The animals paid no heed to the guards as they searched, with their noses to the ground and then in the air, for something that eluded them.

Tipeeke were such nervous, testy animals that the two men evidently did not take their agitation very seriously. Devon was devoutly thankful for their lack of confidence in the beasts. Perspiration trickled down his neck and down his forehead into his eyes as he sought some answer to their dilemma. He looked at Louke, who shrugged and pointed at the ground firmly. There was nothing they could do but wait. One move and the already excited beasts would be on them. Devon was almost ready for it to come to a fight. He felt sure that he could take the men and the two tipeeke. However, he didn't know if Louke knew how to defend himself. He did not want the boy to be injured, nor did he want a lot of noise. The minutes passed. The moon rose in the east, spreading its light. Both the tipeeke and men became quiet.

<hr />

Meanwhile, a small party of men with torches, bows on their backs, and knives at their sides was following the tracks of a wagon down the lane. Sometime earlier in the day, the wagon had traveled toward Tnasaelp. They found footprints coming out of the forest, and farther down the lane they found animal tracks that had to belong to tipeeke. Then they found tracks of several men wearing boots, which could only mean Blackrobes or soldiers. Lavel's eyes became hard as rock and his face rigid.

They all had hoped Devon's disappearance could be easily explained: perhaps a broken wheel or an injury to the horse. Any one of a number of different things could have happened to delay him. Under ordinary circumstances, Lock would not have sent anyone to look for Devon until the next day or perhaps the next, but the circumstances of the last few months had been anything but ordinary.

A confusion of tracks made it difficult to determine exactly what happened next; however, it did not look good for Farmer Uoy's horse. It appeared that tipeeke had attacked the animal and that, some time later, the wagon and horse had been led toward town. The tipeeke had then turned into the woods. In the damp soil, they found boot tracks again. The men put out their torches. It was difficult to follow the trail in the thick undergrowth. Under the trees, the light of the rising moon was frequently blocked.

Devon and Louke must have dozed in their hiding place. They jerked awake at the sound of low growling and whining from the tipeeke. Louke squirmed; his leg had gone to sleep and was like a block of wood. If they needed to run, he would be in a sorry fix. Devon listened intently. The men were speaking in excited whispers and holding the straining tipeeke back. Whatever the animals sensed, it was evidently not him and Louke. He squeezed the restless young man's arm in warning. *What is the matter with the child? He is squirming like a two-year-old.*

Before Louke could explain, the night exploded into the full howling of attacking tipeeke and the cries of confused men. None were more confused than Louke and Devon, who did not know if they should take advantage of the diversion and run, or stay to discover what was happening. They decided to creep closer and see if they could learn something of the noisy conflict. In a small, dark clearing, men and tipeeke were fighting hand to hand. The moonlight cast some faces in bright light while others were in deep shadow. One of the men looked familiar to Devon. In spite of the mask the man wore, Devon recognized him as Sher. Then he also recognized the large man fighting beside Sher as his brother. He groaned inwardly. Devon joined the desperate fight, and Louke came limping after him. With their help, it was quickly over.

Louke felt relieved to see the tipeeke were dead. He loved animals, but there was something very wrong with this animal. The Blackrobes soon recognized they were outnumbered and dropped their weapons. Vikk and Tumo tied the Blackrobes' hands securely and gagged them. They also put blindfolds on them even though the Glidden men wore masks and Devon and Louke had covered their faces with mud, making it doubtful their own mothers would recognize them. Sher grabbed Devon's arm and started to speak but then held up his hand for silence. In the distance more tipeeke were answering the howls of their dead brothers. "Blast the beasts!" he muttered.

There were four men in Sher's search party. Devon and Louke made their number six—six men who needed to find an entrance to Glidden quickly. They discussed going back to the road, but that path of escape was promptly rejected. It would take them closer to the approaching enemy. They decided that the entrance Devon had been seeking was their best bet. They could not take their prisoners into the mountain with them, so in the end, they decided to bind the Blackrobes' feet and leave them. The Blackrobes' approaching fellows would find them. They were sure the two Blackrobes could not identify Devon or Louke because of their blackened faces, though their size might be remembered.

At least Sher knew exactly where the entrance was and how to get there. Sher spread a powder on their trail that would madden and confuse the tipeeke and then led the way. They followed him without question and as quietly as they could. He led them swiftly through a bewildering number of meadows, streams, and ravines until they reached their goal. Devon realized with dismay that never could he have found this place in the daylight, much less in the dark. They moved a large rock and entered a tunnel. Sher did what he could in the dark to hide any tracks they left. As the howling grew louder, he and Lavel quickly closed the opening. Sher lit a widgeon torch. A supply of torches was kept close to all entrances because the tunnels were utterly dark. The small group sighed. They were safe ... until the next time.

NOT A RUMOR

LOUKE HAD HEARD THE STORIES OF COURSE—
everyone had heard them: stories of fugitives in the Glidden area who lived hidden on the border of the Bitterroot Range. In antiquity, the mysterious Bitterroots had been formed by cataclysmic changes that had thrown down whole mountains and ripped apart others. There were no roads in the rough, untamed country, only game trails. Because of heavy rain and fertile soil, verdant forest and attendant wildlife flourished in the mysterious land. There had always been rumors of fugitives there, but Louke had thought the stories mere fantasy, wishful thinking by dissatisfied people. Never had he dreamed of this! Within Glidden there was an organized community that functioned just as Tnasaelp did, better perhaps. There were no Blackrobes or soldiers snooping and interfering in Glidden.

Lavel, who turned out to be Devon's brother, escorted Devon and Louke to a healer, named Shonar, to have their wounds tended. *I don't like the sound of this. My scratches are just fine, thank you.* Louke's experiences with healers had not been positive. Lavel, it seemed, was none too happy with Devon at the moment. Louke grinned to himself, in spite of feeling sick and light-headed. Trouble was brewing between the two, but since little brother was even bigger than big brother, it would be hard to predict the outcome.

Shonar carefully removed the strips of Devon's undershirt from Louke's wrists and hands. The scratches were shallow and easily cleaned and bandaged. The healer evaluated Louke's condition quickly with bright blue eyes. The young man was exhausted and had a hungry look, as if he had not eaten well for a very long time. His eyes were full of suspicion and showed the strain of shock.

Shonar asked Devon to lie down on a cot that he pointed to across the cluttered room. The large monk complied and groaned as he lay down. "Lavel, help me out of these wet boots. We're likely to never get the things off." He acted as if nothing were wrong between them. Lavel glared at him but started tugging one of his boots. He only succeeded in moving the cot with his brother on it across the floor, knocking over some baskets. The boot did not budge. Devon hid his amusement and eyed his brother with some misgiving; this added frustration would surely cause him to explode.

Shonar casually pointed to another cot and asked Louke to lie down also. For a moment, the young man looked as if he was going to bolt, but there was no place to go. He would only get lost in the maze of tunnels out there. Since Devon seemed to trust this man and since he had little choice, he, too, lay down. Truthfully, it felt good to do so. His scratches from the tipeeke were on fire now, and he felt limp as a wet rag. In spite of a strong desire to close his eyes, Louke watched the healer closely as he worked.

Over his small brazier, Shonar heated water and poured some of it into two heavy cups. While he waited for the herbs he had added to steep, he sat on a small stool and rested.

By this time, Lavel was red-faced and angry from his tug-of-war with Devon's boots, but he had managed to get them off. Devon knew he was on dangerous ground and wisely kept silent. Shonar gave one of the steaming mugs to Devon and told him to drink it. Then the healer gave the other to Louke, who fully intended to pour its contents on the floor when the man was not looking. His small experience with medicines was extremely unpleasant. Among all these baskets and jars, who would notice the puddle? So far, these people seemed kind, but Louke had learned from experience that people were not always what they seemed.

A young man with curly blond hair and incredibly blue eyes pushed back the weaving that covered the opening to the cave. He called out to Shonar, "I've heard our padre needs some stitches, and I've come to help!" His face was serious, but his eyes were full of laughter. He nodded pleasantly at Louke as he crossed the room to Devon's cot.

"Ah, the wages of faith breaking," the young man cried sorrowfully when he examined Devon's arm. The abbot swung a ham-sized fist to cuff him, but the young man anticipated the blow and ducked. "Add to disobedience *that* unruly display of temper," he mourned, shaking his head with disappointment.

"Dare, you disrespectful young cub, be still! Don't you know how to treat your spiritual counselor and an abbot at that?" Devon asked with an attempt at dignity.

"Aye, I do, but a man of the cloth who has been involved in *two* fights in one day, as I understand it—" Dare retorted sadly.

"And what could I have done to prevent that, I'd like to know?" Devon responded with irritation.

"Perhaps you could have not been out there in the first place?" Dare suggested, smiling sweetly.

"You—you," Devon spluttered.

"Careful, careful, my lord abbot," Dare warned, holding up an admonishing finger. "I think your tongue is about to utter something unworthy of your holy calling."

"True, very true," Devon gasped and lay back on his cot, laughing. Lavel's stern face cracked into a smile in spite of his wrath, and the tension between the brothers relaxed somewhat.

While watching this strange scene, Louke forgot to pour out the contents of his mug. He still had a full cup in his hand when Shonar noticed he had not drunk it. The healer's eyes were stern. "Drink up," he ordered.

With real fear clouding his mind, Louke rebelled. "I don't want it, and I won't drink it," he declared flatly. *No one is going to make me drink this … this … whatever the stuff is.*

Shonar said thoughtfully, "Do you see those three men over there? Do you really think you could resist all of them?"

Louke looked. Though Dare was not big in his present company, among most men he would be. Despair filled Louke's heart. "You wouldn't … force me!" he faltered angrily.

"Aye, I most certainly would," Shonar said. "You need that to fight any infection that has started and to dull the pain."

Louke looked into the merciless blue eyes and knew that he had lost. Devon and Lavel alone could hold him down, even without the other one.

Devon was letting out mock cries of pain as Dare treated his injury. He called Dare "clumsy" and a few other descriptive but uncomplimentary names, which seemed to amuse rather than offend the young man. Lavel smiled at their banter. Their genuine laughter caused the fear and distrust coiled in Louke to relax a little. He drank the potion quickly. It was very bitter. He gave the cup to Shonar and lay back, as stiff as a board, with his eyes closed. A warm lassitude crept over him, and he fell asleep.

Shonar looked at his young patient with curiosity. What profession had developed his upper body to such an extent? And why was the Maker giving them another man of such size? He looked at Lavel and Devon and then Louke with wonder.

Dare left, and Lavel, who had restrained himself for all this time, was about to tear into Devon. Shonar broke up the impending argument by examining Dare's work on Devon's arm. He declared it well done.

Devon was growing very sleepy. "Don't be angry, Lavel. I was just in time to save Louke, after all. Of course, then he had to save me … and you and Sher had to save us … but it all turned out well in the end, didn't it? So why worry?" he mumbled. His voice trailed off into sleep. Lavel shook his head in disgust. He looked at his brother with a mixture of frustration and affection and left.

But that was not the end of it. Lock was also mightily displeased. Having people under his command who were used to their own command and not familiar with Glidden's ways was proving to be difficult. He would have to take more time in the future to explain the rules of Glidden to new members of their community, like Devon. Had he known that Sher had barely saved Lavel from making a like mistake, he would have been even more frustrated.

Glidden used a very simple chain of command. Everyone was in someone's band, and all bandleaders reported to the council. Bandleaders could certainly give approval for any member of their group to do something without council permission, but with any important or dangerous request, they were expected to seek the council's advice. The band members felt a strong sense of responsibly for each other and always reported their trips outside of Glidden to the bandleader. That it had not occurred to Devon to do this indicated to Lock that he needed to do a better job of educating new people, to state his thoughts mildly.

After hearing that the patients were awake, Glidden's leader strode down a winding tunnel toward the healing room with ire in each stride. The guards came quickly to attention and wondered as Lock passed what had happened to anger their chief. Lock greeted Louke calmly, but his mouth was grim and his attention plainly elsewhere. Louke was certain he knew where. The young man felt great relief that he had not incurred this warrior's wrath. It was not that Lock was particularly large or ferocious, but his five feet and eight inches were comprised of compact, hard muscle. His face, with its high cheekbones, could have been carved out of redwood, and an aura of power hung about him. He was used to command, and there was something in his attitude that said he would tolerate no interference or disobedience.

Devon sighed and raised himself up a little on his good arm. He still was feeling the effects of the herbal drink and the last harrowing two days, but he knew there was no putting off this conversation. Lock wasted none of his precious time on courtesy. "I find it hard to believe that you were the leader of anything, much less of our only monastery!" he said caustically, his face stern and his black eyes glittering.

"Well, sir, to tell the truth, my high position had little to do with my ... er ... qualifications," Devon admitted with regret. "In fact, there was talk of sending me home at one time over a certain, shall we say, 'incident.' We don't need to go into that," he quickly added. "Truly, I think the king's trade council selected me as abbot because they thought I was the least spiritual of the brothers they interviewed. They assumed I would be less likely to spread the infection of our faith than any of the other monks and the most likely to produce a quantity of quality leather goods. I have a good head for business, you see," Devon confided with a twinkle in his eye. "I think they also meant my young age to gall the older members of our order and cause them to feel humiliated at having to take direction from a twenty-six-year-old. They were quite right; the brothers certainly did resent me."

"The *trade council* selected you?" Lock asked, astonished that this unlikely body would elect a spiritual leader.

"Aye, the council lists Saint Fauver's as a leather goods business. That way we are, or rather were, hidden from view, so to speak. Also they could tax us, just as they would any other business," Devon explained. "They are, after all, supposed to have wiped out all followers of the Maker and destroyed all churches, monasteries, and schools."

Lock absorbed this information thoughtfully. In spite of himself, the Glidden chief said with an amused twist to his mouth, "I would like to hear about that *incident*." With a quick return to his former severity, he abruptly asked, "Well, what kind of an abbot did you make?"

"To tell the truth, a rather unconventional one," Devon replied, his eyes far away, a slight smile on his lips. "But after a rough first year, in which nobody took me very seriously and I made a lot of mistakes, even the older brothers came to appreciate me. My size and strength, you see, intimidated the merchants and soldiers. They were in the habit of giving the brothers a rather hard time: hazing, cruel practical jokes, that kind of thing. Their officers and the trade officials just looked the other way; monks were fair game. After I knocked a few heads together and threw three of the chief offenders in a vat of rinse water, they seemed to understand how one is to act in a monastery."

Lock gave a shout of laughter and responded appreciatively, "I'll bet they did!" His anger toward this roguish young abbot melted. It was useless to pretend he was still exasperated, so he said firmly, "Do not leave these caverns again without discussing it with me or the head of your band. I will attach you, the rest of your group and Louke to one of the bands today. It is the band members' responsibility to take care of each other. Understood?"

"Aye, sir," Devon replied, but there was laughter in his eyes. Lock sighed and left, feeling less than satisfied with the interview.

Louke looked at the young abbot with awe. "You never did punch king's men, did you, Devon?" he asked hopefully.

"Well, aye, I did, but I don't advise anyone else to do so, unless they are prepared to run." Devon laughed. "After all, the trade council elected me to the post, and the bullies didn't want to tangle with them. As much as they hated it, they had to keep their hands off me."

"You don't really pray and believe in the Maker and all that religious stuff ... do you?" Louke asked fearfully.

"Well, aye, Louke. I'm afraid I do."

Terribly disappointed in his hero, Louke lay back on his cot and closed his eyes. Devon followed his example and was soon asleep.

—————◦◦◦◦————

Farmer Uoy knew that Glidden folk used his farm. He suspected that there were secret entrances somewhere on his land, since people who did not arrive by the lane or forest path popped in with regularity. Yet he did not know for certain that there were such things and certainly did not know where they were. He pretended that the men and women of Glidden arrived by normal methods; the people of Glidden pretended also. It was much safer that way.

The next day, Blackrobes put Uoy through some rough questioning, because the people in the village had identified the horse and wagon as his. A farmer on his way to town had led the frightened horse and wagon to the local stable. Two of the village's stable hands had put the horse in a stall and given him water and oats; however, the animal hadn't made it through the night. The stable owner had kindly returned Uoy's unharmed wagon. The old farmer told the Blackrobes that he'd loaned his setup, as he called it, to a passing stranger who said he needed it. The man had promised he would return it. His grief over the loss of his horse was real, and he railed at soldiers and Blackrobes alike for allowing their vicious animals to attack it. In the next breath, he declared with anger that he hoped they caught the young rascal who had borrowed it. He played his part so well that they believed him, but they still set a careful watch on his farm in case the rascal came back.

A New Recruit

No! NO! I won't go back with you! Louke screamed. Uncle Nesen, with avenging tipeeke, was chasing him through the dark and clinging forest. He shuddered as he shook himself free of the terrible dream that made his heart pound in fright. In spite of the fact that his clothing was soaked with sweat, he felt an icy touch on his skin and shivered. *It was only a dream,* he assured himself. He sat up and looked around Shonar's unusual healing room. Drying herbs hung from the ceiling, baskets of seeds and roots marched in uneven rows across the floor, and pottery jars lined the shelves.

Louke was enjoying the comforts of food, warmth, and other human beings, but he felt weighed down by all the rock. He felt disconnected from the world of sky, sun, and wind. The caverns were always lit by torchlight— one could not tell if it was night or day.

He'd been miserably sick for the first two days in Glidden with a fever that Shonar said the tipeeke's claws had started but that his days of living outside in the early spring had deepened. Hunger and cold had weakened him. Louke knew it was true; there had been many days when he had been unable to catch or find anything to eat. The sons of stonecrafters were not taught to hunt, and he knew precious little about the business. He had a firestone, but he had been too afraid of discovery to make a fire very often. His uncle, he knew, was obstinate enough to search for him a long time. Also, he'd listened with respect to the natives' stories of soldiers, tipeeke, and Blackrobes. The local people had not known he was listening, of course. Anyone of Louke's size would be remembered, so he'd avoided villages and even main roads. He'd quickly decided, after overhearing some of the local folk, that he did not want these sinister men or animals to find him. However, there were problems with traveling cross-country. As a stonecrafter, he knew nothing of woodcraft, and he had gotten lost repeatedly. His plan was simple. He wanted to get far enough away from Redwater that his uncle could not possibly find him. Then he would seek work with a local builder. This had seemed logical at first.

But my plan has taken a strange twist, he thought as he gazed around this haven of dark granite. *I am not even entirely convinced it is a haven.* Louke forced himself to be honest. *Aye, I am sure.* After spending two days in Shonar and Devon's company, he was convinced that these people were sincere. *I am still uncomfortable. No. I am afraid, afraid to trust again.* He had trusted before, and his trust had been betrayed.

And now I will have to talk about it! The thought made him clench his fists in frustration. He could understand why they were being so careful. Usually, people's stories were tested *before* they were allowed to know the truth—the truth that there really was an organized group hiding in the mountains! *I not only know that the rumors are true; I also know how to get inside Glidden. It is dangerous knowledge.* He had skipped important steps each man and woman usually passed through *before* they reached Glidden itself.

Two days later, Louke went through the same process that Dare, and perhaps others, had endured before him. The Glidden council asked very pointed questions to determine if he could be trusted, if he could stay. *I am not sure I want to stay!* His mind avoided the difficult question of what they did with people who did not pass the test but knew too much.

He told them he was from Tnasaelp but had left the village when he was twelve. He and his mother had moved to the port city of Redwater, where he'd been apprenticed to his uncle Nesen, a member of the stonecrafter guild. Huge quarries in the mountains near Redwater contained the finest granite and marble on Ree.

Just as they'd tested Dare's account of his life, the council ordered that

Louke's story be checked also. Glidden contacted their spies in Redwater. They would soon know whether Louke had told them the truth or not.

The young stonecrafter awaited the council's verdict in Shonar's room, which was really a large cave. Louke relived the telling of his tale. He had calmly related to the council the experiences that had led him from his village to Redwater and then to the forest near Tnasaelp. As he sat at the healer's high worktable, bitterness brought on by his thoughts flooded through him again.

He and his mother had left Tnasaelp and their friends so eagerly. The village was full of happy memories of their life together, but since his father's death in the spring, the memories had become painful. His father's brother had invited him and his mother to come to Redwater and offered to teach Louke the stonecrafter's trade. Nesen had no family … no son to instruct.

They gladly accepted. Louke, at twelve, did not yet know enough of his father's craft to make a living for him and his mother. His father had gathered and worked with elong vines to create the tought fibers used to make things like hammocks. His mother kept house for their unmarried, stern, and rather humorless relative. For the first year things went smoothly, but then his uncle, a confirmed old bachelor, fell unexpectedly in love with Falaron, a young widow who had two sons of her own. To make a long and painful story shorter, Falaron wanted her sons, not Nesen's country nephew, to inherit her new husband's profitable business.

After his uncle and the widow's marriage, Louke's mother became little more than a servant in their home, and Louke became the object of Falaron's hatred. His uncle was too flattered by the pretty widow's affection to see what she was doing. Louke was punished for her sons' mischief and slowly, purposefully discredited in his uncle's eyes. It was true that Falaron encouraged his uncle to think badly of him, but it was Uncle Nesen who gave in to his harsh nature. Life grew constantly wretched. Louke endured accusations that were untrue, beatings that were undeserved, and belittling comments that became unbearable. At his mother's encouragement, Louke had run away. Falaron had won.

Louke remembered telling the council regretfully, "I feel awful for leaving my mother in such a miserable household, but one day I'll go get her. It is my hope that now that I'm gone, Falaron will have no reason to trouble my mother. She is a marvelous cook and housekeeper. Both are qualities that Uncle Nesen values highly and that Falaron does not possess."

Louke had fled to his former home, to familiar territory, knowing as he did so that it was unwise, that he could not stay. It would be the first place Nesen would look. However, it had turned out that a strange animal, a tipeeke, had almost caught him, not his uncle.

Two weeks later, when Devon came into the room, Louke was sitting, elbows on the high worktable with his head held in his hands, feeling depressed. "Your story checked out on all points and even a few you didn't mention," Devon said cheerfully. Relief washed through Louke. *Even if I don't choose to stay, it is good to know I can, if I want to.*

"Your uncle is looking for you. He has been to Tnasaelp, but they had not seen you, so he left … yet he has not returned home. By now he may be in Redwater. Our report is days old already. What do you choose to do, my young friend?" he asked with a searching look.

What indeed? Louke thought in frustration. *I am not at all sure I want to be involved with these people. I have only my uncle chasing me. The folk of Glidden have the king, all his soldiers, and creatures I don't even like to think about after them!* Finally, Louke decided to stay, partially because he did not have the energy to go. *That's a really bad reason,* he thought, *but there it is.* "I'll stay." Devon seemed sincerely pleased.

It is difficult to think of leaving this place, friendless and unsure of where or when I will find work. Perhaps, he admitted to himself, *I am also curious. I would surely like to see the rest of Glidden.* He did not acknowledge that his affection for Devon and Shonar influenced his decision in any way.

A few weeks later, Devon watched as Louke trained with Bardon's small company, or "the Pack" as the Glidden folk called them. The young stonecrafter was powerful but used to tools and rock, not weapons. It would take time to develop a warrior from a stonecrafter. Oster, Tier, Dare, Chea, Louke, and Bar worked under Tal qua in the mornings. They perfected all skills that would make them better warriors. Bar spent each afternoon with Lock, learning the ways of command. The others spent this time with whomever they chose, as long as it was someone who could teach them a skill. Bar also spent time with masters of each craft and each member of the council in order to learn their skills.

Dare went to Shonar to further his knowledge of healing. Oster went to Wasatch to train and care for Glidden's horses. Chea worked with Lavel on sorting and evaluating reports that came in constantly from contacts and spies all over the island. Tier, after spending time in many different areas, spent most of his afternoons with Devon. The large monk, with Tier's help, resumed his crafting in leather. Those who followed the Maker in Glidden often gathered around Devon to discuss the scrolls and the prophecy. His friendships were not limited to followers of the Maker, however. Many who believed in other gods or none at all still came to Devon to discuss their problems. While his hands were busy working with and sewing leather, he would listen carefully.

Louke used his afternoons to craft in stone. There was no one in the mountain who knew as much about his craft as he did. There were many, however, who were interested in making their caverns more comfortable and useful. Louke found himself teaching others all he knew. Sometimes the woods called to Louke, and he went with Sher to hunt and fish. These skills he found very easy and enjoyable to learn.

Chea, Lavel, and Acostan, who was a member of the council, were deeply concerned about a pattern they began to see in their reports from the western side of Ree. Villages there reported that young men were being conscripted to join the king's service. If they refused, they were bound and taken by force. If the villagers tried to defend their young men with arms, they were beaten and imprisoned. So far, there had been no reports of this happening on a large scale or in any of the big cities, certainly not in Feisan. But they wondered what the king wanted with the young men. The king already had a large volunteer army in place. He paid them well and was experiencing no trouble, that they knew of, with recruitment. Yet the pattern was there, and it puzzled them all.

Soon, Chea knew, it would be time for him to return to Meggatirra. *I no longer feel like an outsider, and I am not ready to leave Glidden. My work with Lavel is fascinating, and I will miss my friends. Lock has shown me great honor and trust in allowing me to work with the underground's information network. I know more than most in Glidden about its operation! That knowledge, added to what I know of Meggatirra's network, has made me dangerous to our enemies and valuable to my friends.*

Tal qua sat on a bearskin thoughtfully gazing into the flames of a small fire. Lock, Shonar, Devon, and Lavel had joined him. "They do well together, I think," Tal said finally, in answer to a question from Lock. "Louke has fit in, despite the fact that the others have been together longer. It will take him time to forget what he has been through. I have warned the hishua not to push him too hard in combat. His strength is great. I fear he may forget whom he fights and inflict more damage than he intends. He is still angry and bitter about his time in his uncle's home and feels great guilt about leaving his mother."

"Is he dangerous?" Lock asked.

"I don't think so … not from what I saw when he was with me," Devon said reassuringly. "He remained calm under pressure and fought with common sense, if not skill. In spite of that," he said with a quick smile, "I'm glad you warned the others … Best not push him too far for a while."

They talked far into the night of daily events and their plans for the future, unaware that even as they enjoyed the warmth of the fire, the enemy was at their door.

BETRAYED!

FOR A SIGNIFICANT HALF HOUR, A RAM'S HORN
wailed imperative warning from high on Hawks Dell. Then, midcry, it
suddenly fell silent.

If it had not been for that one lone sentry, now surely captured, they
would have had no warning at all. As it was, they were hard pressed.
Somehow, the lookout on Hawks Dell had escaped the fate of all the other
sentries. Perhaps their attackers did not know about her new post. At least,
that was their guess. It would be a long time before the council, or anyone,
had time to investigate or to think about anything but running.

At the first wail of the ram's horn in the middle of the night, Lock and
his friends still sat talking around the embers of their fire. They froze in
shock. Lock had hoped he would never hear this cry echo through Glidden's
dark tunnels.

He sprang into action as his scouts poured a stream of grave reports
and urgent questions into the dimly lit cavern. The threatening chaos turned
into barely maintained order as each member of the underground took over
his or her area of responsibility. The well-trained band chiefs calmed the
families and other members of their groups. Wakened from sound sleep at
the warning horns' piercing blasts, many Glidden folk were bewildered and
disoriented. Their leaders, at council direction, quickly started evacuating
the people. Glidden folk responded, as best they could, to the pounding,

well-organized attack—an attack that was breaching their defenses as if they weren't there. Long years of careful training induced order, and the bands fled, for the most part, in an organized manner. After the bands departed, designated men and women activated traps in darkened corridors and carefully covered exits. They took some of the torches that brightened the tunnels with them; the others they extinguished. Tunnel by tunnel the torches went out, and Glidden became dark and difficult to navigate.

During a dreadful night filled with repeated alarms, terrified screams, numbing confusion, and violent capture, the dwellers of Glidden who broke free of the mountain fled into the Bitterroot Range. They went farther than any of them had ever been—farther than any of them had ever wanted to go. At least it was summer and the temperature in the forbidding, uncharted wilderness was more temperate than at any other time of year.

The hishua bolted out of their hammocks as rams' horns within Glidden were sounded in response to the one on Hawks Dell. The horns' eerie, mournful cries reverberated through the tunnels. The bellowing noise bounced off walls until the shrieking seemed to be within their heads. Bands were fleeing through the passageways, most to exits on the south side. The assault, of course, was coming from the north and east. There was no way to attack Glidden on the southwest side because it was protected by the treacherous Bitterroot Range. It would be a foolish endeavor indeed to march troops into such impossible territory. The Pack knew the urgency of the warning by the repeated wail of the horns, but suddenly, there was only one horn wailing. Then it too stopped. They froze as they realized what this meant for Glidden and its people. Their refuge was not only under attack; it would never be a refuge again. They were all in grave danger of capture. The young men did not take time to grab anything other than the essentials: weapons, packs, water bottles, blankets, and a little food.

Those who did not heed the horns' warning or who were too slow or too close to the attack to escape were captured and imprisoned in Glidden's largest cavern.

Trying to buy their companions time, many of Glidden's warriors barricaded themselves behind anything they could quickly move to block a tunnel. These brave souls made the Blackrobes and soldiers pay dearly for passage. Many were wounded, but few died. Captain Tori had plans for the surviving warriors.

The rest of Glidden's folk went into the cold, dark night, where soldiers were hunting them. The soldiers had been instructed to capture when possible, not kill or wound. Their leaders wanted many prisoners to use as hostages.

Even as Lock ran deeper into the mysterious, formidable Bitterroots, his mind sorted intelligence they had recently received. *Who has betrayed us? How did this happen? According to current reports, Tori and Lotu are supposed to be with Duke Roth in Ravensperch, but surely this attack can be traced to their door!*

Fleeing with Lock were those who had been around the fire with him and remnants of two bands they'd picked up along the way. Before they'd left, they'd taken time to burn all the documents in Acostan's workroom. The information his scrolls contained would have betrayed their networks from one end of Ree to the other. No real names were used—such information was committed to memory—but the enemy would have gained much knowledge. That knowledge would have caused terrible reprisals. Also, the king would have started an investigation. He probably still would but with fewer facts. Thank heaven and one sentry for that! Lock did not know where the hishua were, but he did know they had heeded the horns' warning and gotten away. He had stopped at their rooms on the way out and found them empty.

As Lock pushed his way through heavy undergrowth in impenetrable darkness, he heard a terrible explosion somewhere behind him. The ground under his feet trembled, and fire roared high into the night sky. Lock stared at the flames in horror, trying to think what the explosion could mean, and started back toward the blaze, toward his people.

This explosion must have been caused by our enemy … That means they have come through the tunnels and traps we left to confuse and slow them. Now they are on this side! We are only minutes in front of them! Mighty Maker, defend us! How can this be?

Shonar stepped in front of Lock, his eyes glittering in the flames' bright glow. "You cannot go back. You cannot help them! We are too few. Most surely—hear me, Son—most surely you will run into a trap. Long have we studied their ways. Remember what we have learned! They will take you, they will give you their terrible drug, and you will talk. Then ... they will know *everything,* including names and places."

Lock knotted his fists in anger, not at his father, but at his helplessness. *We do not have twenty arrows among us! Who of these can we afford to lose? They are Glidden's leaders ... They will be badly needed.* Lock scanned the faces around him. The members of his group looked at each other in frustration and grief and waited for Lock's command. He hardened his will and did what he knew was wise. "We will go on," he agreed in a choked voice. *The enemy is too many, too well armed, and too organized. We would be throwing our lives away.* Lock felt like a father deserting his children and groaned as he turned his face from the bright inferno. They pushed deeper into the Bitterroots.

He reminded himself that he had checked all the main tunnels on his way out and calmed, as best he could, the frightened people. They knew what to do and were, for the most part, handling the emergency very well. Long ago, the people of Glidden had worked out a plan of escape, and they'd practiced it many times a year, so that even the children knew what to do. They had always known this could—and probably would—happen. Too many people were a part of Glidden, and it took only one—one to betray all. Yet Lock had grown secure, overconfident perhaps, because in all the years they'd lived there, no one had come close to finding them. Of course, it had helped that no one believed they existed ... until now.

A haunting memory pierced Lock's heart as he stumbled down a game trail. Before they'd fled through Glidden's corridors, he had watched from a high vantage point a scene far below him. He'd been able to see little in the darkness but the dim contours of the land and the flickering torches his people carried. These pinpoints of light had poured from the tunnels of Glidden in a narrow stream and fled into the Bitterroots in different directions. Each group of bobbing lights had represented a band. They'd formed fantastic patterns and then, one by one, winked out.

He reminded himself that the people, unlike the lights, still lived and that their separation was part of the plan. The underground hoped to confuse and divide their pursuers by sending each band to a different haven. In spite of his attempt to be encouraged, grief overwhelmed him at the memory of all those specks of light disappearing into the night. *How many will survive? How many will die or be captured?* One thought kept him going. *I will live through this for those who are still alive. Heaven willing, we will find each other and begin again.*

The hishua roomed together. They were all a part of Shonar's band, but in the assault on Glidden, only Dare understood the meaning of the horns and knew what to do. He had been in a drill the last time he was in Glidden. They did not take time to find Shonar; they simply grabbed what they could lay their hands on and fled. The Pack followed Dare through a tunnel that led down and down. Behind them, they could hear the pounding feet and urgent voices of others fleeing. The sounds grew more distant. They felt that, wherever they were going, they were suddenly very much alone. The small band passed a silent pool that glittered black and still in the flare of Dare's torch. He stopped to fill his water bottle, and the others silently followed his example. They looked at each other a moment in the short pause. Their faces were pale and grim but composed.

Dare thought, *We have lived in Glidden for a few weeks without fear. Now we are on the run again. It took us so long to reach this refuge! We focused on it for the long, miserable weeks of our journey, and now ... it is destroyed. There is no safety anywhere!*

He rose without a word and went on, farther down. The warmth of the tunnels turned cooler and then cold. Silent as the moon rising in the night sky, a smooth, shiny dome rose out of the inky water of the pool. Bright eyes watched them with interest as they disappeared into the darkness. After a short time, the small being slipped beneath the surface without leaving a ripple.

Since the companions could hear no sound of pursuit behind them, they stopped to organize their gear and put on warmer clothing.

"Dare, where are we headed?" Bar whispered.

"In a minute we will come to a stream, and then I must put out the torch. It will be very dark, but if anyone is outside waiting for us, they will see it. We will follow the watercourse until we are outside. Watch your head! The top of the tunnel is very low. The water is not deep, but it is cold, and the stones are slippery. Stay close together and follow me," he answered softly. There was no debate. Normally they would object, just on principle, to taking orders from one of their own, but this night they knew their lives depended on what Dare and Dare alone knew.

The water did not flow strongly, but in complete darkness, it was very difficult to maintain their balance. Dare trailed the fingers of his right hand along the wall and stepped cautiously forward. *I have done this before,* he reminded himself. It had not seemed nearly so far the last time, when someone else had been leading the way, and at that time, it had not been night.

A breeze, which carried the scent of pine, blew gently on their faces. That, in addition to a slight lessening of the darkness, told them they were near the outside world. Instinctively, they moved even more quietly. As they stepped out of the tunnel, they could see bright stars high overhead through the tree branches. Carefully, they moved out of the water and onto pine needle–covered rocks. The Pack listened intently to the night around them. On this side of Glidden, it was as if nothing had happened; all was normal. They followed Dare as he threaded through the trees in a southern direction.

Suddenly, behind them, the night erupted into thunderous sound and raging flames. Bewildered screams and cries of fear filled the air as an explosion of fire raged high into the sky. They stopped and stared numbly at the leaping blaze. How had the enemy come through so quickly, and what was the purpose of this explosion and fire?

Oster said softly, "For the light alone it would be worth doing! This way they can see us running from the tunnels like scared rats and capture us more easily. Otherwise, many could slip away in the darkness. It will cause fear and confusion, and that also will make it easier to capture those fleeing."

Bar whispered, pain in each word, "The screaming! They have wounded or captured some of the bands. We must go back and help them!"

"Wait! It could be a trap, Bar. It's just the kind of thing they would do. If it is Tori and Lotu, and who else could it be, they will not be content until they have you and Dare. Finding Glidden is a nice brand on their headbands, but it is not the purpose of this raid. They want *you*," Oster said forcefully, wanting Bar to think. He did not touch his friend, but his gaze held the shocked prince as firmly as a hand. The rest looked stunned. No one had taken the time to think about who was behind the attack or what its purpose might be. Now that they were thinking about it, what Oster said made sense.

Dare watched the thought go through Bar's mind: *This is all because of me!* He knew Bar so well. But he was in no mood to deal with this problem tonight. Grabbing Bar by the front of his tunic, he brought him scant inches from his face and hissed angrily, "Don't even think about it, because I'll follow you and catch you. I want your promise!" Dare shook his friend hard to emphasize his point.

Bar's rage and fear calmed a little. "Are you going to do this when I'm king?" he asked mildly, humor glinting for a moment in his eyes. He did not struggle, even slightly, in Dare's fierce grasp. "If you are, I think the citizens of Ree are going to be shocked. They might get the wrong idea."

Dare was not amused nor deterred. "Promise or I'll bind you," he threatened coldly. Neither was Dare fooled. Behind the teasing in Bar's voice, he saw bitter despair in Bar's dark eyes and the thought *People are dying again, because of me.*

The others were too bewildered to interfere. They seriously thought Dare had lost his mind, but they trusted his instincts enough to stay out of the altercation. Of all of them, Dare knew Bar best.

Bar dropped the pose of lightness. "Dare, it will end it," he cried passionately.

"That is for the Maker to decide, not you. Promise!" Dare whispered with anger and another fierce shake.

Bar knew there would be no moving Dare, and now was definitely a bad time for a fight—a fight he could win but that would take time and make too much noise. "All right, all right, you stubborn rockhead," he whispered, giving up … for the moment. "I promise."

Dare let him go with a hard look.

Chea whispered sarcastically, "It would be really interesting to know what this is all about, but there are *other* things we need to decide right now."

As if to emphasize his point, the distant sounds of tipeeke and men grew closer. Tier interjected, "Such as, is that a trap back there, and even if we don't get caught, can we help? There are only six of us."

Louke broke his long silence with a simple, forceful statement. "We *must* go now, or we'll not save even ourselves. I hear those tipeeke animals baying not far behind us."

Chea looked at him in admiration. "A man who uses his brain! Astonishing, in present company." Bar had the grace to flush. The others agreed with Louke quickly and chose Chea as their leader. He knew no more than any of them about the Bitterroot Range, but he was at home in both forest and mountain. More importantly, he had years of experience hiding from pursuers and leading men.

They stumbled through the night with shrieking tipeeke on their trail. They did not know where they were going. They had no plan and no time to formulate one. They simply plunged forward in growing exhaustion and fear.

Dare had no idea where Shonar's group was supposed to go once they fled the mountain. That information had been part of the drill he'd participated in, but they hadn't actually gone to the place. Shonar had explained where it was and told the band to stay there, saying someone would come and tell them when it was safe to return or give other instructions. Dare could not remember the place, and even if he remembered, he doubted he could find it in this confusion and in the dark. There had been something about a large, reddish rock shaped like a ship, but that was all that came back to him.

When they broke from the trees, they found themselves on some kind of a narrow trail that ran a twisting pattern between high cliffs. They followed it and climbed steadily upward. Suddenly the trail split in two. Chea looked at each rocky, narrow path and then back over his shoulder. He was drenched with sweat and gasping for air, as were his companions.

The tipeeke were definitely closer, and their hysterical baying announced that they were on the scent—*the Pack's* scent.

Bar grabbed Chea's arm and said softly, "I have an idea." The moon's pale light occasionally brightened the rough terrain around them. For a quick second, Bar had seen a ledge above them on the left side. It might offer them an alternative to the steep and very obvious paths. Though the ledge was tangled with stunted undergrowth, he thought there would be room for them to double back and find a less obvious direction and perhaps even a hiding place. Chea scanned the ledge. It was the only chance he could see. They planned quickly.

Tier and Oster, who were their fastest runners, each took one of the paths and ran up it a short distance to leave a trail the tipeeke would follow. Hopefully, this would split and distract their pursuers ... for a time at least.

Meanwhile, Chea got on Louke's shoulders and grabbed an emaciated branch that he hoped would hold him. The young Chi pulled himself up and then onto the ledge. Louke threw him the rope that Chea always carried in his pack. Now they could hear men shouting to one another as well as tipeeke. Chea tied the rope to a tree with fingers that trembled with exhaustion and tension. "Hurry!" he cried softly.

Bar's heart pounded with fear. *We will never get everyone up in time. What a stupid idea! I should have kept my mouth shut.* He shook himself mentally. What was done was done. They were committed.

Each hishua worked frantically for the next few minutes to get the two heaviest members of their group, Louke and Dare, up the steep wall to the ledge. Bar suffered a few waves of nausea, but by keeping his feet firmly against the cliff wall, he managed to make it to the top without triggering full-blown queal. Bar, Louke, Dare, and Chea waited impatiently on the narrow ledge for Tier and Os to return. The sounds of pursuit grew steadily closer.

Os came flying down the slope. He quickly grabbed the rope and was hauled up by strong hands before he could even attempt to climb. They lowered the rope again just as Tier came pounding into view with a wild grin on his face. Bar wanted to shake him. He was cutting the time much too closely. How far had he gone anyway? Tier grabbed the rope and was literally jerked off his feet and up onto the ledge in seconds. Chea motioned them to quiet while he coiled the rope and placed it over his left shoulder. Then he moved quickly down the ledge, seeking better cover.

The mad howls of tipeeke reverberated off the rock cliffs around them. Torchlight flickered crazily on the cliff walls as a stream of men and animals flowed through the canyon below. They would soon reach the split in the trail. The hishua moved stealthily along the ledge, perhaps three man heights above their pursuers, in the opposite direction. Any noise they might make would be easily covered by the unbelievable noise their pursuers were making. They did not wait to see if their diversion worked but trotted, as fast as poor light would allow, down the widening ledge. In the distance, they heard the roar of a rock bear. His sleep had probably been disturbed by all the noise in his usually quiet territory.

Chea gasped and called out "Halt!" more loudly than he intended. He had almost tumbled into a deep ravine just at his feet. They gathered at the edge and looked down, but no one could see the bottom. It could be twenty or two hundred feet deep. During a whispered conference over what to do, they heard a soft but insistent whistle.

While the others were planning, Louke had found a profusion of elong vines hanging from the cliffs above them. He chose a sturdy one and swung across the ravine to the other side. He grinned at their amazement, very pleased with himself. Then he noticed his friends' expressions change from amusement to wide-eyed terror. They made frantic signals for him to come back. Just as he looked over his shoulder to see what all the excitement was about, he heard a loud roar behind him. With the fearful sound ringing in his ears, he pushed off the ground with all his might and swung out over the gorge. But he was too late.

The large, angry rock bear lunged for Louke and then lost its footing when he swung away. The frightened creature grabbed for Louke to save itself. Enormous, furry paws caught frantically at Louke's waist. He cried out in fear and sharp pain. His hold on the vine broke because of the animal's great weight. The two of them, boy and beast, plunged into the blackness below.

No! No! This cannot be happening! Chea thought. There was total silence. The companions found themselves hanging over the edge in horror, peering into the dark ravine. They urgently, softly called Louke's name.

The pounding of their hearts echoed loudly in their ears as they anxiously searched the quiet, ominous blackness below. After a few moments of total silence, Louke answered them. His voice was hoarse and shaken, but he was alive. They looked at each other in wonder and disbelief. "I landed on … the … bear," Louke called up to them. There was a note of mild hysteria in his voice. No wonder.

The words "landed on the bear" took a few seconds to sink in. Chea breathed, "He what? He couldn't have, could he?"

"Are you hurt?" Dare called softly.

Louke had been too close to death to lie, but he did understate things a bit. "His claws did some damage, I think, but nothing too bad. It was not a very long fall, perhaps thirty feet. The bear is dead … I think … At least, he's not moving." His voice sounded strange, but no one could wonder at that. In their relief, they began to see the humor in the situation and would have laughed, if they had the energy or time.

They were jerked back to reality by the sounds of their enemy. The clamor, instead of growing more distant, was now coming closer and growing much louder. Bar whispered, "They have discovered our trick, I think. We must decide what to do quickly. The moon is riding high now, and the clouds are gone. They will find us very easily, out in the open like this."

"At least the trick gave us some time. As it turns out, we need it," Chea replied.

Dare said irritably, "A rock bear! What *else* can happen? Well, do we bring Louke up, or do we go down?" What a night! They had wakened out of sound sleep to terror and had been running for their lives ever since.

"Let's grab the vine and go down. This has to be as good a hiding place as ever we'll find. The bear's scent should throw them off, if they track us this far," Tier said. Too numb to think of anything else, they agreed. Tier and then Os climbed down the vine to join Louke. Bar looked at Dare. This time, it was too dark in the ravine and too steep for Bar to be sure he could keep his feet on rock for the whole descent.

Understanding the problem, Chea uncoiled his rope and tied it around Bar's waist. "Try it. I will hold this end. If you lose your grip, I will lower you the rest of the way. You will have queal, but you won't be injured. Dare will use one of the other vines and stay by you. If there is a place you must swing out, he will help you get back to the wall." For the first time since they'd met, Chea saw fear in Bar's eyes. Bar nodded woodenly, and with hands that trembled, he lowered himself over the side. As it happened, the descent was rough, but between the rope and Dare's help, he made it quickly.

Finally, it was Chea's turn. He grabbed the same vine Dare had used. As he turned to face the cliff wall and began his descent, his heart jumped in fear. A flickering torch was coming toward him. The tipeeke, he noted, were making only moderate noise—for them. Perhaps they, too, were growing tired on this long night.

At the bottom, he found himself in a deep-sided gorge choked with boulders and bushes. The moon's light poured over the landscape above them, but it was inky black down in the gorge. Even when his eyes adjusted, the others appeared as shadows to him.

O'HATCH?

SUPPRESSING HIS PANIC, CHEA STROVE TO speak calmly. "They have found our trail and are on the ledge! Dare, Bar, find Louke and help him; then stay close to me. Oster, take up the rear and signal me when you hear or see the enemy. Tier, scout ahead and see if you can find a place to hide. We must move quickly and get away from here. They will surely lower someone with a torch into this place to seek sign of us. Move quickly now! We haven't much time."

Groans met his command, but everyone moved to obey. For the first time in this long night, Dare felt despair. *It is simply too dark down here to move quickly, and we cannot light a torch. Though a hundred refuges may be available, we can see none of them.* Long hours without rest or drink were taking their toll; they could not keep this up much longer. Dare and Bar quickly found Louke, but suddenly, he slumped to the ground between them.

"Louke! Quickly, tell me the truth. What's wrong?" Dare demanded as he removed a hanging vine from his hair.

"The bear tore me ... fairly badly. I'm losing ... blood," he gasped. Dare fumbled for his water bottle as he called softly to Chea.

The Chi came back to them quickly. "Louke is fainting; we must stop and bind up his wounds," he whispered.

Chea answered, "Aye, but quickly!" He had been afraid of this; Louke could not have gotten off so easily.

"Os, do you hear or see anything yet?" he called.

A disembodied answer floated back. "No, but down in this dark hole, I probably won't hear or see anything until they are right at the edge."

"Pursuit or no, we are all going to have a drink while Dare works on Louke." He heard fumbling for waterskins and then grateful sighs. "Dare, I cannot give you light; you must work by feel," Chea said, anguish in his voice.

"I understand. I'll work quickly," Dare said. Between them, Bar and Dare bound wounds they could only feel in Louke's sides. Dare was sure Louke needed more attention but not now. Louke guided them to his hurts in a weak voice and then drank deeply from the offered waterskin. In the almost total darkness, Dare did not trust himself to find the right leather pouches in his pack, so he did not give Louke any of the medicines he needed. *Later, when we have light … if there is a later.*

In spite of his decision, Chea had to force himself to wait the few minutes it took to bind Louke. His nerves were at the screaming point. All his senses told him they were in a trap and needed to run.

At Chea's command, they moved deeper into the ravine again. Louke gasped in pain when they raised him. Sweat was pouring down his face and body from the effort it took to stay on his feet. The stonecrafter promised himself he would remain conscious, but pain and weariness made him long to give in to the threatening darkness. Bar tripped over something and bumped Louke's throbbing side. Before he could stop the sound, Louke cried out. They both whispered "sorry" at the same time. Chea repressed a desire to rebuke them. *It is no use to scold. We are all exhausted and cannot see the hand in front of our face. Louke must be at the end of his rope.*

Tier called softly with whistles to guide his friends. Then behind them, Tier heard Os's owl hoot, which meant "enemy sighted." He felt panic. *We cannot see where we are going … or anything else. What can we do?* Strangely, thoughts of his father flashed through Tier's mind and steadied him. He spoke to the Maker for help, an idea, something!

Unexpectedly, a small shape, smelling strangely of moss and pond water, loomed in front of him. He almost cried out in his shock. Holding tightly to his shredding self-control, Tier signaled "halt" and then "unknown," which would thoroughly confuse his friends. *What is this little … this little person?*

A strange voice, hoarse and deep, said softly, "Do not fear, oh large, pur

44

sson. I will help." Words sounded strange in its mouth, as if they did not quite fit. It spoke slowly and with painstaking care.

"Who are you?" Tier asked shakily.

"I—I am of the O'Hatch. Do you kn-ow?"

"No, I do not." *Who or what are the O'Hatch?*

Tier heard tipeeke baying tumultuously and felt trapped. His heart began to pound. He signaled, "come."

Chea appeared beside him and said, "What is the pro—" but then he scented and saw the diminutive shape. It was perhaps the height of a seven-year-old child but much stockier. Chea gasped. *Enemies behind us and this, whatever it is, in front of us.* Out loud he said with exasperation, "What … who is it!"

Tier wondered at Chea's acceptance of the bizarre as commonplace. Were they so tired that they no longer cared? Had they seen so many strange things that one more did not surprise them? Tier answered with only a slight tremor in his voice, "It—he says he is an O'Hatch and wants to help us."

The small being listened with patience while they talked, but now he seemed agitated. "Mu-sst come quick. Down they co-me." He pointed with a stubby arm. "Ssee lights?"

They looked and did indeed see flickering torches that looked as if they were falling into the ravine. Chea whistled a shrill "come." When everyone arrived, they reacted to the O'Hatch with varying degrees of shock. Chea held up his hand to stop their questions and explained, "This being is an O'Hatch. I have no idea what that is, but he has offered to help us. I do not know if we are jumping out of the boiling pot and into the campfire, but I do know this: we must vote quickly, or it will be too late."

"We elected you our leader, Chea. You decide, and we will follow," Bar said urgently. The others agreed. Chea was grateful; they did not have time for discussion.

"We have no choice really. Lead on, great O'Hatch!" he whispered.

The being turned and said simply, "Fol-low." They stumbled after him as quietly as they could. He seemed confident and able to see in the darkness that to them was almost impenetrable. Screeching, frantic baying told them that the tipeeke had been lowered into the ravine and somehow persuaded to leave the dead bear alone. The horrible, cunning beasts had found their trail ... again!

The small company of fugitives swallowed cries of distress as they barked their shins on unseen rocks and were slapped in the face by tree branches. Brambles tore painfully at their clothes and skin. They turned their ankles in holes they could not see and fell repeatedly over logs and other obstacles. On and on, the O'Hatch led them for what seemed like hours. Breathing hard and trembling with exhaustion, they continued to hear pursuit behind them. If the enemy was not gaining on them, neither had the beasts and soldiers been left far behind. The darkness was growing lighter in the east. Sunrise was not far away.

The O'Hatch stopped suddenly and motioned them to come closer. They approached him cautiously; he glinted strangely in the growing light. "No-ow, we must enter water and ssw ... sswm ... You can do thiss?"

Chea answered, "Aye, we can all swim." Of course, he had no idea if they could all swim. He *hoped* they could.

As the O'Hatch unwound a rope that was coiled around his waist, he said emphatically, "Hold tight thiss rope where I ssay. Do *not* un-hold. I guide yous to a ssafe place on other sside wa-ter." Their tired minds struggled with his meaning. "All sswm down to big ho-le in rock, go through, and th-en up to ledge and air! Aye?" No one answered, but this did not stop the diminutive being.

Taking Chea's hand, he led him into a quiet pool that lay just at their feet. The scent of the moss and grasses surrounding the pool filled the air. They had not seen the still water until the O'Hatch had pointed it out.

However, we probably wouldn't notice a lake at this point. Chea's mind was full of questions, but it was too late to ask any of them. The O'Hatch placed each young man's right hand on the rope. They were spaced about six feet apart. Vaguely, they understood his plan, but they did not like it. "Hold with right and sswm with lef ... also kick fe-ets. Aye?" They nodded exhausted, dispirited agreement. The O'Hatch took a few steps into the shallow water and then silently sank out of sight beneath the surface. Evidently the pool had a small ledge, and then the bottom dropped off. The O'Hatch pulled the startled Chea, who was next in line, firmly after him. Chea spoke to the Maker sharply about the situations he got them into. Then the Chi struggled to control primeval panic that threatened to overwhelm him as the inky water closed over his head.

One after the other, they each entered the water with the soft rope gripped tightly in their right hand. Once underwater, they pulled down with their left hands and kicked their feet strongly. The O'Hatch was pulling them down toward a glowing green light. The light greatly encouraged them. The little being swam powerfully through an opening in what appeared to be a rough rock wall and then angled upward. The green light grew stronger and stronger as they followed. Once they went through the large hole, they could see a granite wall ahead and then wide carved steps that went up and up out of the water. It had taken all of Chea's resolution to maintain a firm grip on the rope, but now that he could see where they were headed, he was relieved. There was air and light just ahead. They surfaced in what was probably a very short time but seemed an age to him.

The hand that drew him to the surface was rock hard and seemed much like his own. Beyond that, he could tell little about their rescuer, except that he moved and breathed like a man, albeit a small one.

The O'Hatch stood on the bottom stair and quickly, hand over hand, pulled the others in with his rope. Chea turned and counted dark shapes as they popped out of the water. Gasps, coughs, choking noises, and expressions of thanks and amazement filled the air. Chea counted again quickly. There were only three! "Quiet!" he said forcefully. "Two of us are missing. Call out your names." Dare, Bar, and Louke answered him.

"Tier and Oster broke away and went back," Bar said, gasping.

The O'Hatch grabbed his rope and slipped beneath the surface. He returned a few minutes later with Os and Tier in tow. As Os and Tier climbed the stairs, the others greeted them with joy and relief. Evidently they were in a cave of some kind. Sounds echoed back to them from walls they could barely see.

Softly, the O'Hatch scolded Tier and Oster for letting go. He could not understand why they would do such a thing and was incensed. Their companions could understand, though, only too well! A voice behind them made the hishua jump. These folk made no sound at all when they moved.

"Do not ssco-old them, Wassh. They not of water and cannot ssee as we can in darkness. Nor do they know and trust you," a deep voice said gently enough, but Wassh's reply sounded mortified.

"You right, Ssash. I forget that they have been fro-ogss a loong time and do not re-member tadpoole wayss."

This logic made the hishua smile, in spite of everything uncomfortable they were feeling.

"They not like uss. They never really were tadpo-oless. Well, oonly for sshoort time," Ssash amended. Wassh asked if the "oothers" of his people had covered their trail, and Ssash assured him that they had.

Dare was feeling disoriented, as if he had stepped onto another planet. He finally said, "One of us is injured badly and needs help."

The O'Hatch were immediately concerned. "Coome, with friend, and foolow uss." Dare and Chea helped Louke get to his feet, no easy task, and carried him between them, up widely spaced stairs. The others followed in trepidation. There was no light of any kind here, and they had to be led.

Green light appeared somewhere ahead of them. As it grew brighter, they could hear low voices and laughter that inexplicably comforted them. It sounded so very normal in this very strange place. They stumbled into a cavern that was filled with a subdued greenish hue. Rich, intricate weavings covered the walls, and beings like Wassh turned to gaze at them. They, unlike Wassh, wore flowing fabrics in bright colors. The hishua and O'Hatch stared at one another with mutual curiosity and astonishment. The O'Hatch were shaped as men and women of the outer world, but there were important differences. None had hair, except for eyelashes, and their skin was palest cream. While their eyes were enormous, dark, and strangely luminous, their ears were small, flat, and slightly pointed. They were all about Wassh's height, around four feet tall. They were a handsome people but different ... very different. By the simple act of fainting, Louke ended their mutual inspection.

Two O'Hatch moved quickly to help and led the guests to a cave room where they could rest and care for their injured friend. Wassh followed them.

Quickly, Dare and Bar stripped Louke of his soggy clothing. He was pale and unresponsive. Chea asked Wassh for hot water, hot food, and dry blankets. Undismayed at this list, Wassh gave soft orders to some O'Hatch waiting in the corridor and then rejoined them. He was dismayed, however, when they unwound the awkward bandages and exposed Louke's injuries. There were wounds at his waist where the bear had pulled him to it with claws unsheathed. Louke woke suddenly; he was frightened and bewildered. It took them some minutes to calm him.

"Woould you like our—what you call …"

"Healer?" Dare supplied the word as he inspected his soggy pack.

"Aye, right woord," Wassh said with satisfaction.

Dare looked at Bar and pondered his answer. Bar shrugged and said, "We are something alike; perhaps he could help."

"Aye, Wassh, please send for him. We would appreciate his knowledge and aid," Dare replied politely with a formal bow. Wassh bowed also and left immediately.

Bar executed a neat bow that mocked his friend's courtly behavior and then grinned. Dare glared at him, but his mouth quivered before he pressed his lips firmly together.

Bar turned to Louke and asked him peevishly but with laughter in his eyes, "Do you have a thing about being clawed? Your body is beginning to look like a hide map. Children and women will scream with terror at the sight of you!" Louke glared at Bar. However, he kept silent. He was afraid to open his mouth for fear groans might escape and sound very unmanly.

Meanwhile, Chea, Tier, and Os began to dry their weapons and unpack all their soggy gear. By mutual agreement, they left the Gin'hana covered until they knew these people better. Water would not hurt the swords. Fatigue and hunger were affecting them all, and they became abrupt and short-tempered with each other.

"I will dry my own bow," Tier said as he jerked his precious possession out of Chea's foreign grasp. Chea knew a sudden, strong desire to leave the room … cave … whatever it was called and go find a place to be alone for a while. He realized with frustration that he didn't know where that place would be in this strange underground world. He took a deep breath and tried to calm down.

Tier said, "Sorry, Chea. That was rude. I don't know what is wrong with me."

"I do," Chea said with a frown. "Our world has been turned upside down.

As helpful as the O'Hatch have been, we want to know what happened last night and where everybody is."

Os shook his pack with frustration; its wet and swollen straps resisted his every effort to untie them. If it had not been for the presence of the O'Hatch in the hall, there would have been some heated shouting. All of them were tired, cold, and hungry. Now that they were no longer fleeing the enemy, the significance of the night's events weighed heavily on them. Who of the Glidden folk were left? Where were they? Would these strange people let them go? Go where? They had many more questions than answers.

A very shy O'Hatch brought them dry clothes and left quickly, before they could thank him. As Bar stripped out of his cold, wet clothing, he asked Oster what had happened to him and Tier at the pond. Oster said with a rueful grin, "The spirit was willing, but the flesh refused. I followed Tier underwater, but about halfway down, I panicked and broke for the surface. Tier followed me, thinking I was injured or something, but I … I was just terrified. I am not comfortable in the water at any time, and with the darkness …" He dropped his head in embarrassment.

It was quite an admission from a Basca'. Wishing he hadn't asked, Bar reached out a hand to grip Os's arm and said, "It was like diving in ink. I was afraid too."

Chea said grimly, "And I." The others agreed.

Looking at Bar, Oster said, disbelief plain on his face, "I have never seen you show fear—ever."

"I have it on good authority that princes are not allowed to be afraid," Bar said. He looked at Dare, who ignored him. "Nevertheless, I have been afraid, often. I was afraid to climb down into that gorge out there, just a few minutes ago. I could not see anything, much less where to put my feet so they would be on solid rock. I just knew that I was going to trigger full-blown queal and be a burden to everyone." He scowled at the thought and then continued, "I think different things frighten different people. I know many warriors who are afraid of … spiders or snakes, for example. They would never admit it, of course, but they are." The others grinned in spite of their gloom. They had a conversation concerning private and, until now, never-mentioned fears that would have been very interesting to their enemies.

Fortunately, no one was listening, except a delighted O'Hatch, who thought this sharing of hidden fears extremely entertaining. He had much trouble keeping his mirth to himself. *It is very important to stay quiet,* he reminded himself. His hiding place did need to remain secret, after all. *To be afraid of swimming in dark waters, of little insects … how foolish!* He chuckled softly.

The O'Hatch were incurable eavesdroppers. They had secretly listened to others' conversations for so many years that they no longer had any compunction about it. They never listened to other O'Hatch—well, hardly ever—but they listened to the rest of the races whenever and wherever they found opportunity.

The O'Hatch were few in numbers. Once, they had been a numerous people, but that had been long ago. Unlike the Chi, they did not have a sophisticated system of trails, hiding places, and spies aboveground as well as tunnels and caves underground in the mountains. However, they traveled the prolific underground rivers and springs of the Bitterroots with ease. Because the Glidden folk had chosen a retreat so close to them, they had listened often to conversations within the mountain. There was little they did not know about Glidden's, and therefore Ree's, affairs.

QUIET REFUGE

WASSH WALKED IN WITH AN OBVIOUSLY reluctant healer in tow. The five uninjured young men rose to greet him and dropped their heads respectfully. Gripping his brown fiber bag tightly, the healer looked them over. Irritability and suspicion were written plainly on his wrinkled face. He was smaller than Wassh, and his posture was bent and his head bowed, giving him a furtive look. His nose was shaped like a bulb, and his eyes squinted. In the hoarse O'Hatch language he spoke to Wassh with palpable animosity. At the sound of his voice, the hishua lifted their heads, though this was not formally correct.

"Tatis knowss little about yous diss-tin-guissh racess," Wassh translated, rolling his eyes. This was probably not exactly what the little healer had said. Looking at Dare and Louke, Wassh explained, "He not happy to give medciness that may harm not help, but he examine and give O'Hatch healing herbss and ssal-vess, if you want." They were truly impressed with Wassh's remarkable grasp of their language.

Dare replied diplomatically, "Many of my medicines were destroyed by the water. I would greatly appreciate your help and any herbs or salves you can give us."

Louke groaned and whispered, "Heaven help me," as he closed his eyes in genuine distress. Hiding a smile, Dare motioned the O'Hatch to the other side of his injured friend. The grumpy little man bent down to inspect the wounds, interested in spite of his crankiness. He muttered to himself in his language, which was full of the s sound. Wassh translated Tatis's quick comments and questions.

"Aye," Dare replied, "they have been cleaned, and I have given him something for pain."

"But he iss sstill wake!" Wassh translated in shock.

As it turned out, Louke did not have to endure two healers closing his wounds. The O'Hatch gave him something that quickly put him to sleep. Through their interpreter, Dare and Tatis had a lengthy discussion of herbs and treatments. The O'Hatch healer was a little testy, but Dare was so deeply interested in his knowledge that he did not mind.

The others smiled at the two healers: one large and blond, the other small and bald. They were deeply engrossed in conversation over the body of their unconscious patient. Cantankerous Tatis might be, but he was also generous. Dare's medicine packs were soon filled with many new substances, including a wonderful green salve that could be used to cover and protect an injury.

After baths and food, the hishua slept but restlessly. They could not quite forget their anxieties, and they were unused to hard mats on a rock floor. However, they rose the next morning rested and in a much better frame of mind.

Over the next two days, they learned much from the O'Hatch. These small, sturdy people were entranced by water; they needed it and were never far from it. They harvested the plants that grew in and around pools, streams, and springs for food and for the fiber they used to make mats, beautiful wall hangings, and clothing. Both male and female O'Hatch were explorers of subterranean rivers, lakes, springs, and pools. Their large chest cavities evidently held powerful lungs, for they could hold their breath three times as long as any of the six hishua. They swam with ease, and only the coldest waters discouraged their exploration. They liked to try the different flavors and colors of certain pools and streams, whether aboveground or belowground. The six tasted water that was flavored with this or that mineral from the rock it passed through. To their surprise, they found the different waters strange but good.

In caverns and hidden valleys, the O'Hatch lovingly constructed delicate waterfalls and fountains. In their homes, one was never far from the sound, smell, or sight of flowing, spraying, or splashing water.

When a woman conceived, it was cause for great rejoicing because the O'Hatch had few children. Their numbers had dropped drastically in the last hundred years. Women gave birth with their bodies immersed in special pools of warm water where the heat comforted and eased their labor. Fresh water flowed into the pools continually and drained out the other side. Their little ones were eased into the world submerged. After they had taken their first breath of air, just as any overland child would, they were placed in their mother's arms and stayed in the water with her until they were ready to nurse for the first time. No O'Hatch child could remember a time when he or she couldn't swim. Children were shared with the whole community because there were so few of them. No parent would have dreamed of keeping a child all to himself or herself. Consequently, their offspring considered the whole population their family and grew up bathed in attention.

The green light in the caverns came from a mossy plant the O'Hatch nurtured and grew wherever light was wanted. They simply planted their lamps. To the hishua's surprise, the O'Hatch did roam aboveground often, but they did not stay away from their precious waters or temperate caverns for prolonged periods. The sun did not particularly bother them as long as they were not in it too long. The Bitterroots had been so isolated from the world of men and there were so few of this small people that no whisper of them had reached civilization. The young men could not help but wonder what else these mountains might hold that had never been discovered by the people of Ree.

The O'Hatch had agreed to seek out other Glidden folk for the six hishua. Without any explanation, they understood who was friend and who was foe, which seemed strange to the fugitives. How did these people know so much about everyone, hidden away as they were in their pools and caverns? In fact, how did Wassh and a few of the others know their language? Whenever the young men asked these questions and others like them, the O'Hatch smiled and changed the subject.

Fortunately for the hishua, Glidden's fugitives sought retreats from their enemy that were well protected and near water. This made it easy for the O'Hatch to find them, for those were just the kinds of places they liked.

———◦◦◦———

The summer day was filled with bright sunshine, gentle warmth, and the songs of birds. The pines bent in a light breeze that spread their pungent scent over the mountainside. There was no sound, other than those made by nature, to break the sweet peace that filled Lock and his friends' high and rocky camp. Yet Lock was consumed by anxiety as he stared into a pool that a small waterfall had created. As he sat near the shore deep in thought, he tossed pebbles into the water and watched them sink out of sight. Gradually, he became aware of being watched. Searching the shore and surrounding rocky ground, he could detect nothing unusual with his sharp eyes. His glance passed over the waterfall and then quickly returned to it. A pale face, partially hidden by the water, stared at him! Large, dark eyes watched him cautiously, ready to dart away if he should yell or attack. Lock controlled the startled jump of his nerves and asked quietly, "Who are you, and what do you want?"

Wassh knew who Lock was from his days of spying in the hidden waters of Glidden, yet suddenly, he was afraid to approach him. It was not because he feared the man himself. He knew Lock was an astute, capable leader, as well as a kind one. Now that the moment had come, he realized with sudden clarity that, for his people's sake, he wanted no commerce with these men. If the O'Hatch came to know the overlanders, they would become entangled in their struggles. That made him afraid. No, it was a stronger feeling than fear—terror was closer to the truth. He had heard them speak of Blackrobes, soldiers, Choack, demons, watchers, and tipeeke. What could his simple people, so few in number, do against such strength? Till the moment came to speak, he had not fully realized their danger. He quickly slipped under the water and fled back to his home. His mind was so preoccupied with conflicting thoughts that he took a wrong turn underground and had to retrace his steps—an unheard-of mistake for an O'Hatch seeker to make. He flushed with embarrassment to think he had been so careless.

Back at the pool, Lock found himself doubting he had ever seen the pale face with large eyes and no hair. He wondered if his troubles were affecting his sanity. There were plenty of those. He sighed and reviewed again the events since that awful night.

The attack Glidden's enemies had launched against Lock's people had been separated and then crushed by the vast ruggedness of the Bitterroots. Deep gullies, high cliffs, dense stands of ancient trees, boulder-choked passes, and large, aggressive animals had all conspired against an organized, thorough search. After a few hours, tipeeke, hounds, and men were exhausted and footsore. The royal forces climbed steep, broken slopes, then inched down hillsides choked with towering trees and bushes that might hide bears or mountain cats. They often found they had to climb with the aid of ropes, which was painstaking work and slowed them. Frequently, they were buried in shale slides up to their hips. Swift ice-melt streams were flowing everywhere in the early summer warmth, and they were forced to cross them very carefully or slip and receive a cold dunking.

There was no level land, no place to camp free of rock or choking vegetation. There were no paths, much less lanes or roads. There was only strenuous up and stressful down. Boots were gashed; tender paws were cut and swollen. Uniforms were ripped, ropes frayed or broke, and supplies were lost, dropped, or smashed. Men and animals were continually separated and then lost from one another. Finally, a dispirited and fuming army limped out of the Bitterroots. They were smaller in number than when they entered, yet their enemy had not shot one arrow or launched one rock at them. In fact, after the first glorious day, they had not captured or even seen any people of Glidden. What the Glidden folk had been unable to do for themselves, the Bitterroots had done for them, very effectively.

Lock and his temporary council of Lavel, Devon, Shonar, and Tal qua had begun to make forays into the wilderness to seek others. They'd organized their group to maintain a continuous watch from two high places. The acting sentry would warn their small band if Tori, Lotu, or any soldier tried to enter the Bitterroots again. Camp life had fallen into an orderly pattern as members of their group volunteered to cook, hunt, gather, and clean. Yet there was so much more that needed doing. Lock knew that on a dark night soldiers could slip into their new territory without being seen.

They needed scouts on the ground nearer Glidden, as well as in the high places.

Also, as much as the Bitterroots had confounded their enemies, it now obstructed them. All their efforts to find fellow refugees had met with dismal failure. But what most concerned Lock was not knowing whether Bardon and Dare, as well as their companions, had been captured or injured or were in hiding. Lock threw a last rock into the clear water and returned to camp feeling burdened.

"I find Lock and other coopanionss," Wassh told Bar proudly. His large, dark eyes were shining in his round, animated face. The O'Hatch had allowed six of their best young seekers to attempt to find the Daross, which in their language meant "people above." The hishua were delighted.

"Can you lead us to them, Wassh?" Bar asked.

"Aye, I can lead you, but for yur ssakess I musst go over-land, for you not sswm and climb underground as I do. My path iss clossed to you. Yet Daross musst not ssee me, for the peoples decide againsst it." For a moment, Wassh felt intensely guilty. He was one of those who had encouraged, if not forced, this decision. "Wes go at night, and yous musst let me sslip in pool near frenss' camp and flee before yous call thems. Dos undrsstan?" he asked.

"We understand, Wassh, but we … we do not want to lose your friendship. Will your people let you come visit with us, at night when no one can see?" Bar asked.

"Oh, aye," he replied. "Six sseekerss may see yous six, for thiss way we help you find yur others. I not think you will find them without our help. Frenss very sscattered, and Yadot—Bitter-rootss, as you call it—is terrble maze—aye?" The hishua were amazed at Wassh's rapidly improving ability to speak their language.

Quickly, they packed their gear and prepared to leave Wassh's underground home. They had become attached to his people and, for a time, had envied their quiet, peaceful life. The O'Hatch hunted, they fished, and they sought new and unusual waters. They lived in harmony with their surroundings. Their caverns bloomed with green light, beautiful fiber weavings, and melodious waterfalls. It was a good life for these gentle, artistic folk, but the hishua were anxious to find their friends and discover what had happened that terrible night and since. Who was left? What were they going to do now? As night approached, they grew anxious to leave.

Wassh had a companion with him this time, a youth named Achos. When it was dark but the Creator's lamp had not yet been hung in the night sky, as the O'Hatch put it, Wassh and Achos led them through a labyrinth of steep ravines and boulder-choked valleys and up many steep cliffs to a place near a noisy waterfall that had created a large pool. The water must have drained away underground, for there was no visible outlet to the pond. Achos pointed to a ledge higher on the cliff. "Yur peoples there. We musst return. Fare you well." They both bowed, and before the young men could thank them for all they had done, Wassh and Achos slipped into the water and disappeared.

It was, perhaps, a good thing that they left so quickly. On their way up the hill, large, menacing men armed with bows surrounded the hishua.

"Do not harm us," Bar said quickly. "We are Glidden folk!"

"We'll have a look at your faces before we believe that, we will," a gruff but not unfriendly voice answered.

"Lock, we has guests, we does," the man holding Dare by the arm called out as he approached the fire.

When Lock saw whom his conscientious guards had brought him, he closed his eyes for a few seconds as a great weight slipped from his heart. He exclaimed softly, "Maker be thanked!"

The hishua grinned at their mentors, whose faces mirrored happiness and also enormous relief. There was a hush while the others waited respectfully as Lock greeted each one with a quick word, an arm shake, and an embrace. To the hishua's amazement, his eyes were suspiciously wet. Then everyone surrounded them, all talking and laughing at once. There was joyful chaos for a time as the Glidden folk made the Pack welcome. But soon the need to know what had happened caused them to quiet. They sat around the fire to talk. It was late before each group had shared their experiences.

"We need your little friends' help badly," Lock said thoughtfully after a period of quiet. "They are quite correct in thinking that without them we are not likely to find other Glidden folk who may be hidden in the Bitterroots.

We organized havens in other places, like the forests near our mountain, but the attack was so unexpected! They broke through with such speed that many of our people probably did not have time to get to those places, as we did not. We simply fled with all the speed we could muster into the closest hiding place … the Bitterroots." He thought for a few minutes and then asked intently, "Did you arrange to meet with them again soon?"

"No, sir, we did not; they left too quickly. I think we must wait patiently until they contact us. They are not a warrior people. I think they are very frightened by what we represent. Yet I am confident Wassh will keep his word and help us, just in his own way," Bar said. Lock, he knew, liked to have everything tied down. Bar understood Lock's temperament well by now and was aware of how much this lack of a definite meeting time and place would irritate him. He was quite right.

Lock's eyes narrowed, but to Bar's surprise, the expected rebuke did not come. Lock suppressed his exasperation and said simply, "Let us rest. The Maker is good, and tomorrow is a new day."

They went gratefully to their hammocks. It was good to sleep in a hammock again and not on the O'Hatch's hard mats. They fell asleep under blazing stars, more at peace than they had been in many days. Yet Bar felt the bonds of tsurtne gently reassert themselves, and he sighed. The others to a lesser degree felt the same thing; they were under authority once more. In some ways it was a real relief.

A Meeting

Through the warm months of summer, the six O'Hatch seekers, under the direction of their elders, brought the scattered people of Glidden together, in awareness if not in reality. For safety's sake, many of the groups remained where they were and appointed runners to keep communication open between themselves and the various bands. Some of the bands were moved to safer locations deeper in the Bitterroots and nearer to the council. There was no location the council had yet found that would comfortably accommodate all their numbers. Lock and his council's respect for the O'Hatch minds that guided them steadily increased. The O'Hatch were slow and deliberate, but everything fell into place just as planned.

Though the O'Hatch elders would not allow anyone to enter their caverns again, not even the six young men they had rescued, they did agree to meet with the council. No member of the Glidden community, except the hishua and the council, had ever seen the seekers, and they would certainly not be allowed to view the O'Hatch elders. The meeting was arranged with care for a dark night in the second month of growing season.

Excitement grew among the council members and young men as the time approached. Finally six hishua, six seekers, five members of the council, and four diminutive elders were seated near the waterfall pool. They sat around a low fire. The cranky Tatis was among them. It was a magnificent night. Stars burned in the clear sky overhead, and the air was warm and fragrant with the scent of flowers. As night birds sang in the towering trees, the waterfall played its soft music behind the diverse group.

Dare marveled at the elders who were so ... well, old. How could these frail, bent, thin little men lead the O'Hatch? The seekers helped them out of the water, half carried them to the fire, and eased them to the ground to sit on woven mats. However old they might be, the elders' eyes were bright and alert. Soon, Dare came to suspect that they understood, some part at least, of the language he and the Glidden people spoke. Wassh interpreted carefully, but sometimes the elders seemed to be well aware of what was being said before Wassh spoke the words in O'Hatch. Dare hoped everyone was being cautious about any whispered comments.

After the formality of introductions, the council expressed their gratitude for all the O'Hatch had done, first to aid the Pack and then to find the scattered people of Glidden. The elders accepted Lock's thanks graciously and began to ask questions of their own. Their questions suggested an intimate understanding of Glidden and the rest of Ree as well, which surprised and then deeply troubled Lock. When asked how they'd come by their vast knowledge, they refused to answer, but amusement glinted in their large eyes.

The O'Hatch's information, of course, came from the Glidden folk themselves. They had spied on Glidden for years. They knew nothing of Ree that they had not learned from Lock's own intelligence network. The O'Hatch traveled underground by way of rivers, caverns, springs, and pools, just as overlanders used roads, but they went no farther than Glidden. The fugitive stronghold was their closest and only neighbor. They listened at Glidden's washing and bathing pools and at the cold springs used for drinking and cooking water. They traversed tunnels and ledges to overhear conversations, below or above them, of the most secret nature. No one had ever suspected or seen what could not possibly be there. No wonder Lock's question amused them!

What would really have interested Glidden's stern leader was the fact that the seekers were still at it. They knew that Tori and Lotu had stayed for a while in Glidden, searching its nooks and crannies for information. A troop of Blackrobes, soldiers, and tipeeke were secreted there now, in case any of the mountain's residents returned. Royal soldiers guarded the

Glidden captives who were being treated fairly well. Captain Tori had warned the soldiers that these prisoners were important to the King and not to be harmed. The curious little people had already gathered much interesting information.

Tori and Lotu had been ordered to return to King Bardock and his councillors, to report on their "absurd failures to capture uneducated rebels and peasants." This particular choice of words had an ominous sound. They rode the king's highway back to Feisan with an apprehension that bordered on terror. Their sovereign did not understand or excuse failure. That the prince and his party had slipped through their fingers again was a source of continuous outrage to both soldier and prelate. They had been so close to victory! It was inconceivable, preposterous really, that this simple group of children and rustics had escaped yet another well-laid trap.

With Tori and Lotu traveled a new addition to their group, a man who had proved to be extremely useful and would be even more so—they hoped. *Perhaps*, Tori thought optimistically, *the king will vent his violent fury on the Glidden betrayer and be less vengeful with us, his faithful, loyal subjects.* Tori trembled, and his stomach cramped at the thought of what his powerful sovereign was capable of doing to those who failed him—loyal subjects or no. "Gods of Ree! May Bardock be pleased with our gift of the traitor," Tori entreated softly.

Sudden, unexpected pain blinded him, and he grabbed for his throbbing head with a sharp cry. *Boer's bow! How careless of me.* Perspiration beaded his forehead as he pleaded, "Forgive me, Master." He cursed his stupidity and the envious god's spitefulness equally. Choack was treacherous and wicked; one never knew when he or one of his servants was listening, but it was usually when you least wished it. Yet Choack had power, undeniable power, and Tori hungered for that power. He resolved to watch his comments more carefully in the future.

Lock found himself in an awkward situation. He very much wanted to know how the O'Hatch had come by their very accurate knowledge of

Glidden and Ree. The elders had told him that the O'Hatch were few and lived only in this isolated, difficult section of the Bitterroot Range. If this were true, how had they gathered their information? What little the hishua had been able to tell Lock of their short visit belowground had given him a fairly accurate hypothesis. *Glidden is their only available source, unless they lie.* Lock brought his mind back to the conversation.

One of the O'Hatch elders was warning the Glidden folk not to return to their mountain refuge, because a detachment of Blackrobes, soldiers, and tipeeke were secreted there waiting to capture them. He also told them that there were over a hundred Glidden prisioners being held in the largest cavern. They were being treated well but continually guarded. It would not be easy to free them.

Lock made a quick decision to test his conclusion that the O'Hatch spied on Glidden. "Will you continue to watch this group within Glidden and learn all you can about them—names, passwords, codes, and anything else that might help us? It is in my mind to defeat the soldiers holding our people imprisoned in Glidden and to bring our folk to camps in the Bitterroots. I think it is time we went on the offensive, instead of waiting like rabbits to be pulled out of our holes," Lock said quickly. Surprise widened the O'Hatch's large eyes but only for a moment.

Yevnoc laughed softly, causing his pale skin to break into a thousand wrinkles and his austere expression to soften, but he did not respond to Lock's question immediately. This ancient was emerging as the elders' leader, or at least their spokesperson. In Ree's own language, he disclosed dryly, "We know place deep in Yadot that large enough to hold yur peoples in comfort. There, yur peoples not sscattered as now. Yous interesst this?"

"A-aye," Lock stammered in amazement. *What will this tiny person say next? And in our language, which he obviously speaks as well as understands.*

"We sshow it yous to-morrow if wissh. Once there, no more con-tact with O'Hatch—clear?" he inquired politely but firmly.

Lock was thunderstruck. They were being courteously offered a new home, which would get them off the water people's hands, but refused friendship or collaboration. Lock stared long into those dark eyes. He did not like it—they needed these people. But he answered, "Clear."

"King'ss men, thiss once we watch," Yevnoc said grudgingly. "Wassh and the other seekers were not happy, but they remained silent. "Tatis hass requesst. Come, yur healer, to sshare his sskill for time? We learn from Dare?"

In this request, Lock saw hope for the future. He asked Dare politely if this would appeal to him. Dare realized what his answer had better be and responded appropriately. It would have been interesting to refuse, just to see Lock's reaction ... explosion more like! With deference, Dare explained that Shonar was more skilled than he and would, perhaps, be a better choice. Yevnoc included Shonar in the invitation. Lock strove to hide his delight.

Yevnoc gazed at Lock for long minutes. The silence around the small fire was growing uncomfortable. Almost against his will, Yevnoc asked intently, "Would yous al-low me to ex-amine the two marked child-ren?" His people stared at him in shock. This was evidently not part of their original plan. The O'Hatch had never, in any way, mentioned Dare's and Bar's markings up till this moment. Did they know of the prophecy? From what the young men had been able to discover while with the O'Hatch, the water people believed their ancestors had long ago known, *personally* known, the Creator. However, the Maker who had walked, talked with, and taught the old ones was unknown to them. These people evidently predated the first five tribes by hundreds of years!

Lock saw another way to tie the O'Hatch to those of Glidden, and the door of his hope opened a little wider, but his face showed nothing of his inner feelings. "That is their decision to make," he said gravely.

"We did not assk when theys were with uss. It wr-ong to do thiss without their elderss' per-mission. Yous not know O'Hatch well yet. I promisse before Cre-ator that I will not harm thems," Yevnoc assured Lock.

Suddenly Lock suspected that "examine" had a different meaning to these folk than it did to him. "What do you mean when you say 'examine'?" he asked sharply.

Yevnoc spoke quickly in his own language to Wassh, who then tried to explain. "Yevnoc hass sspecial gift, given to one elder at time. He tell much about persson by touch thems, not factss al-wayss, but atti-tudess and fee-lingss. For ex-ample, he know immediate if ssomeone he touch lie, not loyal, or angry. Iss hard ex-plain be-cause I do not unders-stand very well. When he ssay 'ex-amine,' he meanss assk quesstionss while he touch-ing. Then he know if answerss true and much more besidess," Wassh disclosed candidly. Hishua and Glidden folk digested this in shocked silence.

Lock was unsure of his answer. *What if that is not all of the truth? What if he can exert control over their minds or implant ideas as well? It is hard to believe Yevnoc or his people could do anything so reprehensible, but it is naive not to consider it.*

Bar took the situation out of Lock's hands, not impulsively, but with sure confidence. "I will allow you to examine me on one condition," he said simply.

His friends moved uncomfortably, and Lock almost spoke but changed his mind and remained silent, his eyes hooded.

"Con-dition iss?" Yevnoc asked quickly, before one of Bar's elders could object.

Bar answered with all the dignity he was capable of but rarely displayed, "I ask that Wassh be allowed to stay with us as long as he wishes but for at least two years. He has become a friend. We trust him, and we need his help, his knowledge."

The Glidden folk gasped at this bold move. Two years! The O'Hatch stared in shock after Wassh's stuttering translation. They broke into sibilant conversation that was plain to understand, even though the people of Glidden did not speak O'Hatch. They thought this was the worst, most terrible idea they had ever heard!

Yevnoc ignored them as he stared at Bar. He then turned to Wassh and asked a soft question. Wassh's answer was prompt, hopeful, and affirmative. "Agree, Wassh and I," the elder said simply.

His folk were stunned and began to remonstrate with him. He spoke one sharp word of rebuke that silenced them immediately, though they were clearly dismayed and unhappy. Lock thought, *So he is their leader, not just their spokesperson.*

Bar looked at Lock, who nodded permission, and rose. The marked prince sat on the ground in front of Yevnoc. Bar realized he had taken the situation into his own hands. Seeking Lock's permission was only a courtesy, and they both knew it. Tsurtne aside, E Clue had given Bar alone the words of instruction: "and a water seeker—that makes ten." He had not forgotten the words, and he must follow their cues. At the time, he had not known what a water seeker was or who it might be; now he knew both.

The fire's bright warmth was at his back. His own body shadowed Yevnoc's face from the fire's flickering glow. Even with Bar sitting, the old O'Hatch had to rise to his knees to reach Bar's face. Yevnoc's dark eyes swallowed Bar as he touched, with a gentle hand, the hishua's face. He put his right thumb on Bar's brow bone where it sloped to become the bridge of his nose; his other fingers lightly pressed Bar's forehead. Bar swallowed heavily. *It begins. How many times ... have I answered these questions ... these same questions?*

He felt no sensation. He could hear Wassh translating quietly for his people and for the Glidden folk also as he and Yevnoc spoke. Most of the time, Yevnoc was able to make his questions clear with little help from his interpreter. Three times Bar felt the O'Hatch elder respond with emotion to his answers, and at those moments, he glimpsed some of Yevnoc's feelings. Evidently this door opened both ways, but Bar did not push against it; he only glanced when the other was not guarded enough.

Bar learned that E Clue and his instructions awed Yevnoc. The O'Hatch elder was stunned that the instructions mentioned a water seeker. The prophecy itself evoked no reaction, though—it must be one of the things he already knew. He recognized Choack's evil and was terribly frightened that foolish, weak men would treat with him. This reaction came in response to Oster's experience at the Mirg Rorroh.

Finally, Yevnoc was finished. Overwhelmed, the elder sat back on his heels. *Much we learn from listening, but not ... not this!* he thought fearfully. He wanted to take his people and run, but where? Surely there was no more hidden place on the island than Yadot. Soon the King and those who served him would seek this child, marked by his Maker, and no one who helped him would be safe—*anywhere.* Yevnoc pulled his thoughts together and met Bar's dignified, questioning gaze. The young one had endured his scrutiny, his searching, calmly. He had even refrained from returning it, which Yevnoc sensed he could easily have done. The old O'Hatch touched his heart lightly and inclined his head to Bar in thanks and respect for that restraint. Suddenly tired, Bar bowed also and rose to return to his place.

Yevnoc spoke solemnly through Wassh. "The O'Hatch not know

Maker; we know only Creator. No king we acknowledge, for wes ssep-arate; wes not of yur world. But now I know what I not be-fore, and I glad, very fear but glad. Wes remain ssep-arate be-cause that iss who wes are, but wes too fight Dess-troyer, as wes are able, for if he comess to power, sspare us, he will not."

Turning his austere gaze to Bar, Yevnoc paused and then said in a clear voice, "I honors yous, child, and offers you fidelity, if yous accept it from sso ssmall and humble a peoples as wes." Then Yevnoc bowed his small head to the earth.

His people and Glidden's as well were stunned, but none was so astonished as the prince himself. He had met with much negative response: disappointment from Meggatirra, distrust from Glidden's council, and dismay that one so unworthy as he should be marked from Morin and Amray. Sincere, immediate acceptance surprised and touched him deeply.

Yet he knew it was time. The new confidence that had been growing in him was small but rock solid. He answered, "I am grateful for the honor you do me and gladly accept your fidelity. The O'Hatch have amazed us with their knowledge of the land and waters under the mountains and also with the beauty they create. I am young, Yevnoc. Teach me what you know. My time to rule is a long way off, I think, and a terrible battle may come first. We welcome your assistance."

Yevnoc nodded understanding and acceptance, but his exhaustion, which was apparent, kept him from further speech.

Lock was amazed by this turn of events. Never would he have predicted such an outcome to this meeting. Though the Glidden folk invited Yevnoc and his party to spend the rest of the night with them, he politely refused. The elder told Dare that his turn to be examined would have to wait until he was more rested, perhaps when Dare visited them. Dare agreed to this with unspoken gratitude. The O'Hatch silently disappeared into the water of the pond. Surely Yevnoc, and some of the others as well, were so tired that they would have to be carried the whole way.

Before Wassh left, he told them quickly that their betrayer, along with Tori and Lotu, had left Glidden and that the king's men had been overheard talking about taking the southern road to Feisan.

"Who is the traitor?" Lock asked.

Wassh's beautiful eyes were sad. "Verona," he whispered.

"No!" Lock cried in disbelief.

"I ss-aw him, Lord, with my own eyess," Wassh said firmly and slipped into the water.

Lock looked as if their small friend had struck him. "Verona!"

For long moments he felt nothing but the numbness of shock. It was the last name he had expected to hear. In flashes of memory, he saw himself and Verona as boys growing up together. The numbness melted, and he felt the stabbing pain of betrayal.

My oldest friend! This one man, a member of my own council, has betrayed hundreds of innocent people. He is not a terrified peasant or merchant, not a simple shepherd or coerced fisherman, but a trained soldier! He is a member of one of Ree's oldest families. He has been taught loyalty, honor, and integrity from birth. Why? Why?

This unexpected blow was almost as devastating a loss as that of Glidden.

Then another blow struck. *There is nothing about the underground, about Glidden, that Verona does not know. Nothing!*

Lock had to make sure his oldest friend never reached Feisan, no matter the cost.

THE SPARK

OW COULD A MEMBER OF THE INNER *council—one of my oldest friends—betray us? Did they threaten him or coerce him, capture or buy him?* Lock wondered. He was too grieved, too furious, to speak. His heart ached with painful intensity.

The Glidden council, a blend of old and new members, and the hishua stood around Lock, aghast. Verona! Shonar spoke quietly in the stunned silence. "This night has held much excitement and now, terrible sorrow, for all of us. Let us go to our hammocks. Tomorrow, before the O'Hatch come, we will meet and discuss Verona. Now, I suggest we rest." Lock agreed numbly, and they all went to their hammocks.

"Bar, wait! Come back for a moment," Lock ordered. Clenching his fists, he forced himself to focus on Bardon and the amazing meeting with the O'Hatch. This new problem—*What an inadequate word*, Lock thought— would have to wait. Uneasily, Bar returned to his liege's side. He had been afraid he would not get off so easily. Shonar bowed and left them. Before he went, he squeezed his son's arm in sympathy, and their gazes touched in shared pain. Verona had been like one of Shonar's own sons.

The moon was rising, and a warm summer breeze began to sing in the trees. At the time, Bar had been certain of what needed doing, confident even. Now he was not so sure.

Lock sat down again by the dying fire and spoke calmly. "Join me. I know you are tired, and I am also, but I must know more about what happened to you tonight. I am not sure what tomorrow will bring, but at the least, there will be very little free time." Shutting his eyes, he rubbed his temples with his fingers. Bar sat next to him. Lock looked burdened and troubled yet very much in control again. Bar realized that the weight of what he carried was almost crushing him.

"What did Yevnoc learn from you?" Lock asked after a moment.

This was not what Bar had expected him to say, but he answered after a second's hesitation, "Everything he wanted to know and more. Wassh perhaps understated his gift. It is possible Wassh does not really know the extent of it. I felt strong emotion from Yevnoc three times but small surges all along. He observed—perhaps *sensed* is a better word—my feelings concerning what I did say and even emotions concerning things I did not talk about directly. I could feel his compassion, anger, or whatever emotion my answer evoked in him." Bar frowned, looked away a moment, and then said candidly, "Sir, the man knows how I feel about everyone and everything we touched on. He may not know the exact facts, but I am sure he has a good idea of what my entire life has been. I could have examined him also—I realized that after only a few minutes—but I refrained. Yet the glimpses I had were of a quick mind filled with a growing fear of the O'Hatch's association with us. He is ancient, his age far beyond what our normal life span would be. He found it impossible to believe that people would willingly associate with Choack and was horrified that the evil spirit's power has grown and reached as far as Glidden. He was delighted with E Clue and astonished that he knew of 'water seekers.' Overall, he was terribly disturbed. More quickly than anyone else we have encountered, he recognized the danger Dare and I represent, yet ..." He hesitated, then said in wonder, "He committed not only himself but also his people to help us ... immediately." He shook his head in disbelief. "It is hard to comprehend."

"Indeed," Lock said absently as he analyzed Bar's experience.

After a few minutes of silence, he smiled faintly; it made years fall away from his face and filled his eyes with warmth. "Now tell me, my prince, how you came to act like one tonight. All that you did was well done." At Bar's shocked expression, he said, "You thought I would be angry because you did not seek my permission to negotiate with Yevnoc ... because you are tsurtne?"

Bar answered with an emphatic "Aye."

"E Clue's instructions come first; they must."

Shocked by praise and approval—twice in one night!—when he expected a lecture at the least and more probably a reproof, Bar found Lock's question difficult to answer. He took a few minutes to think about it. *Why was I so certain that I knew what to do? As for acting like a prince ...* He shrugged his shoulders and said seriously, "My instructions spoke of a water seeker. We need the O'Hatch's help. I trust Wassh. He and I have spent much time together in the last few weeks, and Wassh thinks Yevnoc hung the moon. It seemed no great risk, and we had much to gain."

Lock nodded approval but said, "I think that is not all."

Bar sighed. *True, and there is no escaping giving the man an answer.*

One eyebrow lifted over Lock's dark, thoughtful eyes, and he waited.

Bar admitted cautiously, "When it comes to E Clue's instructions, I am responsible. I know the rest of you will help me, as Shonar did when I was trying to decide about tsurtne, but in the end it is up to me. That idea has grown inside me and changed me a little, I think."

"I think so too, and I'm glad," Lock said simply and got up. He stretched. "Great Gant, I'm tired!"

As they walked back to camp, Lock asked, "Wassh is a water seeker, but how can you be sure he is the one?"

"Basically, because he really wants to join us and he is the only seeker, the only O'Hatch, who does. He and I had spoken about him coming with us, but he was sure his people would never allow him to leave. He told me he was very shocked tonight and very pleased when Yevnoc gave his approval."

Weary and exhausted, Bar and Lock both went to their hammocks. Much to both men's surprise, they slept soundly.

They rose early the next morning to sit around the council fire with their comrades. While sipping bowls of hot tea, they discussed Verona. Slowly, the council came to the only possible conclusion. Their fugitive band would need O'Hatch advice first and then their aid.

When the seekers came, Lock asked them to delay the arranged trip to survey a new location for the Glidden folk. Then he explained what they needed. The seekers returned to their home for permission from the elders and for supplies, and two returned, Wassh and Lassh. The two O'Hatch would be their guides, and afterward, Lassh would carry a message back to Rednu, the O'Hatch community.

From the O'Hatch, they'd learned that Tori and Lotu, along with Verona, had left Glidden the day before the council meeting and were traveling the king's highway south to Feisan. Lock, Wassh, and the council formulated a plan. Wassh would lead their party through a pass in the mountains that would cut off many leagues that Captain Tori and his troop would have to travel on the royal road. The royal highway stayed close to the sea, where the land was much more level; however, it was a much longer road than the shortcut through the mountains. Once through the pass, Lavel could lead his warriors to the royal highway, hopefully before the king's men got there. If the plan worked, Tori and Lotu, along with their spy, would ride into an ambush.

Lavel predicted it would take the king's men at least seven or eight days to get to the spot he had in mind. He remembered well how Tori liked to travel: good camps, secure tents, and hearty meals. However, if their enemy really pushed and did not stop at Rave or in any city, they could possibly get to the designated spot in six days.

After the planning was complete, Lock faced his most difficult task. He sought the Maker's wisdom as he gazed at the ardent faces around their council fire. Hardening his resolve and his heart, he put on his sternest face, yet he knew there would still be an outcry. Sensing his mood, each man wondered what had displeased their leader so much and hoped it was not something he had done. The group grew quiet and uneasy.

With an implacable glance around the circle, Lock said severely, "I have decided who will go on this raid, and I want no argument. It was very difficult to choose, but I have strong reasons for my choices, and you will abide by my decision. Is that clear?" He received dutiful bows all around the circle and thoughtful frowns as well. "I am going on this raid myself, because I must." His shocked councillors started to voice immediate objections.

"Silence!" he ordered harshly, and he went on forcefully before they could regroup. "I selected Verona to be on the council. I have known him since we were seven. It is my duty to capture him and to confront him as well. Wassh and his companion, Lassh, will guide us through the pass to the border and then wait there for us to return." The small seekers bowed acceptance.

"Only seven of you will go with me." Shock spread through his men like a wave. "Lavel, Tal qua, Oster, Evarb, Tsaf, Sher, and Traeh will go with me. With a small party, we have a better chance."

Disbelief! Outrage! Pending uproar! All Lock's councillors and warriors, including the Pack, began to protest and appeal this terrible decision. Bar and Devon were on their feet, eyes blazing.

"My lord, it is because of Dare and me that you are in this mess! They want us! Please reconsider," Bar protested passionately.

Devon objected with a frown, "Only eight men! Surely—"

Before their swelling objections could get out of hand, Lock commanded, "Sit down and be quiet! Now!" His quelling glance raked the circle of men, young and old. Embarrassed at their loss of control, they complied, but with difficulty. Tier and Dare pulled Bar down to a sitting position again and dug their elbows into his sides to keep him quiet. Lock noted the prince's shock and anger with an intense frown, and Bar subsided, realizing his danger. Eyes flashed and cheeks flushed around the barely subdued circle of men, but they did manage to keep their mouths shut.

Lock's withering gaze rested a moment on Devon, who should have known better. The large brother flushed at the unspoken rebuke. In strained silence, Lock continued, his displeasure apparent, "Wirth, Shils, Shonar, and Devon will be the council in our absence. I ask Devon, Wirth, Wasatch, and the hishua to go with the O'Hatch to evaluate Yad Thgil, this place they have found for us. Are there any questions?"

There were many, many questions, but none were spoken out loud. Few were pleased with their leader's plan.

"That is all. We will leave in thirty minutes."

Lock rose and went to oversee the packing of their supplies. *All in all, that did not go too badly. However, I have not heard the last word from one large monk.* He maintained a rigidly unapproachable front.

In spite of their disappointment, the Pack did not dare to plead with Lock. They had no doubt he meant what he'd said, and they did not wish to become the objects of his wrath. For such foolishness, one could end up with weeks of unpleasant tasks, like cook's helper. The Pack, except for Oster, went to the pond, which had become their meeting place, and discussed the situation.

Bar fumed, "I have been trained all my life to be a weapon. It is the only thing I am good at! They will never let me go on any raids, because it's 'too dangerous.'"

Dare wasn't listening. He had his own concerns. "They have no healer. Shonar is too old, and Odnu is no warrior—he can't even ride! I guess they could take Pleh, but his wife is due to have a baby soon. I suppose I am 'too young,'" he complained bitterly.

Chea and Tier knew that their hidden peoples and their relationships to the rulers of their clans left them out, but they were still stung by Lock's rejection. Louke had never had any hope that he would be allowed to go. It would be a long time before he was a warrior, if ever, but he listened with understanding to the bitter complaints swirling around him. Finally, the hishua ran out of steam.

The Pack went back to camp to see the raiding party off. They envied Oster with all their hearts but tried to be pleased that he, at least, was going. They did not succeed too well. Os knew the reason he had been included. He had over a year of experience tracking and fighting with Tal qua, the most famous of the Basca'. This would not be new terrain for him.

Lock was speaking with Shonar, Shils, Wirth, and Devon while the rest of the group waited. Apparently, Devon had contained his chagrin and accepted Lock's reasoning, though his mouth still had a mulish look. As Lavel waited with the rest of those leaving, the Pack noticed that the brothers did not speak to each other at all. Evidently big brother was not happy with Devon's outburst, and little brother was really angry that he wasn't included the search party. They felt bad for the brothers but could think of nothing they could do to help. After the hishua said goodbye to their friends, an emotion they were well-acquainted with hit them—worry. Their eight warriors would be up against a whole troop of the king's soldiers that included Blackrobes as well as the uncanny Lotu.

Lock joined them. "Report to Devon, each of you, while I am gone." Then he said softly to the whole group, "I know how much you want to go. Your time will come, soon." *Too soon*, he thought.

More like never. Will anyone ever let me fight? Why is Devon in charge? Bar wondered resentfully.

The Pack's anxiety deepened as they watched the small raiding party disappear into the forest. Their friends were leaving on a fourteen-day mission—fourteen days at the least! The mission would take them first into an unknown section of the Bitterroots and then into enemy territory—*if* everything went according to plan. When did it ever?

AMBUSH!

GLOOM SETTLED OVER THE BITTERROOTS CAMP. It would be two long weeks, perhaps longer before the raiding party returned. The Pack's disappointment and anxiety were making them sullen and irritable. They snapped at each other and everyone else.

Ssom and Shsif arrived after midmeal to lead Devon, Wirth, Wasatch, and the remaining hishua to view Yad Thgil, as Lock had ordered. Before they were out of camp two hours, Bar's friends knew the marked prince was headed for trouble. His caustic comments were undermining their new leader's authority. Bar intensely resented what he considered to be Lock's high-handedness in placing one of their own over them. Of course, in the mood he was in, he intensely resented everything. Bar was looking for a fight. Dare could understand his desire to vent his anger on someone, but he thought Devon a poor choice. However, he was too troubled and distracted to do more than warn Bar of his fate if he kept taunting the good brother. *Why didn't they take a healer? Any healer?* he wondered over and over.

Unaffected by the general depression around him, Louke was, unfortunately, amused by Bar's clever tongue and let it show, which only made Bar worse. Tier and Chea were far too deep in their own disappointment to knock some sense into their friend before it was too late. They were having difficulty reconciling themselves to being treated like children when their own clans treated them as warriors and had for years. *How humiliating to be sent on this tame sightseeing mission,* Chea thought with a grimace.

Wirth and Wasatch watched the contest between Bar and Devon with interest, as did the two O'Hatch. Devon's authority had been tested for over a year by young monks, old monks, and all ages in between, as well as by the king's officials. Bar was no match for him.

However, the marked prince, caught in a whirlpool of seething frustration, didn't even know that he was engaging in a contest of wills. *Will I never be free to do what I want to do? Will someone always be in control of my life? I have gone from Bardock to Lock! A change for the better certainly, but still, I am under authority ... Meggatirra was right! I always follow someone else.* Then an old refrain, an old pain, intruded and clung. *How many died this time? We still don't know the number. They estimate twenty in the mountain, six watchers, and perhaps fifty to sixty outside in the explosion? Did Tori and Lotu take prisoners? If so, where are they? In time, the O'Hatch will find out for us. Maker, protect those who live!* His heartache and his guilt grew until he could feel nothing else. Immersed in his own misery, he ignored Devon's firm warning to bridle his tongue. Bar had always contained and hidden his real emotions. It was a new and intoxicating experience to express anger, with the sure knowledge that only he would suffer for it. He was unaware of the growing discomfort of his traveling companions.

The party stopped in a small, rocky clearing for a meal. They ate flatbread, squirrel stew, and cheese in uneasy silence. Bar wasn't uneasy, because he didn't notice the silence. When all were finished, Devon assigned various tasks. He asked Bar to scrub the stew kettle and use it to fetch water for tea from a stream close to their camp. Bar glared at him and didn't answer, but he rose to obey. As the others scattered to their work, they heard Bar grumble, "Some people think now that they are in *charge* that they are too important to take watches or do chores." Dare groaned softly and glanced at Tier, who shrugged in resignation.

Devon sighed and rose slowly to his feet. "Bar, could I speak with you, privately?" he asked gently and stretched.

Bar nodded irritably. *Now what? More chores probably.*

"Wasatch, would you keep watch until we return?"

"Aye, Devon. *Gladly,*" he responded with a grin. Wasatch rarely grinned. In fact, Bar wasn't sure he had ever seen the man smile before. He wondered at this uncharacteristic display of emotion.

Devon led the way to a steep, rocky glen where they were out of sight of their camp. He leaned against a craggy wall bathed in the golden glow of the setting sun and gazed at Bar from under the rim of his floppy hat. Bar frowned. He hated the hat; it didn't fit Devon's otherwise very appropriate warrior dress. It didn't fit the dignity of a monk either. It didn't fit anything. Suddenly, he became aware of where he was and Big Brother's stern countenance. Anxiety finally pierced his self-absorption. "Devon, what did you want?" Not the best beginning, perhaps.

Devon was quiet for long seconds, and Bar's vague discomfort grew. It occurred to him that Devon was angry and seeking to control it before he spoke. "I am waiting," Devon said, his voice and face cold.

Bar almost snapped. *Waiting for what?* However, some vague instinct for self-preservation made him refrain. With a puzzled frown, Bar reviewed his day. At first, he remembered nothing except his own tangled thoughts. Then, he recalled Dare's sharp warning to stop taunting Devon. *What did Dare mean, "taunting"? I made a few observations, nothing more.* His friend's groan when he'd grumbled about Devon assigning tasks to the others but taking none flashed through his mind. Vaguely, he remembered his sarcastic comments and also Devon's firm warning to bridle his tongue. *Perhaps …*

As he looked at the day from Devon's point of view, his frustrations boiled up again and resulted in an intense internal argument with himself. *But it isn't fair! When is life ever fair? It isn't right. How often are things right? I wanted to go! So did Devon. How many? How many more deaths? If Lock finds out how I've behaved this day … Maker have mercy, what an awful thought.* Viewing the day through Devon's as well as Lock's eyes brought his rudeness into focus. He had been looking for a fight with a good friend, which was the problem in a nutshell. Now, Devon was more than a friend, much more—he was in charge.

Bar knew what Devon was waiting for, but the words were slow to come. "Devon, I'm sorry. I've been sarcastic and insulting all day. I am disappointed and furious, and I took it out on you."

"Why?"

"Why?" Bar exploded. "I resented Lock putting you in charge. You are not much older than the rest of us, and you are one of us! I resented not being able, *ever*, to do what I want to do. They will never let me fight or be in danger. Never! Because we are 'the marked,' Dare and I will be kept safe and protected forever. Why does somebody else always have to be in charge? I am tired of being under someone's authority all the time, day and night. When will I ever be free?" Bar exclaimed with heat. He was surprised and a little embarrassed at his outburst.

To Bar's amazement, Devon chuckled softly. He took off his ridiculous floppy hat and laid it on a rock. "Well, I feel much the same way, to tell the truth. I wanted to go too, and I am tired of hiding in these rugged, forsaken mountains, waiting, and we don't even know for what! It is frustrating and difficult. I had grown used to being in charge at the monastery and am struggling with being a follower again, especially with keeping my mouth shut."

Bar was amazed at this look into Devon's real feelings; the large monk always seemed so cool and controlled. Remembering a conversation with Dare, he had to grin. "Aye, Dare and I have talked about having too many leaders! We've been waiting for an explosion, but so far there hasn't been one. We've been really disappointed."

Devon laughed in spite of himself and said, "As I hope you will continue to be! We have enough to worry about with out that kind of thing."

After a moment, Bar said, "I thought you were reconciled and perfectly, disgustingly content."

Big Brother smiled ruefully. "Lock gave me a piece of his mind I won't soon forget for my 'loss of control' at the council fire, and my big brother added his bit before he left. So you see, I've been lectured by both, when I am used to doing the lecturing." He paused a minute, then added, "I hate to tell you this, but you will probably be under someone's authority much of your life, and if you're not, you'll wish you were." He shook his head. "Lock leads Glidden. Think about it! Can he do what he wants, when he wants? Do you want his responsibilities? He gets to decide, but I wouldn't want his position, would you?"

Bar stared at him resentfully. *Devon can be a real pain.* Against his will, scene after scene flashed through his mind. He remembered the times when he'd been aware of the crushing weight Lock carried: after news of Verona's defection, for instance, or after the raid on Glidden. *He felt responsible for not keeping his people safe … for not seeing what Verona was planning. Everyone was so discouraged; he had to pull us back together. I wonder if he wanted to quit.*

Even when I pledged tsurtne, he knew what he was getting into, though I didn't. He knew he was becoming the leader of a resistance movement that could last years. His life is no longer his own … no longer simple. Every time something goes wrong, he gets the blame. He gets to fix it. He is responsible for people's lives … worse, their deaths!

"He rarely says anything, but I know it's a terrible weight," Bar acknowledged.

"One day you will carry a worse weight, Bar—the weight of a whole kingdom. He wants you to live to see that day. The Maker made you a warrior. Never doubt that your time to fight will come, but you will need to be much more than a simple warrior. A king needs other qualities, one of which is patience, a quality that isn't easy for any of us." Bar recognized the truth in what Devon was saying, but he still hated it.

Devon arched a brow and said, "Now, my disrespectful prince—" Bar groaned. Devon continued, "There'll be no more 'remarks.'"

"Agreed."

"And lots of respect, including 'sir.'"

"Aye, *sir*."

"And no discipline, this time."

"Alati, Dev—I mean sir!"

"If there is a next time, you'll spend many days in silence. Understood?"

"Aye, Dev—sir."

In the deepening twilight, they walked back to camp. Their companions were merrily discussing something around the fire. Bar's face flushed when he realized he was the subject of their conversation. He managed to keep his tongue in check for the rest of the trip. Even so, he continued to be an irritable, difficult companion. He was not where he wanted to be and could not reconcile himself to his least favorite role, that of waiting. Guilt remained a pervading ache.

It took them all the next day to reach their destination. Without the clever seekers, it would have taken a week or longer, even if they had known the way. Yadot was difficult but not impossible for those who knew the area well.

The O'Hatch entered Yad Thgil, the high valley, their way. They had found a narrow tunnel created by water that seeped down to the ground below from a waterfall up in the valley. The water was snowmelt from the surrounding mountains and was still icy cold. They climbed up this passage with ease, though even for them, the tunnel was sometimes a tight squeeze. Once the small seekers reached the top and found the right steep cliff, they tossed an elong ladder they had hidden there down to the ledge far below. They also dropped a rope of elong with a woven net attached to the end.

Under the cover of towering trees, Devon and the party followed a steep game trail up and up the mountainside until they reached the wide ledge where the ladder and rope net were gently blowing in the wind. Bar sighed as he swallowed a bitter Bani herb. It would help him endure being pulled up in the net without suffering too severely from his queal. Of course, he would then suffer the effects of the herbal mixture, but they would be short-lived. Devon secured the ladder at its base and began the difficult ascent. The O'Hatch did not think it so difficult a climb, but the others found it arduous. The world below them looked miniature when they finally arrived at the top.

The climb was worth it, definitely worth it! As they explored the land, Devon wondered how they could ever thank the O'Hatch for such a gift. It looked as if the valley could sustain life with no outside help. Water was abundant, both hot in the form of geysers and cold from snowmelt. Wildlife, fish, forests, elong, and arable land were ample. There were long hours of sunshine as well. The only problem was the valley's inaccessibility. Yad Thgil was a wonderful place to disappear but a terrible place to launch a fight, unless you had the O'Hatch.

Louke drew plans for a platform that could be hoisted with rope. The workmen would come first to erect it and other necessary structures, and then the people of Glidden could come and finish building their new homes. The water seekers' secret way would remain unknown to all but a trusted few. The enthusiastic seekers pointed out to the awed fugitives the advantages of their new hideaway. Though the fugitives appreciated the seekers' explanations of the vale's benefits, the advantages were readily apparent. They all had spent much of their time seeking or living in places of concealment.

The impossibly rugged Bitterroots surrounded Yad Thgil. The valley itself was high and vast. There were no passages in or out, except the one the

O'Hatch used, a way no one but an O'Hatch would ever find or could ever use. Of course, there were weapons that could overpower any stronghold, treachery chief among them. It would work here as well as it had in Glidden. Yet, so far, they were more than pleased with Yad Thgil. Plans for the valley started to develop in each man's brain, influenced by his special interests or abilities ... or fears.

The O'Hatch insisted, and the people of Glidden agreed, that no one would ever make maps of Yadot. The seekers maintained that all ways through the treacherous, difficult mountains must be memorized. Those who were adept would become guides for others who found the skill difficult. All reliable paths to and from Yad Thgil would be kept secret. The high valley was well protected by the rugged terrain surrounding it, and the Glidden refugees as well as the O'Hatch wanted to keep it that way.

The plans they made and the enormous energy needed to prepare a scattered people to move helped the time pass. Yet their thoughts returned again and again to Lock, Lavel, Tal, Os, and the others in the raiding party. They counted the days and spoke to the Maker often concerning their friends.

Lock's desire was to take Verona prisoner. He wanted—he *needed*—to ask why, and most importantly, he needed to stop Verona from revealing all he knew to the king. Lock positioned scouts along a deserted northern section of the royal road and waited. A day passed slowly and then another. They worried that perhaps they had missed Captain Tori's troop.

Finally, on the third day the lookouts saw the troop at a great distance down the road, and each galloped quickly to his assigned place. After what seemed like hours, the royal troop entered a sharp curve in the king's highway and trotted right into the Glidden warriors' trap. Unknown to the soldiers and their leaders, there were warriors on both sides of the road. Lock's men and their mounts were hidden behind huge boulders. At Lock's signal, they rose quickly from their hiding places, bows drawn, and shouted the Bani battle cry continuously while shooting a swarm of arrows over the top of the troop. Their intent was to cause confusion and fear, not to harm anyone. It certainly worked! At the same time Lock and Tal qua rode out into the middle of the road with bows ready and Lock cried out, "Halt now! Or we'll shoot!" Lavel, mounted on his huge horse and armed with a bow, was behind the troop, Sher by his side. That left two warriors on top of a boulder on each side of the road. All four pointed bows armed with arrows at the troop.

Chaos broke out! Horses shied wildly, whinnied with terror, and tried to run. All in Tori's troop struggled desperately to quiet their frightened mounts and regroup. Some of the Blackrobes were thrown from their horses. Verona, Lotu, and Tori quickly tried to break free of the carefully prepared trap, but there was no way out. They were surrounded.

Tori's mount stumbled, and he was thrown into the road right under the terrified horses' hooves. His right shoulder was injured. In spite of great pain, he rolled to the side of the road and watched for a horse with no rider. One plunging bay was near. He quieted the horse as best he could and mounted it awkwardly. He managed to trot away, half in, half out of the saddle. In the confusion no one noticed. The attackers' whole attention was on Verona.

The traitor and prelate were sick with apprehension. They gave up quickly and quieted their animals. Verona's face was harsh as stone and grim. Lotu was pale and shaking with fear. They realized Glidden's leader could not let them escape; they knew too much and had done too much. The Blackrobes and soldiers followed their example and stopped all efforts to escape. At Tal qua's order they all threw down their weapons. Not a single member of the royal troop had shot an arrow or drawn a sword. The king's men were surrounded and had given up without a fight! The ambush was a success.

Lock ordered Tal qua and Lavel to bind Verona's and Lotu's hands in front of them. He would have preferred to bind their hands behind them, but they needed to be able to ride. As a further precaution he ordered Tal and Lavel to tie a rope around their waists and hold it tightly enough to pull them off their horses should they try to escape.

Oster suddenly noticed Captain Tori's absence and quickly told Lock, who decided not to risk pursuing him. They were too far from the safety of the Bitterroots to take time to chase Captain Tori. Hopefully he and Verona had had little chance to talk about anything but the attack on

Glidden. After questioning the soldiers, Tal learned an encouraging bit of information. Captain Tori had told his lieutenant that the king had given strict orders to leave the questioning about the resistance and their organization to him. It seemed he trusted no one with the knowledge but Draville and his other advisors. Did he fear spies in his own ranks? He was wise to do so. Lavel had many listeners in Casterray, and some were close—very close—to the king.

Sher was one of the warriors guarding the soldiers and Blackrobes. To his surprise, two of the royal soldiers approached him hesitantly. They appeared to be frightened but determined. He could not imagine what they wanted.

"We want to join you! We have had enough of Blackrobes and the king."

Sher was speechless. This was something that did not happen often. He quickly called Lavel who questioned the two soldiers. It seemed they sympathized with the resistance and were ready to leave the king's service. Neither feared retaliation, because they had no family members who would suffer for their desertion.

The soldiers gladly shared what they knew about the attack on Glidden. They said it had been well planned and had come so quickly that many of the guards and watchers had been captured before they could fight, sound the alarm, or flee. Verona's detailed information had been invaluable to Captain Tori.

They also shared what they knew about the results of the attack. Bad as the death toll was, it was not as bad as the Glidden folk had feared. Ten Glidden men and women had died in the initial assault and ten more who had stayed at their stations to protect their friends' flight. Some may have died in the explosion, but the soldiers didn't know if any had or how many were injured. As Lock and Tal had suspected, the explosion had been meant to light up the darkness and terrify the people fleeing into giving up. The light had also made it easier to capture those who had continued to run in wildly different directions. Captain Tori had imprisoned at least a hundred of the wounded and captured, who were now being held in Glidden Mountain. Lavel and Sher knew they would be used to coerce Lock.

The soldiers seemed to feel that they'd imprisoned most of the insurgents, but there were over four hundred people in Glidden at any given time. Surely Verona had to be aware of the misconception. The O'Hatch had counted three hundred Glidden folk who had escaped into the Bitterroots, and they weren't through searching. Perhaps Verona had allowed the misconception to make his information and aid look better to the king and to Tori and Lotu as well. If they knew the true total of those who had escaped, it would certainly make the raid look even more ineffective to the king than it already did.

Lock ordered Evarb and Traeh to gather and bundle up all the discarded weapons. Then he let all the soldiers and the Blackrobes go. He even allowed them to keep their horses. They were stunned but grateful. The Glidden band had few warriors and no time to take so many prisoners with them. They also wanted the soldiers and maybe even a few of the Blackrobes to remember their mercy in the future. It did not help their cause to wound, kill, or even imprison their own people. They wanted the citizens of Ree on their side.

The Glidden folk's small ambush ignited a blaze that burned larger and spread farther every day thereafter. Bardock's fury knew no bounds. Not that he deeply valued Lotu, but he badly wanted Verona for the information he could give him. The *rumors* of a resistance had become an embarrassing reality. All the soldiers and Blackrobes that the foolish Glidden warriors had released were eyewitnesses. Though he ordered them not to speak of the incident, word got out. It more than got out! It spread like wildfire in dry timber.

The king paced and raged in the royal capital of Feisan. *My former battle commander is leading the resistance! How could he do such a thing? He's supposed to be dead. A small group of men, women, and, aye, children— peasants for the most part—are refusing to be part of my kingdom, to obey me, or even to return my traitorous son.* He suspected that his subjects laughed at him behind his back. *The people are undoubtedly astonished that my own son defies me—a mere sixteen-year-old that no one seems to be able to capture!* He was quite right.

His people were also mystified and enthralled by strange stories and rumors of Moor ha Chi and little people—the O'Hatch, though none of

85

them knew that name. The citizens of Ree became interested in their own history and searched their shelves for old scrolls, which told even older tales. Long-forgotten things were spoken of again. In taverns and marketplaces, people made bets on the existence, or not, of old clans thought long dead. They also placed wagers on who would capture the marked ones or the resistance's battle commander, for they would surely be captured in time. Who could stand against Bardock? The strange tale of E Clue marking the prince was remembered and woven into the whole. There were rumors that Bardon's marked companion spoke with wolves, and it was said that the marked ones' friends who fought with them were called "the Pack." It was a tale that delighted the young and old alike. Bardock's people badly needed hope. His tyranny, like drying elong bonds, squeezed ever tighter.

Near Lock's camp in the Bitterroots, Bar sat, knees hugged to his chest, watching from his high perch for any sign of their leader and his company. Devon searched the rugged landscape from atop a boulder not far from him. The ambush party was already one day late. It was the evening of the second day with no Lock and company. Glorious color filled the sky in the west as the sun slipped behind the mountains. Birds, insects, and a soft wind from the south sang among the trees and grasses. All was peaceful, except the two who watched. Their anxiety was reaching the breaking point. Another night was coming quickly, and no one traveled the Bitterroots at night. If Lock and the others didn't get here soon, it would be the next day before they arrived. Where were they? What had happened? Did they need help? The tension was almost unbearable.

Suddenly, Bar glimpsed movement in the canyon below them. He watched the spot intensely and finally was sure. It was the ambush party working their way up the torturous ravine. "Devon, look! There they are!" he cried joyfully. "Alati ma, gracious Maker," he whispered softly and ducked his head to his knees. For a moment, relief made him weak.

Devon searched the group. "All the original group are there and seem, at least from this height, uninjured. Do I see four more in the band? They have prisoners!" They scrambled joyfully down the rocks to their camp.

Lock and his party returned to their people in the Bitterroots exhausted but victorious. Not a man had been lost or even wounded. Verona and Lotu were their prisoners and could not betray all they knew to the king. They'd also added two of Bardock's soldiers to their numbers—if the men passed the council's testing. It had been a good raid.

The next day Dierald and a small band of warriors took the traitor and Choack's priest to Meggatirra. They would be held captive deep in the Chi king's mountain stronghold. It would take many long days for the Glidden warriors to get there and back, but knowing there was no way the two could escape the Chi labyrinth gave Lock and his people peace.

With O'Hatch help, Lock and his warriors freed the captives in Glidden Mountain and led them to a safe place in the Bitterroots. Shonar and his healers cared for the wounded. They freed the few Blackrobes and soldiers Captain Tori had left behind in Glidden to secure the prisoners. Lock and his people were pleased and grateful for these successes, but they were now irrevocably committed to fighting. Bardock would ruthlessly seek them—to smash the prophecy and all it intended and to salve his injured pride.

——◦◦◦——

Later that week, Tori dragged into Casterray. He appeared before his sovereign in a sorry state. Blood from his wound had stained his uniform, and he was pale, exhausted, and weak from fever and terrible pain. His clothes and hair were covered with road dust and wet with perspiration from the long, hot ride—a far cry from his usual meticulous appearance. Normally confident and amusingly sarcastic, he now trembled with fear that he sought desperately to hide as he approached the royal throne. A rigid body of councillors stood around Bardock and stared at Tori coldly. Tori gulped as he glimpsed his father among them. *By the gods, what more could I have done?* He agonized as the last few months flashed through his mind.

Incomprehensibly, the king, to whom he had been so loyal, ordered that he be thrown into Casterray's dungeon for his failures, as an example to Bardock's other subjects. His father and the rest of his family were exiled to their home in the country in disgrace.

Perhaps, when the captain has suffered enough, Bardock thought, *I will use him again. What an effective weapon he will make by that time.* He laughed for the first time in many days and then forgot his faithful servant. A young, promising prelate in Draville's service replaced Lotu, and his absence was not mourned by anyone.

The Glidden folk knew, of course, why Lotu had helped with the attack, but before being taken to the Chi, Verona had repeatedly refused to speak to Lock or Shonar and explain his terrible treachery. So they tried another way. Lock pieced together from Mitora, Verona's wife, the mystery of his old friend's betrayal. Traeh, Verona's son, sat beside her, grief-stricken and shamed. Against all advice, Lock had allowed Traeh to join the raiding party. The man had a family of his own and had begged Lock to allow him to go. He'd wanted to clear his name and prove his loyalty to Glidden. Lock had accepted him because he was one of their best archers and because he trusted him, in spite of his father's defection.

What they learned seemed an impossibly inadequate explanation for what Verona had done. From various things he'd said, Mitora and Traeh put together what they'd thought had so changed him. Neither had taken his grumbling seriously. How could he betray longtime companions to their enemy for prestige? It appeared that Verona longed for the power, status, and wealth that he and Lock, once aristocracy, had possessed. He wanted his high position in Ree's society back. Living in a mountain stronghold with few luxuries and surrounded by simple people had apparently at first bored and then angered him. He'd grown bitter. He felt cheated of his rights and regretted following his friend into oblivion. It had been only a small step from grumbling discontent to blaming Lock for his vast losses. He felt that Lock had deprived him of the life he should have led.

Apparently, the next step had become possible: to betray the person he blamed for ruining his life and to take back his rightful inheritance. What did it matter who else was hurt? That he'd caused the death and imprisonment of trusting friends and Glidden's people, that he'd endangered the two marked young men did not seem to bother him. But for a lone sentry, all Glidden folk would be dead or captured. That was what Verona had helped plan.

Without question, Lock knew that neither Mitora nor Traeh could have possibly guessed where Verona's dissatisfaction would lead him. *Was I not just as close to him as they? And I never dreamed my friend*—at that word bitterness flooded his being—*was capable of such callous treachery.* Heartsick, Lock accepted Mitora's and Traeh's renewed pledges of loyalty to the people of Glidden. He wondered if he would ever feel good again, if the pain would ever go away. He remembered an old proverb: "The betrayal of a friend is a knife in the heart."

<hr />

Tori lay shivering uncontrollably in a stinking hammock deep within the dungeon of the ancient keep. His royal lord evidently wished him to live, for he was given plain food and clean water. A healer even put salve on his cuts and bruises and changed the dressing on his wound every few days. Though the healer was allowed to give him nothing for pain, still Tori appreciated these short but uncomfortable visits, because they were his only human contact.

How he hated being alone! Terrible memories haunted him, yet there was little he could do to distract his mind. Visual images from the multitude of Mirg Rorrohs he'd attended filled his dark cell with terror. Grasping for something, anything pleasant and real, Tori tried to maintain his sanity by focusing on agreeable memories.

A particular one comforted him. When he remembered the farmer and his daughter who had helped him after the ambush, the creeping horrors in his dank cell seemed to retreat. He could not imagine why this particular memory brought relief, but he was too feverish to think it through. After the farmer had carried Tori into their simple kitchen, he and his daughter had gently cared for him. They'd bandaged the cut and terrible bruise on his right shoulder from the horse's hoof, cleaned and rubbed ointment on his other less serious injuries, and given him remedies from their small supply for pain and infection. Much to his discomfort, they'd also prayed for him, revealing themselves to be followers of the Maker. How foolish to betray their belief to a king's man! Their modest room had been a cool shelter from the sun and full of pleasant smells and peace. All that day, he'd watched the daughter, Liras, go about her duties with grace and skill while he lay, weak and unable to speak, on a pallet in the corner. Somehow, she'd seemed to know his needs before he could ask.

When he'd left the small farm, Tori had been surprised at the depth of his emotion as he thanked them for their aid. The glow of Liras's beauty in the bright sunshine had taken his breath away. Though they had not spoken twenty words to each other, her face and that small farm had become rocks of refuge in a world that swam with terrible apparitions.

It struck him, in the terrible, haunted darkness of his prison, that he had met with much kindness in the long days it had taken him to return to Feisan. Farmers, shopkeepers, and an occasional housewife had offered food and water, for his horse as well as for himself. He would have been surprised to know that many of them were also followers of the Maker. Much of the kindness could be directly attributed to his rank and uniform but not all.

The king held all the five provinces tightly in his grasp, but the mountains were no-man's-land. There were places there that belonged completely to the underground. He was well aware that spies riddled his territories, and he became ruthless in his attempts to flush them out. His road, the king's highway, had become a battleground. Because it circled the island, it was vital to commerce. It was also vital to his ability to keep order in the realm. Soldiers guarded it and traveled its length continually to maintain Bardock's authority with the threat of might. Resistance raiding parties swooped down from the mountains like ferocious hawks to ravage the merchant caravans protected by the king's soldiers. They harassed, ambushed, and disrupted all royal traffic and then disappeared.

Yad Thgil in the north, Meggatirra's capital in the middle of the mountains, and the Bani's Glimmervale in the south became centers of the insurgent movement. The insurgents were few in number and always subject to infiltration and betrayal. Every man and woman who joined them had to be carefully tested. Yet, for all their lack of size, they were a terrible thorn in Bardock's side. His wonderful plans for the complete domination of his people were becoming frayed. He desired to control all wealth, to be the only authority on his island, and to be revered as a god. Choack promised to fulfill all these aspirations. Yet neither his god nor he had counted on Bardon's defection and marking or the emergence of a forgotten ancient prophecy or the growth of an insignificant insurgent movement capable of standing against them.

Over the next year, the Glidden folk, now in their new home; the Bani; the Chi; and the O'Hatch worked together to defeat their enemies' attacks and attempts to dislodge them. In certain locales, their domains touched. By joining forces, they held a bar of territory down the middle of Ree that almost extended the length of the island. There were few areas they could not reach to harry their enemy and then flee back into the mountains to hide, leaving no trace, no clue. The people of Ree called them the Resistance or the Alliance or simply the Alli.

Unfortunately for the royal army, three individuals who had begun to unravel the insurgents' devious weaving were lost to them. Tori was fighting to stay alive and sane in prison. The king thought Lotu and Verona were Lock's prisoners, but no one knew where Lock had taken them. All the three had learned, with much guidance from darkness, would have to be rediscovered. They also did not know where the few men left behind after Captain Tori's attack on Glidden Mountain were, now that the Resistance had freed the prisoners being held there.

Meanwhile, the O'Hatch seekers delighted in the new waters to explore in the beautiful Yad Thgil. The Glidden refugees fell in love with the wild, tortuous, and beautiful Bitterroots.

A Captive Set Free

BAR RODE AT BREAKNECK SPEED TO INTERCEPT the lead horses of a runaway wagon. His black hair flew out behind him as he stretched over Charger's neck to catch the flapping reins. Drawing back on them, he was able to slow the terrified team. Billowing dust blinded his vision and filled his mouth and nose. His horse snorted and shied nervously, not liking his proximity to the noisy wagon and frightened workhorses. Suddenly, Charger's right front foot plunged into a hole, and he stumbled. Bar was hurled forward over his neck. Letting go of the wagon's reins, the young warrior grasped at his mount's neck in an attempt to stay in the saddle, yet all he managed was to slow his fall. Stunned, Bar lay on the ground trying to regain his wits. He knew he must get to his feet before one of the other horses trampled him. *I have not been thrown from a horse since I was six!* Disgusted with himself, dazed, and bruised, Bar pushed himself to one knee, gasped in pain, then looked around.

Because of his efforts, the trembling team had stopped, so the passenger, whoever he might be, was safe. The soldier driving the wagon had left it to join the hand-to-hand fighting, and his frightened team had evidently galloped off down the road without him.

Bar's vision suddenly blurred, yet he could see well enough to observe mounted warriors engaging mounted soldiers in furious combat up and down the road. *We never intended for this ambush to result in hand-to-hand fighting!*

He remembered the moment when sullen surrender had turned into a

92

fight. Unexpectedly, a few of the cumbersome wagons and their drivers had made a desperate attempt to break away. They'd almost succeeded. To stop their flight, Tal and Oster had risked their lives to pull up the horses. In spite of the Alliance's desire to take no lives, fighting had broken out. Enraged, the guards on either side of the wagons had rushed at the rebels furiously with their swords drawn. Unfortunately, their comrades in arms had joined them with a vengeance and loud battle cries, screaming encouragement to one another and abuse at Tal's warriors. Evidently, the royal troops were tired of being rounded up like cattle. This time they intended to fight back. In spite of the Resistance's best efforts at containment, lives were sure to be lost in their enemy's determined attempt to break free.

We must overwhelm the soldiers quickly and force them to lay down their weapons, or this raid will become a total failure. There is still hope we can take command and stop the fighting; we have more men than they. Our main force is ranged in trees and rocks along the highway. There are scouts both north and south on the road and others guarding our retreat. We thought the king's soldiers might be unwilling to fight us because they've been so easy to defeat in the past. Not today!

Ready to rush into the fight, Bar pushed himself to his feet. He cried out in agony and fell, rolling on the ground in anguish. His left foot had been twisted in the fall and was either broken or sprained. Something else radiated misery higher up his leg. Unable to stand, he scrambled off the road, crawling. His vision blurred again, and he found the gully mostly by feel. Perspiration ran down his face and back as he struggled against the agony caused by his various injuries. *You will not ... not pass out*, he ordered himself sternly.

It was cooler in the bushes, and he rested a few minutes. He tried to control the trembling in his limbs and to slow the pounding of his heart. He found a stout stick and used it to pull himself to his feet. Bar clenched his teeth, but a groan still escaped him as he fell, unconscious, to the ground.

Tal gained control of the battle finally and gathered his party together to flee back to Glimmervale. They had most of the horses, weapons, and supplies secured; the wagons would be destroyed. The soldiers were stripped of their arms but otherwise allowed to flee down the road. They carried their wounded with them. Two of the soldiers who had continued to fight instead of throwing down their weapons might not make it. Never had the Alli run into such determined resistance.

Tal's raiding party was larger than normal this time. The king had grown cautious after a summer of harassment and interference and had increased the number of soldiers and Blackrobes on the royal road. The underground had responded by increasing the number of men in their companies. This particular supply train had been well guarded, and the king's soldiers had been extremely determined not to have their goods taken. They'd put up a fierce fight, in spite of the strong odds against their breaking free. Tal hoped this was not a trend. They had almost lost control of the raid.

Tal carefully scanned the road and countryside. All seemed to be quiet. There was a deserted wagon on the road north of him, but he let it go. Before he could check on his men and their captured supplies and horses, ram's horns sounded a sudden, urgent warning from the road, both south and north of their position. The horns' haunting cries filled the air, but no soldiers were yet visible on the road. That meant they had time to regain the forest—he hoped. Thank the Maker for their sentries! Having served their purpose, they would now flee into the foothills. Tal wondered if the king had posted lookouts somewhere to watch the road. How else could they have known so quickly about this raid?

"Scatter the captured horses! Leave the wagons and supplies!" he ordered as he spun his horse. He was instantly obeyed. His men swatted and screamed at the royal mounts until the terrified horses galloped headlong in all directions. "Y'crem, Ard, hang on to their weapons as long as you can, then dump them down a ravine. I'll not give them back their arms, though they'll regain everything else we've taken this day," Tal shouted bitterly. As Tal surveyed the road one last time, Bar's horse was no longer on it to notify him of his prince's accident. In the confusion, neither he nor Dare missed their marked friend.

Tal signaled forward with his hand, and the raiding party swept like a storm across the plain. Each rider rode like an extension of his horse, crouched low over his steed's neck. Clouds of dust spurted from their mounts' pounding hooves. Driving hard for the safety of the trees, Tal hoped they would not run into a wall of the king's soldiers there. *There are no warning sounds from the sentries hidden in the forest's darkness. We are safe once there.* When they finally were closing on the wood, Tal pulled his unwilling horse, Reef, to a halt and spun to look back. The animal snorted and pranced his nervous displeasure. While Tal patted Reef's lathered neck, he watched two troops converging on the road, their horses raising clouds of dust in the heat. *So many, but they are too late,* he thought with grim satisfaction and whirled Reef forward toward the trees again. As the enemy started across the plain, Tal joined his warriors under the stately pines. He cried, "The Northern Gate! Scatter!" Melting into the forest like startled deer, the men separated to flee in different directions. The forest stood quiet and empty.

They would meet again at the assigned place, but meanwhile their pursuers would have to find and follow thirty separate tracks, on ground that was hard and dry. It had not rained for weeks. Tal thanked the Maker for their escape. He had no fear for his men now. They were well trained and knew what to do, even the hishua. Disappointment and anger gripped him like an ache. *It was close, too close, and utterly profitless. Worse, we seriously wounded some of the soldiers, which has the potential to turn the people against us. The king is growing more devious and clever. We must find out how his men knew about the raid so quickly.* Tal did not realize that he had sustained a loss more grievous to him than those he was numbering.

Bar lay, an unconscious heap, in a bush-clogged ditch beside the road. No one had seen him fall—well, no one in the raiding party. The forgotten passenger on the wagon seat, gravely watched the battle. When the wagon stopped, the young prisoner quickly cut his bonds with the absent driver's deserted knife and climbed swiftly down. The bare blade gleaming in his hand, he drifted into the woods. No one stopped him or even noticed his departure. He had watched Bar struggle to rise after his fall and heard his cry of pain. Though he was grateful to the warrior for stopping the wagon, he knew this might be his only chance to escape, and he desperately needed to escape. Trembling visibly in fear of discovery, he fled into the trees. After running a hundred yards with his elong bonds flapping, he stopped and groaned. He couldn't do it—the man had saved his life after all, and now he was hurt. *Blast!*

Cautiously, he returned to the roadside ditch and found Bar's unconscious body. *I need the horse to get us away and the waterskin to bring him around.* Resigned to the delay, he returned to the road with stealth and led the limping horse into the ditch. All was still quiet, but he had heard ram's horns from the south and then from the north. He didn't know exactly what they meant, but he had a good idea. The king's soldiers would soon arrive in dogged pursuit of the Alli.

I must, must be out of here by then. After enduring years of captivity with no hope of escape, he found it difficult to be so close to freedom and not run. The temptation rose again, only stronger this time. *Leave this man, fool! The soldiers won't find him hidden in the bushes … probably.* He pushed the thought aside. No matter how slight his chance *with* the injured man might be, without him and the other Alli, he would have had no chance at all.

El took a closer look at his rescuer and was shocked to find in his features a strong resemblance to the king. With a look of wonder and a trembling hand, he moved the leather vest aside and found a smoky-blue, triangular scar on the man's right shoulder. *Bardon! Of all the rebels on Ree, why must Bardock's fugitive son rescue me! So the stories are true; he has been marked.* He rubbed the mark lightly. The scar was leathery but a part of Bardon's skin, not something painted on with dye. His heart sped faster.

Suddenly remembering their situation, El dumped water on Bar's face. He meant to sprinkle it, but he was very frightened, and the waterskin slipped. He called to Bar softly, urgently, willing him to wake.

Bar roused, spluttering and anxious. Memory returned in a flash along with a grinding pain in his right leg that took his breath away. "Boer's bow!" he gasped as he fought for control. Bar could see little of the face of the young man in front of him, for he wore a short cloak with a deep hood, but he remembered the slight, brown-clad figure in the wagon. It seemed strange that the lad wore a cloak on such a hot day.

"Your friends have left without you! I'm fairly sure soldiers are coming down the road from both directions," the youth explained hurriedly. "We must get out of here, or we'll be captured."

Left me? Bar was stunned and asked the young man to elaborate. He listened to the tale with dismay. *Wonderful! I am alone, miles from Glimmervale, with an injured horse, an injured leg, and a lad who has soft, white hands. He undoubtedly knows nothing whatsoever of the woods.* Bar noticed elong bonds, like bracelets, around the youth's wrists. The youngster had cut the rope holding them together. *A prisoner, then! When we have time, I will have to remove those—they are chafing the child raw—and find out how he came to be their prisoner.*

He sighed and rubbed his aching head. *Would it be better to stay here and let the soldiers pass us while they race to follow the raiding party, or should we try to leave now? If we do, we could easily be caught in the open, yet if we stay, someone might stop to search the roadside.* He thought the last possibility unlikely, and they hid themselves in the gully as best they could.

Bar gazed at Charger anxiously. "That foot needs tending, but there is no time now. I fear we must ride him in spite of his injury, if we are to escape." His hard gaze slid to his companion. "What is your name?"

"Er … El," the young lad replied. They could hear the thunder of approaching horses and fell silent. El, who seemed comfortable with Charger, stood at the steed's head to keep him quiet. So intent were the soldiers on the Alli that they would not have heard the horse even if El hadn't been quieting him. They swept by in a cloud of dust and charged across the plain in pursuit of their quarry.

Cautiously, El helped Bar to rise. Bar swayed alarmingly but soon righted himself with his young friend's help. El realized with sudden insight that the warrior would never be able to put weight on his injured left foot to mount. He could hardly stand, much less swing his leg across the animal. They looked at the horse and then desperately at each other. "I'll lie over the saddle," Bar gasped, his head pounding with blinding pain. He gagged and willed his queasy stomach to be calm.

Standing on his right foot, Bar grasped the far side of Charger's saddle with both hands and pulled his weight off the ground, with El guiding his right foot into the stirrup. Bar cried out sharply when Charger moved forward. He concentrated on not screaming. El grabbed the reins and led the horse through the trees and out into the meadow, where they were in plain sight, but no one was watching—they hoped.

Later, when they entered the cool, dark forest, Bar relaxed a little. Now, he had to find his way—their way—to safety. He also needed to sit in the saddle, not lie across it.

"What now?" El asked softly.

"Let's see if I can swing my right leg over my horse." With El's help, Bar managed to sit upright on Charger. "Go deeper. Head east," he panted, concentrating on staying conscious and holding himself on the horse. As his throbbing headache increased in intensity, both tasks became more and more difficult.

El knew that, for all his determination, the young warrior could not keep this up much longer. He needed help, now, but El could think of no way to aid him. El steadied Bar with his hand to keep him upright, and they went on.

Many hours later, as darkness spread over the landscape ahead of them, El stopped the weary, limping horse near a rushing stream. He looked around him. "Where are we now, I wonder?" the lad asked softly with a dazed look at trees and more trees marching away into the gloom.

Bar was barely conscious. He started to get down but passed out when he moved his left leg. Quickly, El guided his fall to the ground. The warrior was just too heavy for him to be of much help. Bar came to with his head reeling. It was many minutes before he could think. El gave him the waterskin, and after a long drink, his head cleared a little. It was an unbelievable relief to be off Charger and stretched out on the cool ground. His companion sat not far from him, resting his weary head on his hands. *He has had an exciting but frightening day,* Bar thought with sympathy.

After a few minutes of rest, Bar almost fell asleep. He forced himself awake. *Fool! You'll be caught—and the lad, too—like birds in a snare, if you don't think and plan, now!* "El," he managed to say, "we need to care for Charger and eat something before it's totally dark."

Slowly El raised his head. "Of course. Just tell me what to do." His voice was heavy with fatigue. Awkwardly, the youngster removed the weary horse's saddle and rubbed him down as Bar instructed. He let Charger drink at the stream and gave him grain from one of the saddlebags. Then they started a very small fire, in order to boil some water.

It was dangerous, Bar knew, to light a fire. However, the herbs in his saddlebags worked better when steeped in hot water, and he needed them to work well. Gingerly, Bar searched the back of his head and found a swollen cut. No wonder his head ached! Observing his reaction, El knelt behind him to look at the injury. He murmured something sympathetic and added a cleansing herb to the heated water in Bar's cup. Bar braced himself, but El used a torn piece of his own shirt to make a compress, and the warmth actually felt good. El rinsed the small rag in the cup and put it on the injury again and again. Then he was able to clean it. After Bar explained the salve's use, El smeared the slimy green paste from the O'Hatch over the cut.

Bar gave his gentle companion an approving look. "You would make a good healer, lad. I'd have been in sad shape this day without your help. Thank you."

"And I'd be a prisoner still without yours, so we have helped each other."

Bar smiled for the first time that day and said, "Aye, that's true."

After Bar drank hot water laced with otet from their only cup, they smothered out the few burning twigs. El made a place for them both to sleep and then helped Bar to the stream. Bar had no intention of removing his boot, which held his ankle tightly in place, but he hoped the cold water would reduce the swelling and calm the pain. He lowered his foot into the icy water. His upper thigh was badly bruised, probably by Charger's hoof, as he had fallen almost under the horse's feet.

Bar said softly, "These woods may be full of soldiers tonight, searching for Alli. If so, they could have tipeeke with them. Those blasted animals will find us in a flash. I don't know where in Boer's bow we are precisely." He grinned. "If I did know, I would know places we could hide in safety, but I can't find them tonight in the dark. Yet this is a terrible place to be if they start searching for us."

The dark shape that was El remained still a few moments, and then he said logically, "Well then, why don't we rest here till the moon rises? Perhaps then we will be able to see enough to travel. Until then, I will listen for them, and we will ride out if they come. That way, at least you will get a chance to sleep."

Bar was surprised at the good sense of this plan and couldn't think of a better one. "That sounds good to me; however, I'll take the first watch. I'm hurting too badly to sleep anyway." This was not entirely true. Without another word, the young man lay on Bar's blanket on the pine needle–covered ground and slept. Bar leaned his back against a tree and concentrated on staying awake until his turn came to sleep for a few minutes. No tipeeke cries or any other sound disturbed their rest.

At moonrise, with El's help, Bar got his left leg over the horse and was able to sit astride. They followed the stream's meandering course eastward toward the mountains. It was a beautiful night, full of the sounds and scents of summer. Even full of otet, Bar was miserable. They heard no sounds of a search. Bar knew that they were farther north than the rest of the raiding party, who would have scattered the minute they hit the forested slopes of the foothills. Therefore, the hunt for the Alli should be south of them, unless, of course, some sharp scout had found his and El's tracks, heaven forbid.

When Tal discovered Bar's absence, he would begin an immediate search. Bar grinned a second at the thought of his bodyguard's dismay—Tal had left behind the very person he had sworn to protect.

Where would it be best for El and me to go? Someplace where Tal can find us? Or should we try to make it to the vale on our own? He searched the landscape around him for some clue to indicate where they were. Nothing looked familiar, yet they went on. El was stumbling with weariness when they heard the first distant cry of tipeeke. He looked up at Bar, his face hidden from view by the hood. "The animal you fear?"

"Aye," Bar said, his face grim. They took time for water and dried fruit before they started again.

When El reached for the saddlebags, Bar noticed again the cut elong bonds on his wrists and feet. "Why were you a prisoner?"

"I was a hostage. They move me every year at this time to Casterray but only for a few days. The king looks me over and then sends me back to my prison. I have never had a chance— not the smallest opportunity—to escape before this. I am very grateful to you and the others. Even if we don't make it, I have known freedom for a few hours."

Shock brought Bar wide awake. *Casterray? The king? Who is he, and why is he so important? There is a story here, but it will have to wait.* A distant chord of memory sounded, but Bar could not recall its meaning. As he carefully searched the young face, he said in sympathy, "I, too, have been a prisoner. Let's see if we can manage to outwit them and stay free. My friends, when they realize I am missing, will return and search for me. We must give them time to find us before the soldiers do." El was sure they *would* search for Bar, considering who he was.

The gentle flow of the stream became swift and wild as the rocky terrain climbed steeply. The difficult banks grew steeper on either side. When they came to a rough but sturdy bridge, they crossed to the other side of the swiftly flowing water. Some woodsman, perhaps a Bani, had built it from scraps of pine and elong long ago. Charger balked, but El handled his fears capably and, by turns, petted and bullied him across. Truly the horse was as exhausted as they and had little strength to resist him. Bar's muscles trembled, and fire burned in both his head and leg. Soon they must stop again, or he would simply fall off the horse.

As they turned east on the other side of the stream, they saw ahead of them a huge tumble of rock that seemed familiar. Bar shook his head in an attempt to think. *If I am right, there is a pool formed by the stream on the east side … a big if!* As the eastern sky grew light, Bar explained his thoughts to El. They eagerly urged Charger up a steep slope and around the great cliff. Hope of a hiding place gave them both renewed energy. But there was no pool, just rough rock. Disappointment drained them. "We must keep going. Daylight cannot find us in the open," Bar said huskily.

Bemoaning his luck, the captain ordered his men back to the highway. It infuriated the king's soldiers to return to the road and signal for tipeeke, but what else could they do? The Alli had disappeared into the foothills like smoke. They needed the tipeeke's sharp noses to find this prey that scattered like the wind.

At the landmark called the Northern Gate, Tal's weary company gathered as sunlight brightened the eastern sky. Right before dawn, they'd heard the faint cry of tipeeke, and their irritating noise had continued off and on since then, but the animals were still far behind them.

Everyone was accounted for but one. As they shared information, it became apparent that no one had seen Bar since he'd taken off in pursuit of a runaway wagon. Tal, Os, and Dare—Bar's watchdogs, as the other Alli called them—looked at one another in dismay. They were overcome with guilt and the kind of fear that suspended thought. No one could remember Bar being with them when they fled across the plain into the foothills. That meant he was still near the site of their ambush, long hours behind them. There were only two reasons he would not have joined them: he was either injured or captured. With a grim face, Tal said, "Os, we must go back. The rest of you return to Glimmervale. Tell Amray what has happened and ask him to send a search party for us."

As Tal jumped down from the rock he was standing on, Dare barred his way. "I am just as responsible for protecting him as you are, and I'm going with you."

Tal started to argue and then changed his mind. "Come, then. We might need your healing skills." *Surely only a serious injury or capture could have kept him from joining us.*

Chea and Tier stepped in front of him. "This is Bani country, sir. You need me," Tier said respectfully.

"If you don't let me come, I'll follow anyway," Chea added firmly.

"I suppose I should be grateful that you sometimes allow me to lead this company!" Tal exclaimed. "Come, then. Don't anyone else even think about it," he commanded with a quelling look at the warriors around him. They figured he had been pushed farther than was safe, but no one moved to leave.

"He is our future king also," Dell said softly.

The irrepressible Yrd spoke for them all when he added, with a straight face, "Why should you have all the fun, sir?" His eyes were full of mischief.

Incensed, Tal asked, "Is there anyone who will volunteer to see our wounded home?" One of his lieutenants, a man named Tesz, had a sword slash on his right arm. It was not deep, but he knew he would be of no use in a fight and offered his services. Tal ordered everyone to eat and rest for an hour; then they would start. He and Tier discussed the best plan, for this was Bani country.

The search party followed a deep chasm north for a few miles. Bar had been headed north the last time anyone had seen him, and they hoped the enemy search would be intent on their trails to the Northern Gate and not on his. Their pursuers should be many hours behind them. Thank the Maker the king's soldiers had not brought tipeeke with them at first; they'd evidently returned to the highway to wait for them. The party confused their trail with an herbal dust Shonar had created just for that purpose, but tipeeke were hardheaded. They would keep hunting until they picked up the Alli's scent again. At least it might give them more time.

A quickening breeze teased the trees around them and then grew into a full-blown wind. Dark clouds covered the sun, and it began to rain. Rain was long overdue, but what timing! It could confuse their enemies' purpose as much as the Alli's. Because it was never far from cold in the high country, the company of seven was soon shivering and miserable under their capes. Tier led them to shelter, a large rock overhang, until the rain let up enough that they could see where they were going.

⸺⬦⬦⸺

As the driving sheets of rain pounded Bar's back, he thanked the Maker. Not even the fanatic, single-minded, tenacious tipeeke could hunt in this. All scent of the Alli, as well as any tracks, would be washed away. Bar let out a victorious, if rather weak, war cry. For a moment, he dropped his head back to let the rain wash his face clean of dust and grime. He enjoyed the sheer relief of no longer being hunted and opened his mouth to taste the cold, sweet water.

El stared at him in disbelief mingled with concern. *Has the man lost his senses?* They were soaked and couldn't see two feet in front of them. The temperature was much cooler. They needed shelter of some kind soon, and his companion was acting like a … a madman! Bar explained himself to the startled youngster sheepishly. When El heard that they were safe from capture, at least for the moment, he sat down in the running wetness on a hard rock and wept. One who had been a prisoner for ten years did not take freedom lightly. Bar waited patiently; he understood what relief could do. El had been strong when he'd needed to be.

After the sobs ceased, Bar said more cheerfully, "Along this stream somewhere, there is a hidden cave. If it is not on the other side of that outcropping up there, we will have to settle for any shelter we can find." They moved on again, exhausted still but more hopeful. It was not the place Bar remembered; however, there was a deep cleft in the rock that would shelter them and Charger. It would have to do. There was a narrow opening at

103

the top, but the rain was blowing from the west instead of coming straight down, so the floor was dry.

In this shelter, Bar got off Charger by degrees, with El's help. All cheerfulness fled with the doubling of throbbing pain that movement caused. Gathering dry leaves and twigs from where he sat, Bar explained shortly where El could find dry wood outside to keep a fire alive. It had not been raining long. There should be plenty of tinder and branches that were not yet soaked under the pine needles and leaves that covered the forest floor.

After a few minutes, El staggered back inside with an armload of wood, and they got a small blaze started. He went out again and brought back another load, but each was too tired by that time to do anything but curl up and sleep, wet though they were. Bar did not sleep long; pain and the cold discomfort of wet clothing woke him. He fed the fire, laid out what food they had left, and made tea laced with otet in his cup. Also, Charger needed tending. Somehow Bar would have to manage it, as El was deeply, soundly asleep and snoring softly. Bar doubted if he could wake him.

A Strange Battle

BAR WOKE SUDDENLY FROM A LIGHT DOZE. The warmth of the fire combined with strong, otet-laced tea and the droning patter of rain had relaxed him into sleep. Unease crept over him like a cold mist. He glanced sharply at the opening to their shelter and gasped in shock.

A tall, perilous form filled the entrance and stood there, motionless, watching him. "Who are you? What do you want?" he demanded in a hoarse voice. No answer. Bar sensed a strange, indifferent emptiness from this being, who was cloaked from head to foot in fold upon fold of black cloth. Harsh, cold air invaded their small sanctuary.

Heart pounding, Bar tried to think, to remember where his sword, bow, or knives had been placed in their little cave. *Stripped off everything but my short breeches ... laid my other clothes on rocks near the fire to dry ... My right boot, the one with a knife in it, is there. Kept the left one on because of my injured ankle ... but it holds no weapon!*

Bar rose to a standing position by bracing his hands against the wall behind him and inching his way up the rough granite. He was careful to put no weight on his left foot. He never took his eyes off the immobile, menacing figure, not for a moment. Bar tried to speak, but his mouth was dry, and a nightmarish numbness was beginning to steal over him.

El! El! He tried to call, but no word came from his lips. He raised his hand as if to ward off a blow, and a small cry came from his throat. Then he made a second sound that was only a moan, but these small sounds were so terror filled that El woke. He looked up at Bar, his eyes sleep dazed.

The frozen horror on Bar's face caused the youngster to cry softly, "Bar! Bar, what's wrong?" He rose quickly to go to him and in so doing got between Bar and the strange creature at the entrance to their small shelter. El gently shook Bar by the shoulders, calling his name all the while, and suddenly, with a shudder, Bar glanced down at his new friend.

The numb sensation faded a little, and he desperately fought a compulsion to look up again—up into that awful strength clothed in black. "El, don't … don't turn around! Stay close to me, and don't let me go!" Bar commanded urgently in a shaking whisper. Sick with fear for El and shame at his inability to break the thing's hold on him, Bar struggled with all his strength to keep the monster out of his mind. *How is it doing this! It's not … not even touching me!* El was confused, but he knew Bar's terror was real. He himself sensed a strong feeling of coldness in their previously warm shelter, yet the fire still burned. He could hear its soft crackling and see its flickering glow on the stone walls.

Though El did not turn around to look, he knew something terrible was behind them, something that was shaking Bar deeply and draining his strength. It took strong effort not to turn and see what it was. Instead, El clung more tightly to Bar and searched his face with fearful inquiry, trying to read there what new trouble had come to them, a new trouble in a growing list.

Bar gripped El's upper arms convulsively as his ability to resist the thing was exhausted. Aware that he was sinking into a stupor and losing the battle of wills, Bar cried painfully in a voice nothing like his own, "Maker, help us!" At his anguished cry, the sense of cold, sucking emptiness broke, as thin ice broke when struck. His relief turned to terror as the sinister figure rushed at them with murderous intent.

Bar whirled El against the wall at his back with all his remaining strength and covered the lad with his body, his only thought being to protect him. Inadvertently, he put weight on his injured foot, and pain shot through his left ankle and leg. He groaned and crumpled to the ground, taking El down with him.

With hands outstretched to seize them, the hoarsely panting figure plowed through the fire as if the burning flames were nothing to it. Sparks and burning logs sprayed all over their small enclosure. The being's large hands smashed into the granite wall because its prey was no longer there. Unnoticed for the moment, Bar and El lay huddled at the creature's feet. Finding its hands empty, the dark apparition screamed in pain and fury, for it had cracked its head as well as bashed its hands. Bar heard the furious howls above him as the thing stumbled backward in agony.

Strong but clumsy and not exactly bright, he thought wryly. Pain and exhaustion blackened the edges of his vision. *Now! I must find my Gin'hana now, before I lose consciousness!* He turned and frantically searched the ground for the ancient sword. El was crouched between him and the wall, safe for the moment. His searching fingers finally found the carved handle. He tore the blade free from its scabbard with awkward, trembling hands. Quickly Bar rose on one foot and turned to face his enemy. He held the sword in front of him with shaking hands. Overcoming its pain, the creature charged Bar again. Too late did it see the softly glowing blade the young warrior held before him. The huge being speared itself on the ancient weapon with all the force of its being, doing what Bar did not have the strength to do!

A howl of anguish echoed off the walls and gradually diminished. Bar lay frozen under the huge creature, still tightly gripping his sword. El could not move either, for he was trapped under them both. Bar had no strength to move, to cry out, or even to think. Darkness swallowed him.

Two hours later, Tal found Bar and El's hiding place in the cleft. Charger had wandered out of the cleft to get away from a fearful something he did not like. Being a sensible horse, he'd begun searching for grass and a drink. Tal and his company discovered the animal grazing contentedly near the stream. They searched the area and quickly detected the cleft in a jumble of rock. As Tal and Dare entered it, they felt a bleak sense of evil and became uneasy. Lying crumpled on the floor against the far wall was a huge figure cloaked in black. Their gazes met in inquiry and dread. Fearfully, they lifted the heavy body. Their pounding hearts almost stopped beating.

Underneath lay Bar and another slight figure, both of them pale and cold. Bar's hands still held his sword handle; he had killed or badly injured the huge man. His comrades swallowed with difficulty and found they had stopped breathing. Fear that Bar and the other person were dead paralyzed them both. The silent, tense company watched from the opening. Those in front relayed whispered information to those behind them who could not see.

Dare's training as a healer compelled him into action, and he fell to his knees to feel unsteadily for Bar's pulse. It was there, faint and slow but steady. Relief brought color back into his face and a soft, explosive "Thank the Maker." The young man under Bar was also alive, and neither appeared to have any serious injury. The large being had a wound in his left shoulder caused by Bar's Gin'hana. Dare bent down to see if the man lived and could hear soft breathing. He, too, lived! Tal ordered two of his men to remove the man from the small enclosure. At their gasps of horror, Tal turned and, for the first time, took a really good look at the huge being.

What in Boer's bow? He pushed back the black wool cloak and stared in disbelief. This human being was right out of fireside fables. In a flash of memory, Tal remembered that Oster had described men who looked like this—men he had seen at the Mirg. *To see is to believe. I thought he saw an illusion, but no, this is real.* The man's head was large and hairless. His skin was a ghastly, pale white. Whatever Blalock—and who else could it be!—had given him or done to him had made his limbs, his whole body, thick and large. There were strange twin puncture marks on his neck, as if a snake had bitten him. Perhaps this alien hulk had once been a warm-blooded man—a man who had laughed and cried and loved. "Move him out of here and watch him closely in case he wakes up."

His men obeyed him quickly. He ordered, "Post sentries all around us and tell me about anything—*anything*—unusual. Guard the body carefully." Tal did not know exactly what he feared, but one thing he dreaded for certain was that there might be more of these beings seeking them.

Tal turned to look at Bar and allowed himself to feel relief that the prince and his companion lived. He gave quiet orders to start a fire, boil water, get warm and dry blankets, raise a shelter, and prepare food. The small camp became a beehive of activity.

The rain had stopped, but the ground outside was still wet, so they worked on both patients in the little rock cave. Dare sponged Bar's torso and face but found no injury. As he checked him more closely, he found the bruised thigh. The single boot gave him a clue that something was wrong with his friend's left ankle or foot, but that was not life threatening and could wait.

Tal had started to strip the still-damp clothing off Bar's unknown companion when he made a startling discovery. "He" was not a he at all but a young woman! Tal kept his discovery to himself and wrapped her in dry blankets. He found no injury on her body and began to clean the dirt off her face. Suddenly he stopped and stared at her as if afraid to continue, both hope and fear in his eyes.

Dare felt Tal's stillness and silence and turned from Bar to look at him. "Tal, what … what's wrong? *Now what?*" The Basca's eyes were fastened intently on the face his scrubbing had revealed. His own face was pale and stiff, his eyes filled with conflicting emotions that Dare couldn't even name. Tal lifted the still-unconscious form to a sitting position and held the boy to him in a long embrace, an embrace that startled Dare. Tal reached a trembling hand to the lad's cap and pulled it off. Shining black hair tumbled down his back. Dare was even more startled when he recognized the strangled sounds coming from Tal's bent form as sobbing. *Surely the world is coming to an end! A Basca' weeping?* After a few minutes, Tal quieted, but he still held the lad, who was evidently a lass, and he still could not speak. Feeling serious alarm, Dare went to the entrance and called loudly for Oster, who came running.

Os gave Dare a quick questioning look. The young healer pointed to Tal's still form. Oster knelt next to him, and Tal wordlessly held the girl's body away from his own so that Os could see her face. Wonder spread across Os's countenance. He was speechless for a long minute and then grinned at Tal with joy. Remembering Dare's confusion, he explained, "*She* … she is the Basca' child the king has held prisoner for ten years, the one he threatens to harm if we do not comply with his orders. Our raid on the king's supply train must have freed her. That explains it! That is why the soldiers fought so hard! They knew her true identity and realized the king would be furious if they lost the Basca' hostage." He paused and added with a happy grin, "She is also Tal's daughter."

Dare said blankly, "Daughter?" He took a good look at the small, pale face framed by glorious jet hair and saw a very beautiful young woman.

Strange, it is so obvious now. "Daughter! Tal never told us that the child they took was his. No wonder he stayed in Feisan all those years when the others returned home. It was his only opportunity to see her." He looked at Os in wonder. "And he gave that up rather than harm Bar. He risked his own daughter's safety." Os nodded, his eyes bright with pride and joy.

El coughed softly and started to move restlessly in her father's arms. She opened her eyes, which were wide with fear. "Bar! That creature!" she whispered wildly.

"Look," Tal assured her, pointing at the still form next to her. "He is well and will wake up soon, just as you have. The large man is unconscious and under guard. You have nothing to fear."

She looked for a long moment at Bar, and then her gaze returned to Tal qua. Recognition filled her eyes with warmth and affection and then tears. "Father!" They embraced with fierce delight. She gazed at him a long time before she added with amusement, "I knew you would find us! I was so shocked when Bar told me that it was Tal qua who would search for him once his absence was discovered."

Tal laughed. "I thought yesterday a total waste of time and energy and then something much worse—a total disaster—when we discovered Bar was not with us. Now I have recovered him and gained you also. How impossible it is to predict the Maker's ways." They talked softly for many minutes before El tired. Dare returned his attention to Bar, who surely should have come around by now, but he did not wake that day.

Strangely, everyone in camp felt dreary and discouraged. The men looked over their shoulders continually, prompted by the feeling that someone was watching them ... someone they couldn't quite see. The rain started again and then turned into a wet mist and fog. It swirled around on the ground in strange patterns that confused the eye. There was a heavy overcast and occasional rumble of thunder.

Why, Tal wondered, this strange oppression? Bardon survived a fall from his horse and an attack by a ghastly, altered human and is now with us and safe, instead of lost in this great forest. After being held hostage for ten years, Ellarann is free and with us also. Why do I feel so heavy?

Bar groaned when Dare removed his boot and bandaged his ankle, and then he started to mumble incoherently. Suddenly, he sat bolt upright and opened his eyes. They were dilated and fixed on something dreadful that only he could see. Cautiously, Dare called his name. Bar turned to gaze at him, but his expression was unchanged. Dare grabbed both Bar's shoulders and shook him slightly. "Bar, you've wounded that dreadful creature! We've tied him up. Everything is all right. El is alive and well, and the whole company is here. Bar, talk to me!" he pleaded desperately.

Some of the rigid coldness went out of Bar's countenance, and his eyes focused on his friend's face. He swallowed and took a deep breath. "Dare?"

"Aye."

"Tell me again."

Dare repeated what he had said and added more detail. "I am so cold," Bar said as from a great distance. A chill of anxiety went through Dare that made his heart ache. Bar looked over at El, who was lying next to him still, and she smiled at him reassuringly. It took time, but between Dare and El, they managed to bring Bar back to the living world, yet he was not himself. He showed little surprise that his companion was not the young boy he had thought him to be. El, too, was frightened at the difference in Bar. She and Dare exchanged worried glances.

After they had cleaned up a quick meal and were preparing for sleep, Tal heard a low whistle from one of his sentries followed by whistles from them all. They were surrounded! With every sense alert, Tal gave orders quickly—orders he had been planning for the last few hours. Whatever or whoever was attacking them had waited until dark to make their move, but the warriors had sensed their foe's presence all through the damp, dreary afternoon, and they were ready. They obeyed quietly and quickly. The camp was as full of light as they could make it. They had added wood to the fires, which were now blazing.

Two sentries materialized out of the trees and reported to Tal that creatures like the one Bar had fought were approaching their position. They were in no kind of formation; each was lumbering into their area from a different direction with a single-minded, slow tread. Looking neither left nor right, the beings were making no attempt to communicate with one another or to be stealthy. Such complete indifference to ordinary methods of attack betrayed unquestioning confidence in their abilities—and perhaps an inability to work as a team—and dismayed Tal. He wondered what it would take to stop these strange beings. The company ranged themselves on the large outcropping of rock and all around their small camp. They were well trained, and each knew what to do in a normal attack. As they faced the dark woods, they realized there would be nothing normal about this battle.

Bar grew anxious as large forms disengaged themselves from the shadows beneath the trees and ponderously approached their rocky camp. The things carried no weapons that anyone could see. A vivid memory of his encounter with the large being flashed through his mind. He realized these beings used their arms to batter the object of their attack. Suddenly, Bar knew why they carried no club or sword, no weapons of any kind. Their most useful weapon was their vacant, drawing minds—minds that could suck consciousness from ordinary people before they knew what the focused creatures were attempting. Once people realized what the creatures were doing, perhaps it was not nearly as effective.

Bar recognized that El's intervention had probably saved him from being drawn into a trance of some kind. He must warn everyone, or there would be no battle; it would be over before anyone could raise a weapon.

"Tal! Warriors! Listen to me," he cried hoarsely, fighting for words, for breath, for the ability to think through the coldness gripping his mind. His voice stumbled, and his mind went blank. Breathing hard, Bar searched the darkness around him, trying to recall what he had so urgently wanted to say.

A soft hand slipped into his and pressed it. He looked into El's eyes and remembered the last time he had done so—remembered the being that had drained his thoughts from him. "Their weapon is their mind," he shouted feebly. He continued, his voice gaining force, "Call upon the Maker, and do not make eye contact! Do not even look directly at them! Refuse to be controlled!"

Bar looked around him. For some it was too late. Their expressions were vacant. He and El went to them and shook them with agonizing haste, bringing them back to themselves. Bar's searching gaze finally found Tal, who appeared dazed but was still aware and conscious. "When they cannot win this way, they will attack us physically," Bar shouted. "Be ready!"

Anger surged through Tal that anyone would use such dreadful methods on their fellow men to win a battle. He had just found his stolen daughter. She was a wonderful gift from the Maker; he would not lose her again.

Years of submission to a king and system that he hated exploded into anger. Filled with hot fury against every oppressor who forced, coerced, bullied, and taunted for his own pleasure, he drew his sword and attacked the rigid, cold form nearest him. There was a terrible uproar at his first stroke.

The being howled, as did his fellows, and they turned heavily to attack this foolish, puny man. The Alli poured off the jagged rocks shouting their battle cries, and the battle became violent, noisy, and physical. Though the company far outnumbered the awkward, lumbering men, they were losing.

The things could be injured but not stopped. Bar struggled to think what had been different the last time. Why had his enemy passed out when wounded? He looked at the Gin'hana in his hand.

In obedience to Tal's strict order, neither Bar nor Dare had joined the battle. They were to protect El and stay out of it. Amray's sharp lesson in following orders was still fresh in Bar's mind. His ankle made him useless, anyway. Yet what if the swords were the answer, and what if they needed to be used by those marked, as only he and Dare were—marked for the Maker's service?

He shared his thoughts quickly with Dare and El. Dare responded angrily, his eyes on the terrible battle they could barely see in spite of the roaring fires. "We must try! There is no time for discussion. Soon our men will start dying, if they have not done so already."

Harassed on every side, the strange men were surrounded by superior numbers, yet they were still dangerous and inflicting damage, using only their arms as weapons.

Oster and Tier continually pulled the enemy's concentration from Tal's savage attack, saving him injury countless times, for in this battle, he knew no reason.

Yrd caught a blow meant for Louke with his sword and was thrown ten feet into the air. The warriors tricked, teased, and distracted their enemy in an attempt to get knife and sword thrusts past the oak-thick arms; however, even when they managed to land a blow, it seemed to make little difference in their enemies' strength or coordination. The lumbering brutes would howl in pain and continue to batter at them. Each member of the company was breathing hard and tiring. The battle had changed from all-out attack to quiet, desperate perseverance.

The darkness made it difficult to recognize anyone or see exactly what was happening. El helped Bar down the rough rock face onto firm ground. Then with whispered forcefulness, Bar ordered her back up the cliff. She started to argue, but he said, "Your father will never forgive me, El, if anything happens to you. Go! Please." Guilt at leaving her alone made him hesitate for a moment, yet if they lost this battle, she would share their fate. She fled back up to hide herself and watch, disgusted with men.

Bar hopped forward using his sword like a cane; still, he almost fell. *This will never work*, he thought desperately. Seeing Bar's need, someone left the nearest group and helped him stand. Bar recognized Louke by his bulk. "Alati, brother," he whispered gratefully. Bar, with Louke's aid, and Dare attacked the flailing creatures in hope that the marked swords would make a difference. Their adversaries fell back before the ancient weapons and cried out in dismay. The marked warriors gave each other tight smiles filled with hope. They battered two of their attackers back into the woods until they fled roaring hysterically.

If the remaining enemy joins together to oppose us, Bar thought, *they will be victorious, swords or no!* The two marked could not handle all seven at once with just two weapons, but the idea of cooperation never seemed to occur to their attackers. To the cheers of the company and with the other warriors' help, Bar and Dare pushed the huge men back into the dark forest one by one. The beings shambled with amazing speed and deep rumblings of discontent into the night.

Bar, Louke, and Dare were too exhausted to follow the creatures, and no one knew if it was possible for anyone else to wield their swords effectively against the strange beings. The three young warriors collapsed to the ground, gasping for air, wet with perspiration and spent. Dare thought, *I have fought these evil beings and sent them running into the night with the swords the Maker provided! Thanks be to him!*

Tal's Alli were too exhausted to cheer or even smile. They slumped to rest where they were and stared at each other in grim amazement. Soldiers were one thing; they were men after all, but what kind of enemy was this? Whoever—whatever they were—the Alli felt pity for them, for once they had been normal human beings.

DEATH'S DARK VALLEY

GASPING FOR BREATH, BAR CROUCHED IN THE dust and tried to find a more comfortable position for his injured ankle and leg, but he discovered that his body would not obey him. His head also throbbed with pain, yet worse than his injuries was the return of the empty, cold despair he'd felt on waking a few hours ago. The Alli named their new enemy the *selitper*—a word in Bani for "snake." They all had seen the twin puncture marks on the strange beings' necks that looked like snakebites. The marks were swollen and red. The thought of what Blalock had done to normal human beings made the warriors feel sick. To do this to his fellow men, just to create a better soldier and win the battle for power, revolted them.

Not again, Bar thought desperately. *It is the selitper ... Something to do with these things brings this darkness, but how can it affect me even after they are gone?* Louke saw that Bar was close to fainting, and lifting him gently, he carried him to his pallet. Louke was so tired that his legs felt mushy, and he was light-headed. Bar made no complaint as his body sagged in the strong thirteen—no, now fourteen-year-old's arms. He could not even find enough energy to thank him, yet without Louke's aid against the selitper, he could not have raised his sword arm, much less fought.

Tal talked with his men briefly and set the watch for the rest of the night. El came to him then and assured him she was well. He embraced her tightly for a few minutes and then walked with her to the small cave that held her pallet. Dare was there, having recovered a little, and was pouring otet and other medicines into Bardon, who was in pain. "Good work, both of you, and quick thinking," Tal said. Bardon started to speak, but Tal interrupted him. "Rest. Tomorrow we will discuss this night, but now sleep." Bar wanted to obey him and tried to let go of his worry, for the moment at least, about the strange beings that fled into the night. Tal would have done all that could be done to be ready for the creatures, should they attack again.

Dare had much work to do, and after gathering his various pouches, he gave Bar a quick look, then left to help the other injured. He could barely stand, yet with the aid of those who were not badly injured, he worked on his fellows until all were settled for the night.

Bar found he could not sleep, as much as he wished it. Pain and frenzied thoughts chased one another through his mind to no purpose and kept him awake. Though he wanted to be quiet so that El could rest, he could not seem to keep his aching body still. A small, warm hand slipped into his cold one and squeezed it. After a time he quieted and fell asleep still holding her hand, but he did not sleep for long. He woke a few hours before dawn with a raging fever, and El called Dare to treat him.

They broke camp at first light and traveled toward the vale with Bar tossing and turning in delirium on a litter. There was no one in the company who did not have bruises, and there were some with broken bones. Dare had not rested at all. With Louke's help, he set broken bones, bandaged sore ribs, and dispensed the last of all their combined medicines. Bani and Basca' saddlebags alike were empty of remedies. They limped toward the Bani's refuge at a slow pace to accommodate their many injured and the cumbersome litter that carried Bar.

Heavy gray clouds overhead threatened rain, and something followed behind them. They could feel its malevolence. Then they heard the baying of tipeeke in the distance. Looking at one another in dismay, they wondered if they would ever make it to the vale. The enemy seemed to have endless resources. Dare collapsed, and they stopped for a time, to let him and the badly injured rest.

As the sun sank in the west, the company heard the wild cry of geese overhead. Tier threw back his head and answered the lonely sound with a haunting signal of his own. He grinned wearily at Tal. "Amray is coming," he said. Despite Tier's effort to show no emotion, Tal heard relief in the young man's voice. They waited, and the Bani leader with twelve men emerged out of the trees ahead of them. They and their ponies glowed in the golden light of the setting sun.

With relief Dare recognized one of the approaching group as Sureese, the Bani's healer. Bar needed medicine and more-expert help than Dare's limited training could give him. Also, he was sick with weariness, which made his thinking slow and difficult. There was something about fighting these evil beings that drained the fighter physically, mentally and spiritually—something very different than normal fighting against normal soldiers. Bani ponies and Alli horses mixed in the dying light as the two companies greeted each other.

Tal and Amray conferred in quiet whispers. Then the Bani chief spoke to the battered raiding party. "You are being followed. I know you are tired, but we must go on and not stop until we are in the vale." The company groaned, but they knew he was right. No one wanted another confrontation with the selitper. And also behind them were tipeeke with all that meant.

Amray continued, "Our retreat is guarded by many Bani, yet I would prefer not to engage the enemy. We need to disappear. My men will carry the litter and change runners often. If you find you cannot keep the pace, say so, and we will help you." He searched their faces with a stern eye and then led them east at a fast trot. While Amray was speaking, Sureese examined Bar and gave him otet and wilett, an herb to bring down his fever. As Sureese mounted his horse, his forehead creased in a worried frown.

The twilight of the summer evening deepened into darkness, and Amray was forced to slow their pace. As the air cooled, mist rose from the forest floor and swirled around the horses' hooves. They dismounted and led their horses while night birds called and crickets chirped. Dare was sure that some of the night's noises were Amray's men, who were all around them.

After a few hours of slow progress, Amray called a halt in a small clearing so that they might eat and rest for a few minutes, but he did not dismount. The moon rose and beamed soft light through the branches overhead. They would be able to move more quickly now because they could see somewhat better. Amray listened intently to the chirping and birdcalls, which the company knew were messages from his scouts. His face became grim, and he started to speak but was interrupted by Bar.

The marked prince sat up suddenly from where he lay on his litter. He drew his sword with trembling hands and cried hoarsely, "He's—the selitper is coming again!"

Dare reached out a hand to still him, and their eyes met. "I'll take care of it. Rest." He rose and threw Chea lar Bar's sword, then easily drew his own. *How familiar we have all become with weapons, with fighting.* He and Chea lar waited, watching the dark, shadowed trees that surrounded them. Both were grateful for the soft light from the moon that flooded the clearing. This time they would be able to see their enemy more clearly. Both Tal's and Amray's men drew their weapons and searched the silent darkness under the trees. No one moved; they barely breathed.

"Will I be able to fight a selitper with this thing?" Chea asked softly.

"I don't know," Dare responded with a forced grin, "but we may as well find out now while there is only one of them. At least I hope there is only one."

Bar hoped so too. The numbing sensation, which had told him of the selitper's presence, was gripping his mind. The misery of his body's aches and pains retreated before the attack on his intellect. It took all he had to call upon the Maker and stand firm in his name.

All the soft noises of the night ceased. In the eerie silence, they heard a heavy tread among the leaves and pine needles. Everyone shifted position to face the sound. Chea and Dare raised their swords in preparation. The huge selitper trudged into the clearing. Men grasped their weapons tightly and prayed for strength. The dreaded creature lumbered straight toward Bar as if no one else existed. Their faces grim, Chea and Dare jumped in the selitper's path with the marked swords raised and glowing softly. As he stomped by them, they attacked with all their skill and strength.

A horrible roar rent the night, yet the selitper battered the young warriors aside with his massive arms, without ever looking directly at them. They each landed in a crumpled heap on the hard ground many feet from their undeterred enemy. Amray's experienced warriors gasped, astounded at the selitper's monstrous strength. Chea and Dare lay stunned and bruised.

Dare raised himself to a crouch and shook his head in an effort to think.

Heaven help us! The thing feels pain, but we did not even slow it or harm it in any way! This one is much more powerful than the others of its kind ... others that I fought just yesterday. Why! Confused and shaken, he struggled to rise.

Fear gripped the company at the obvious impossibility of preventing this being from doing whatever he wished. It was like trying to stop the charge of a living rock. The monster's whole focus was on Bardon. Amray watched with an appalled gaze as he fought to control his frightened, plunging horse.

Given strength by sudden pounding fear, those warriors nearest the litter leaped in front of the creature to defend Bar until Chea and Dare could get back to their feet. The selitper tossed aside seasoned warriors as if they were children.

Louke watched with horror and confusion. *Yesterday ... yesterday was so different!* The huge being's injuries did not seem to affect his unbelievable abilities in any way. Quickly Louke darted to the shaken Chi. They exchanged quick glances of agreement—yesterday *Bar* had held the marked sword. Louke took the blade Bar had named Uriisis and ran with it back to the litter, hoping he would be in time to meet the selitper's attack. Bar struggled to stand. Desperately, Louke asked the Maker for help, forgetting that he did not believe in him.

He placed the marked weapon in Bar's cold grasp and covered the marked prince's hand with his very large one. They turned to meet the trudging selitper. Those who had recovered their feet, as well as the still-mounted Tal and Amray, charged to distract the single-minded creature. The selitper plowed through them like a battering ram. Both men and horses cried out in pain as he pounded them out of his way. Weapons, men, and gear flew through the air. Bar slumped against Louke, who managed to get him back on his feet. It was clearly Louke who was holding both Bar and the sword upright and ready, for Bar's strength was gone. Yet Bar had anger and determination to add to Louke's quick thinking and great might.

Meanwhile, Dare pushed himself painfully to his feet and stumbled around the tangled knot of men surrounding the selitper so that he might try to engage it. The creature threw back his head within the deep hood and roared his furious frustration at the constant interference and pain. The woods shook with the sound. Darkness and dread seemed to fill the small clearing and invade their minds. The warriors struggled to fight back and remain positive and ready.

Flinging aside the last man in his way, the creature drew his immense right arm back. He then swung it forward with all his might, intending to smash Bardon into oblivion. However, the strength of a stonecutter's arm, fist wrapped around Bar's own, held the marked sword firm against the mighty blow. The creature howled in bewildered fear and terrible pain as the Gin'hana slammed into his arm and stopped his strike. There should have been a gash in his arm at the least, but there was none. The selitper felt pain but was not cut! Louke felt the shock of the blow through his whole body and cried out also in fury-blended pain of his own.

With Louke's war cry ringing in his ears, driven by terrible fear for Bar's safety, Dare attacked the creature with determination from behind. The enormous brute, who seemed capable of only one emotion—namely, fury—raised his huge fists to the sky and howled. He then whirled with incredible speed and swept his right arm in a backhanded swat at Dare, as if Dare were nothing more than a troublesome mosquito. The warriors gasped in terror, but Dare, who knew his enemy by now, was ready. He ducked the blow, and it whistled over his head, missing by inches. The marked healer rained blow after blow on the mountainous selitper, stunning the creature and causing it confusion as well as pain.

Holding Bar firmly around the waist with his left arm and gripping Bar's hand with his right, Louke attacked also. Bar struggled to stay conscious and keep the thing out of his mind. That comprised his total contribution to the fight, yet somehow he knew it was a vital one. The consciousness holding the sword must be his own, though all the strength was Louke's. The creature backed fearfully away from them, howling, staggering, weakening. For Bar's sake, Louke stopped his attack, hoping the healer's sword would be enough to finish the obstinate selitper.

Perspiration ran down Dare's face, blurring his vision. His breath came in gasps, and his arm trembled, yet he kept on. Finally, the great arms fell from the protective position they had taken across the selitper's chest, and the huge being turned and limped with terrible effort into the night. No one followed. Dare stared at the retreating thing and sank in exhaustion to his knees, unable to hold his sword, which fell to the ground.

There were no cheers. The entire camp was frozen in shock and horror. They stared numbly at Dare's slumped body on the ground. It was long moments before they were able to move and speak again. Bani materialized out of the trees, relieved that the enemy had given up and was retreating to no one knew where. They were appalled that they'd been unable to prevent the creature from reaching their camp. They were ashamed to face their lord, who had told them to guard this party yet warned them not to directly confront the thing, for it seemed only the Gin'hana could harm him. They had failed to achieve the impossible task. They had not been able to slow or to distract the selitper no matter what they tried. Amray silenced them with an understanding gesture and motioned them back out to guard again. They left quickly and hoped against hope that there were no more such creatures in their lands.

Quietly, Tal and Amray lifted Dare and put him on a horse. They reverently sheathed Wolf, his Gin'hana, after carefully wiping it clean. Louke did the same with Bar's sword. His hands shook with the effort, and he did not try to hide their trembling. Suddenly he bent from the waist and braced his straight arms on his knees. Breathing raggedly, he tried to calm his shaking body. *Bar bore the brunt of that thing's mind! I am sick and cold with what leaked through to me. Will he ever be the same?* He shook his head to clear it and straightened. They were all awed and shocked by the battle they had just witnessed.

Shaking his head in amazed disbelief, Amray acknowledged that the Maker had placed their survival in the hands of youth. The marked and their friends seemed up to the challenge. It took great effort to dismiss these thoughts and get the company moving again. One of the Bani warriors gave his horse to Amray, for the selitper had grievously injured the chief's mount. The Bani did not stop, even to hide their trail, but quickly hurried the fainting, battered group toward the safety of Glimmervale.

Dare rode in an exhausted haze and would have fallen had Tier not stayed close to steady him. Bar lay unconscious on his pallet; they could not rouse him. This creature possessed the same unbelievable power as the first one Bar and El had encountered. It had been too much for Bar to stand against in his weakened condition and remain whole. They'd all felt the evil, drawing power of the thing's mind, but Bar had been the object of the selitper's purpose. Had that purpose been to subjugate or to kill? No one was sure of what the creature had intended, but they knew the king wanted Bar alive. At least, they thought he did. No one asked who had sent this grim reaper; they all knew.

Louke grinned crookedly at a shaken Chea as they rode side by side. Their right arms, which had held the Gin'hana, ached from shoulder to fingertips. Tal and Amray exchanged anxious glances, and as one person, both pushed for sanctuary. They reached the vale sometime after the twelfth hour with the distant sound of tipeeke echoing in their ears. Relief flooded both men when the security of the valley's high walls closed around them. They thanked the Maker for deliverance.

Bar woke the next morning with a body that seemed as heavy as a boulder and a sluggish mind. He swallowed scalding tea and felt better for it but still strangely distant from all that was happening around him. Days passed, but Bar took no interest in the activity around him, not in the Bani or in the councils of his fellows. His friends grew more and more worried about his condition. He showed no interest in anything; he simply lay and stared. He spoke only when spoken to and then, shortly. His body was healing well, but his mind seemed damaged. Sureese urged them to patience. "Let nature take its course. Give his body and mind time to heal. Let him rest."

But Bar himself decided in some distant corner of his brain that he could not wait any longer to feel better. The cold, dim world he was living in was unnatural and terrifying. Thinking was like trying to walk upstream in cold, chest-high water. It was hard, weary work. He knew, following a half day of tenacious mental effort, who he must find.

After searching the camp, he found Devon scraping a large piece of leather in one of the workrooms with Tier's energetic help. Strong aromas filled the room, from the herbs and chemicals they used and from the hide itself. It was a sultry afternoon, full of bright sunlight and passing shadows caused by sweeping rain showers. The air was so damp it was heavy and hard to breathe.

"Devon," Bar said faintly with little expression. The huge man turned quickly. His sharp eyes searched the drawn, thin face with haunted eyes. Bar could not seem to go on; finding Big Brother had taken all the energy he possessed. Tier met Devon's eyes, and he nodded in unspoken agreement. The young Bani left quickly with some excuse that wasn't necessary, for Bar was unaware of his presence. Tortured by cold fear, Bar pleaded urgently, huskily, "Help me."

Devon experienced instant panic. Bar's trust that he, of all people, could help with this … what? This undefined illness caused deep fear. The large abbot gripped Bar's shoulders with his hands and sought some spark of life in those strange eyes. He found terrified loneliness and fear instead. Pity filled him. *But what can I do? The selitper are outside my knowledge, and I have not found anything in the few scrolls I have left that discusses the creatures.* Though he'd racked his brain and talked to all the Bani elders, none of them could remember ever having read about or seen a condition like Bar's present one. *I simply don't know what to do,* he thought desperately. He released Bar and leaned on the rough worktable, seeking an answer.

As he gazed out the open shutters at the bright sunshine, a racing bank of dark clouds covered the sun and plunged the valley into shadow. Rain splattered down as far as Devon could see. It made drumming sounds on the roof. Yet he knew the sun was still there behind the clouds, even if it was not visible. He recognized that old enemies—fear of failure and inadequacy— were behind his reluctance to aid Bar.

Quiet assurance flooded Devon. Nothing was too hard for the Creator, and he had gone nowhere. Like the sun, though invisible, he was still there. They would knock on doors, seek information, and ask until they found the answer. He turned to Bar with renewed confidence. "Wait for me here. We will find a way. After all, nothing is impossible for the Creator." Bar sat on a bench and listened to the rain. Devon returned many hours later with an idea he and Sureese had found in an ancient, battered scroll. He shared his news with Bar and sent him back to his hammock.

The Bani gathered that night in the council hall and sat on skins around a blazing fire in the large pit. Everyone over the age of twelve who did not have duty of some kind was there, as were the hishua and Bar. They spoke earnestly to the Maker, both silently and out loud, on Bar's behalf. Devon read from the scrolls. Flutes, a harp, and a stringed bast played gentle, sweet music. The Bani and their new friends lifted their voices in songs of praise to the one who had created them and hymns of thanks for all his gifts. Peace filled the hall and the folk in it.

Amray touched clear oil to Bar's forehead, eyelids, lips, and chest. They'd found this anointing of the sick in the Maker's name in an ancient scroll. It was for physical healing, but they hoped it would work for mental healing as well. As they felt the Maker's peace in their hearts, men and women slipped quietly away. Each touched their marked prince before they left. They asked for healing and release from this strange malady for a brother and a friend. At last, only Devon, Amray, and Bar remained. "Go to your hammock, child, and let us see what the Maker will do," Amray said softly as he pushed Bar toward the door. Devon and Amray exchanged hopeful glances. They could tell from Bar's expression that he felt the same cold emptiness. It seemed nothing had changed.

Yet a small something had. A tiny crack appeared in the solid wall of his cold emptiness. Bar was touched by the Bani's sincere concern, quiet sympathy, and deep affection. Their heartfelt prayers also touched him. A tiny ray of light reached into his darkness, yet the hollowness within seemed even worse in comparison to the tribe's warm vitality. As he drifted off to sleep, he saw a workman's calloused hand reach downward. He tried to waken to see his Maker better but could not drag his eyes open.

The next morning he awoke feeling glad for the warmth of his blankets, intense hunger at the smell of baking flatbread, and a real desire for a cup of hot tea. These were sensations he had never stopped to appreciate before, but now he recognized them with relief and gratitude as a return to normalcy. He had himself back! The distant, vacant coldness that had numbed his mind was gone. He thanked the Maker, Spirit, and Creator over and over again with a full heart.

Reaching out his hand to a ray of sunshine, Bar delighted in its warmth and light. He wanted to ride his horse, take a hot bath, talk to his friends, eat, and tell Devon the good news. He laughed out loud at the joy and vitality filling him. Bar did the last thing he'd thought of first and went to find Devon. Then he saw something he had never seen before: the mischievous abbot wept! For a moment it frightened Bar, but then he realized they were tears of joy. There were many tears that day and great rejoicing as the word spread through the vale that their sick friend was well.

That night the Bani feasted, laughed, and told their favorite tales, both ancient and new. They honored Bar's and Dare's courage, but they gave their highest honor, a white quill vest, to Louke, who blushed with embarrassment and pleasure both. They laughed merrily at his confusion, and he laughed with them, glad for the distraction. He thought being the center of attention was a frightening thing. The Maker's name was honored and praised, for he had proved himself faithful and true.

Bar gazed into the glowing embers long after everyone drifted off to their hammocks. He was himself again, and he was grateful, but he was not the same. He knew he never would be. He had chosen to fight something that evil had created, and it had left its mark on him. *I have gained knowledge and experience but at a price.* He shuddered. *I think that thing was a man once ... a living, breathing human being that someone—I suspect Blalock—has altered, changed some vile way for his evil purpose. Did the selitper know what he was doing, or was he just a shell mindlessly following orders, any orders his masters gave him? What masters? Who has found a way to make a man give up his freedom, his will, and his body for evil's use?*

In a distant cell far beneath Casterray, Tori held on to sanity by a slender thread. The thread's name was Liras, and his memory of her drove back the oppressive darkness.

A BATTLE LOST

H IGH ON A GRASSY KNOLL WHIPPED BY THE
wind, Bar sat astride Charger gazing at the flatlands far below him.
His dark hair was blown back from a countenance taut with intensity as he
searched the winding strip of dusty road. The black leather band that circled
his forehead was etched with symbols in fine script. In wearing this band,
he followed an ancient Bani custom of inscribing significant information
about a warrior, such as his birth clan, on his headband. Each man was
given a band at his twelve-year celebration; Bar had received his when he
was sixteen. It was the only crown the young prince possessed or wanted.
He was much prouder of it than the intricately carved medallion that lay
gathering dust in Casterray.

Dressed in beautifully crafted but worn black leather, Bar wore a vest,
with no shirt because of the heat, and chaps over breeches of a linen-like
material. These were also distinctly Bani. Braced on his stirrup, he held a
tall hardwood spear, a weapon rarely used by any of Ree's tribes. In this
open, grassy place, it made sense to his guards that he carry it now along
with bow, quiver, shield, sword, and knife. Only the spear was unusual, for
a warrior or soldier, in Bar's day.

His horse pranced nervously under him. He controlled Charger's restive
movements automatically, for his whole mind was on the supply train slowly
creaking into view. Soldiers positioned in front of and behind the long,
lumbering caravan guarded the heavily loaded wagons.

His gaze swept the road, the valley, the hills around him, and the mountains behind him for clues, for some hint of how his enemies communicated. The landscape was empty, just trees, rocks, and birds. The birds were tufthawks, two females, hanging high on the currents above him. His gaze quickly returned to the clean black shapes that were the birds. *Could they possibly be used by men to spy on us and to carry messages somehow? Foolish? Perhaps not, considering Blalock's gifts.*

Foreboding gripped him as he watched them, for they could see him clearly and he was far from the cover of the forest. Blalock had created from natural animals the horror of the tipeeke and braith, and from normal men the selitper; at least that was how they thought the huge men had come into being. Had this evil mastermind done something to train a normal bird, say a farseeing hawk, to do his bidding?

Today, the insurgents' intention was to discover how the king's reserve troops were alerted when the rebels attacked a supply convoy. Bardock garrisoned cavalry intermittently, in strategically placed camps both north and south on the royal highway. Bar knew where each camp with its bright yellow tents was located and how many soldiers were stationed there. What none of them knew was how these special troops were alerted to insurgent attacks. Almost always, they arrived in time to disrupt a raid, even though the caravan might be miles down the road from their camp and completely out of sight.

The king's soldiers repeatedly interrupted the Alli's raids and forced the rebels to flee without accomplishing their purpose. The Alli had to abandon the slow-moving wagons, which meant that Feisan was no longer deprived of goods from the outlying provinces. Also, there was rarely time to identify messengers and confiscate their dispatches from the king to his loyal followers. Some goods from Feisan were making it through to other districts.

In spite of many close escapes, the rebels had not yet lost any men, due in great part to their capable network of sentries, but their effectiveness in disrupting royal supply caravans had been completely destroyed. *How are the soldiers signaling for help? Is someone watching the highway from high vantage points as yet undiscovered?* Bar intended to find out. Their harassment of royal traffic was being thwarted, very effectively.

Ree's enraged sovereign was also flooding the mountainous interior of Ree with packs of hunting tipeeke, braith, and the dreaded selitper. Last month, he'd added trained troopers in small bands, who roamed the mountains and specialized in stalking and ambush. Royal resources seemed limitless. The alliance of Bani, Moor ha Chi, and Glidden folk was never safe, even deep in their own territory. Bardock's determination to ferret out and destroy insurgent strongholds made the simplest journey both difficult and dangerous. Alli successes were responsible for the sovereign's new ferocious intensity and ingenuity.

During the long summer months of raids, the Alli had awakened confidence in the people of Ree. Bardon and Dare had become symbols of hope and heroes to the common people, who associated them and their marked swords with the prophecy. There successes kept the ancient words fresh in people's minds, and they were beginning to believe that the prophecy could come true in their time. The Alli alone stood in the way of the king's complete domination of the island.

Quietly, the people talked among themselves about friends who had been hauled off by soldiers and never returned to their homes and about villagers who had been conscripted into the king's army against their will. They talked of troopers who rode good people down in the streets and abused them for no reason. They discussed neighbors who had become strange, cruel, and distant after attending Mirgs. Attending the strange ceremonies *did* gain people higher positions in the government or more business from the king and his noble friends but also strangely hardened their hearts. In the face of grinding oppression and fear, a small green shoot of optimism sprouted. Bardock had been overconfident at first and had not taken the ragtag underground seriously, but now—now he clearly saw the danger they represented.

Bar watched from his high vantage point as the same pattern emerged below that had frustrated them for the last two months. First came a surprise raid by the rebels. Then the Alli bound the soldiers who guarded the caravan as well as the wagon drivers and confiscated their weapons, which they wrapped in a bundle to take with them or dump later. Bar concentrated on the confusing scene below, trying to catch any unusual action.

Mounted rebels in black leather mixed with soldiers in gold-trimmed, gray uniforms and merchants in bright robes. A mounted soldier raised something white to his lips, and Bar heard a piercing whistle that was almost a high-pitched scream. The hawks above him responded immediately with a cry of their own and sped north. They were out of sight in a few seconds. If Bar had not been watching carefully, the whistle's sound would have mixed with the other noises below, and he would never have separated it from the general uproar.

Bar felt elated. This must be the answer! Perhaps the hawks were trained to return to the base camp at the sound of the whistle. When a lookout at the camp saw them coming, he would alert the reserve troop on duty, and they would be in the saddle before the hawks swooped down to receive their reward. Whatever direction the hawks flew indicated the direction the royal soldiers would ride from to stop the Alli. It was hard to believe that birds could be trained to accomplish this task, but Bar thought he might be on the right track. Perhaps they did sometimes fail, for an occasional raid succeeded.

Alli warriors began to drive the wagons, with their supplies intact, off the road and across the meadow toward the trees while others gathered the soldiers' mounts. If all went well, the supplies would be removed from the wagons in the hidden safety of the trees. The supplies would be retrieved later or loaded on the soldiers' horses and taken back to the vale. The Alli would destroy the wagons, because they had no use for them.

Suddenly, a horn blast from their hidden sentries warned of royal troops coming to the rescue of the caravan. The Alli raiding party on the road below fled for their lives again. Bar clenched his spear tightly in his fist as he observed his friends urging their mounts toward cover. He was not really worried, as there was plenty of time, but one never knew when something might go wrong. He calmed his restless horse, who perhaps sensed his frustration and anxiety. His experience of being inadvertently left behind was still a sharp lesson in the unexpected. He had watched the whole raid, was still watching, but now perhaps they knew the answer to their enemies' communication. Bar didn't know how they would stop the hawks, but they would find a way. Lavel would be relieved. His spy network had been seeking this vital information for the Alli, but so far they had been unable to learn anything.

These comforting thoughts were interrupted by an unexpected development. Bar stiffened as he watched and then cried softly, "What are they up to now? No!" Instead of staying on the king's highway, tipeeke and attendant soldiers who had come to rescue the caravan were pouring over the low hills and meadows that bordered the road. He remembered the switchback that avoided a rough place in the dry streambed. The steep banks would be impassable for the wagons but not for horses or tipeeke. The soldiers and tipeeke were taking a shortcut. The royal troops must have left the road far to the north of the location of the actual raid in an attempt to cut off the Alli from the forest and sure escape. They had never done such a thing before, nor had it occurred to Bar that they could do it today. In despair, Bar saw that their strategy would succeed.

I planned this raid for the purpose of discovering the enemy's method of communication, but I have also led my friends into a death trap!

This time the king's soldiers went a step further than simply breaking up the Alli raid; they had discovered a way to capture the raiders. Bar was by no means the only watcher positioned in the hills and forests surrounding the road, nor was he unguarded (leave that to Amray and Tal), but were any of them close enough to the raiders to provide help in time against double their number?

Sick with apprehension and guilt, Bar plunged Charger down the hill and raced for the fleeing insurgent company. All thoughts of spying hawks were gone from his mind. The four who guarded him tore out of the trees, furious with the young warrior, until they reached the top of the hill and saw what was happening. Then they, too, galloped toward their companions who would soon be engaged in a battle for their lives. The raiding party would never make the trees in time to avoid fighting. Those who guarded Bar knew their only hope now was to save the marked prince from being injured or taken prisoner along with the rest. *The young fool!* But in their hearts they did not condemn him.

Bar lost sight of the company each time he and Charger dipped into a valley. At the tops of the gently swelling hills, he could watch them again for a few seconds. *Thank the Maker this ride is mostly downhill. Maker, let enough of us get there in time!*

The fleeing company saw the approaching soldiers pounding down on them from the meadow. Tier gasped in disbelief. Quickly, he ordered half his company to flee, and the others turned to send a barrage of arrows into the charging tipeeke and soldiers.

Along with Tier, Bar had placed Louke, Oster, Dare, and Tal qua in this raiding party. He groaned out loud at the memory. They always appointed an experienced leader to a company with an inexperienced one. Tal would—Tal *must*—hold them together.

Bar watched the unfolding battle as his horse narrowed the distance between him and the fight. The enemies' front line stumbled to a halt and fell, but those behind poured over or around their comrades and continued the charge. In only a few minutes, Tier's group turned again to launch a storm of arrows at the foremost attackers, who were closer this time than the last. The soldiers shot arrows of their own and did much damage, though they were notoriously bad archers. They preferred the sword, but who could miss at such close range! There was no time for the raiders to flee again. They were quickly outflanked and forced to fight with swords that gleamed in the sunshine. The swords the Alli used had once belonged to the king's soldiers.

The other half of the company turned and saw their companions surrounded. They quickly returned to aid them.

The tipeeke created havoc by attacking and frightening the horses as well as the Alli. The numbing sickness in Bar turned to cold rage as he saw insurgent horses without riders fleeing the conflict. Despair and grief robbed him of the ability to think. He knew only speed—action—the need to get there in time to fight, to prevent unthinkable tragedy. Bar yelled the Bani war cry as he swept into the melee in front of him, heedless of wisdom or danger. He hurled his almost forgotten spear through a tipeeke attacking a plunging Bani horse. He threw his boot knife at another tipeeke who had torn an injured Bani from the saddle and was scrambling for his throat. The ferocious animal died instantly. Other yammering tipeeke ripped at his and Charger's legs. Bar cried out in pain as one huge creature tore his right leg leathers from thigh to boot top. The soldiers, who suddenly recognized this newcomer, grinned with delight. What a prize was within their grasp!

The noise, smells, glaring sun, and confusion were terrible to Bar's shocked senses. Soon king's men surrounded him, but he had trained from his childhood to fight, and they were no match for him this day. All his skills were focused, and for the first time in his life he fought with total commitment. Bar held his ground with savage, methodical skill, inflicting terrible injury. He became the definition of his name—a barrier, a deterrent. The ancient sword was an excellent but normal weapon against human men. It seemed to take on special properties only against those created by Blalock's experiments with venom, plants, and who knew what else. In them the Gin'hana inspired terror and seemed to inflict awful pain but often no visible injury. Somehow it hurt not just their physical bodies but their spirits as well. The tipeeke cringed away from the sword, but common soldiers attacked with every hope of winning.

Those who were responsible for guarding Bar thundered into the fray, as did other Alli, who raced to the fight from their vantage points where they had watched the raid and surprise attack. Gradually ten Alli were added to the skirmish. *Where are the others?* Bar wondered desperately. But flesh and bone could only travel so fast, no matter how great the need. These were enough to make a difference but not to turn the tide. Bar's guards sought to keep up with him and turn harm aside. It was in their favor that Bardock had offered a reward only for his son's capture, not for his death. The soldiers were seeking to wound, not kill. The tipeeke knew no difference but feared the bright sword.

Glimpsing a patch of white, Bar fought his way toward it, hoping he would find Louke in his quill vest and his other friends also. He hoped he would find them alive. For a short moment, Bar could see the meadow between the fight and the road. He caught sight of royal soldiers, who had guarded the supply train, rushing on foot across the field. Thank the Maker the raiding party had taken their weapons and horses, but this was still bad news. There were weapons for the taking on the ground and plenty of milling horses without riders. Bar knew with clear desperation that they must get free before these new recruits arrived.

A plunging horse screamed beside him as a tipeeke raked at its legs.

Louke was the horse's rider! An arrow was buried deep in his shoulder, and his right arm hung useless at his side. He defended himself with a sword in his left hand, but it was awkward for him, and he was weakening. "It took you long enough to get here!" he shouted over the din. Bar laughed grimly and fought by Louke's side, his eyes constantly seeking the others and a way out. He found them one by one. They gathered around him, and they fought together, letting their battle cries rip through the air. Fear gripped Bar as he realized Tier and Dare both were pale and wounded. Louke's terrified horse stumbled, and Bar reached quickly to steady his friend in the saddle. While he reached to hold Louke upright, one of his guards stopped a flying knife with his shield, just inches from Bar's back. So much for not harming the prince! Those guarding the prince fought to stay near him and to create a fence of mounted warriors around him and Dare also. But the soldiers' were a determined enemy and broke through again and again. Bar did not have his shield; one of the enemy's swords had hacked it in two.

Suddenly, a group of Bani, screaming their war chant, raced out of the trees. For a moment, their sudden arrival distracted the soldiers and tipeeke, who paused to reckon their numbers and to evaluate the seriousness of this new threat.

A chance! Bar thought. His heart lurched in panic that they would not be fast enough. He grabbed the moment, perhaps their only opportunity, and cried, "Retreat! Retreat!"

Tal was suddenly at his side, and he, too, cried over and over, "Retreat now!" and urged the company back, toward the trees. The raiding party was able to break away from their distracted attackers and put some distance between the royal soldiers and the Alli.

Quickly taking advantage of this opportunity, Tal cried, "Bani! Shoot quickly!"

The advancing Bani saw their opportunity and put arrow to string and let fly. They continued shooting into the raging confusion their missiles caused until the soldiers fled back to the road and out of range. Then the Bani turned their mounts, picked up those Alli on foot, and raced for the trees. The royal soldiers rallied under a new, strong leader and charged once more. But it was too late. The raiding party had melted into the trees. The surviving soldiers decided they would live to fight another day and returned to the caravan of wagons.

Bar and Tal watched from the trees. Bar had received no serious injury, due in great part to his guards. He ordered the fifteen Bani whose arrival had saved them to spread out and watch the enemy. Then he signaled "to me" to the other Alli and headed farther into the trees. Only a few hundred feet into the wood, they took the time to tend serious wounds.

If the disheartened royal soldiers had armed themselves, caught horses, gathered those tipeeke still alive, and continued to chase and press the Alli, the death count that day would have been much higher. They would have undoubtedly taken many captives too. But the idea was firmly implanted in their minds that once the sneaking devils were in the trees, they were impossible to catch. Not this time—the Alli would have been easy to snare.

Anyone who could stand worked feverishly to help those who could not. Bar found Dare conscious but wounded and dazed. "What took you so long?" he gasped with a weak grin. Bar tried to smile but swallowed sudden fear instead and laid his friend on the ground. *Where is the wound? Dear Maker, help me!*

He fumbled in his saddlebags for the herbal kit Shonar made them all carry. His hands trembled as he mixed the O'Hatch's green powder with water from his skin and quickly smoothed it over a wound in Dare's side and a small gash on his upper arm. He also bound his side with strips of cloth. "Easy, clumsy!" Dare said. "I'm not a piece of baggage you know." Bar grinned in spite of his fear. Dare's leather leggings had been shredded by tipeeke claws, but fortunately they had protected his legs from serious injury.

"This is not the way it usually goes, old friend," Dare whispered, his blue eyes twinkling faintly.

"Quiet," Bar commanded with a stiff grin. "Save your strength." After giving Dare a drink laced with otet, Bar searched for someone else who needed help. He found Tal, who had bound a wound on Tier's right shoulder. As he looked around, he realized that all the wounded, including Louke, had been aided. They must handle them carefully if they were to survive the long journey back to the vale. They quickly devised litters for those who needed them and moved out.

Help would find them on their way back, for those who guarded Bani lands were watching for the raiding party's return and would see their distress. Bar had also ordered one of the scouts to ride as fast as he was able back to the vale for aid. At the edge of the great forest, Tal and Bar joined the fifteen Bani warriors who were watching the enemy and guarding their companions' retreat. After observing the royal soldiers for a while, Tal gave Bar reluctant permission to stay with the Bani warriors. It seemed the royal troop would cause them no more trouble this day. They looked completely dispirited. Tal left to join the band of warriors and injured fleeing back to the vale.

What was left of the royal troop drove the wagons back onto the highway and then stayed there, probably at the frightened merchants' insistence. They made no attempt to retrieve lost horses or weapons near the forest, fearing arrows from the trees. When Bar thought it was safe, he and the Bani carefully crawled out of the woods in the deep darkness of night. They went to the battle site to retrieve their two dead warriors. The ride back to the vale was bitter, for they brought grief and loss with them, wrapped in blankets and tied to their horses.

Once in the safety of Glimmervale, Bar slid wearily from Charger's back. Crickets chirped, and a soft wind blew. He smelled cooking food and smoke from the fires and gagged. Grim, quiet Bani took their dead to prepare them for burial. All that Bar had held back during the long, dreadful day—grief, fury, anxiety, and guilt—descended on him so heavily that he could barely stand.

Yet there was one more thing he must do. A soft wind sang among the aspen and cottonwood as he walked the narrow path beside the canal. "Maker, give me strength," he whispered softly. The long stone healer's hall blazed with light, and he could hear the low murmuring of many soft voices. Courage failed him at the door, and he leaned against it, breathing hard, caught between hope and despair. How would he face Amray and Calley if Tier was dead … or Dare, or Louke, or any of the other injured? How would he face himself?

He pushed the door open and was engulfed by light, heat, soft voices, and strong herbal smells, yet all was calm and orderly, because the injured had arrived hours earlier. Small groups gathered around different men in the neat rows of cots, for Sureese allowed family members to stay with their wounded. Os limped to Bar's side, and seeing his dazed expression, he guided him gently to Sureese.

The master healer took Bar to Tier's cot. Calley sat beside her pale, still son. Bar could not meet her eyes. "He clings to life, but it is too soon to know. He has lost much blood." One by one Sureese explained the condition of each of the injured members of the raiding party. Bar touched and spoke to those who were conscious. It lightened their pain to see at least one of the marked well. Dare, who had also lost much blood, was unconscious. "At this time, Dare and Tier are in the most danger," Sureese explained. "The others should all recover, barring infections." Grief and regret expanded inside Bar. He thanked Sureese stiffly but with real gratitude and turned to leave. "Wait, Bar! Come with me, and I'll take a look at your right leg. Your chaps have been shredded by that filthy animal." He quickly treated Bar's few minor scratches. "On your way now, but come back in the morning."

Bar said, "Aye, sir." He was pleased that the leather chaps coated with lacidem had protected his leg much better than chaps that were not treated with the useful substance. *Now, thank the Maker, I can leave—for a time at least.* He was tightly controlling his emotions, but he didn't know how much longer he could contain them. The effort it took made his look grim and determined. He brushed past Oster without a word to him.

The young Basca' recognized the glittering look in Bar's eye as trouble and ran for Amray but found someone better. Lock and Wassh had finally arrived safely from Yad Thgil. *Praise the Maker for good tidings in a day filled with bad.* They had been expected all week, but the king's hunting parties had delayed their progress again and again. Tal and Amray stood in the flickering torchlight talking earnestly with the insurgent's elected leader and his small friend. All took orders from Lock now, except Meggatirra, who took orders from no one. Yet the two leaders cooperated with few problems, for the Chi king was content to let Lock lead.

As Lock's guards took away their tired horses, Os interrupted their conversation urgently. "Lock, Bar is headed for trouble! I know that look. He is beyond reason. Please, come quickly." They all followed him without question. Os was a seasoned warrior and hard to alarm; they did not doubt his evaluation. Also, they knew Bar's rashness when lives had been lost. Os led them to the stables, where they found Bar saddling a fresh mount by glowing torchlight.

Os took one look at Bar and decided not to say anything. *Best leave this to Lock.* He admitted to himself that he didn't want to be knocked down by Bar's too-ready fists.

"Bar, Wassh and I have just arrived. I hear you have been in a terrible and unexpected battle," Lock said.

Bar whirled at the sound of Lock's voice, but he was neither distracted from his purpose nor deceived by his liege's calm manner. "Lord, welcome," he replied coldly and bowed his head for a brief moment. "It is good to see you have arrived safely. We have need of you." He mounted with fluid grace and held back the restive horse. "Do not try to stop me please, Lock ... or any of you." His cold gaze swept the rest of the small group: Wassh, Amray, Tal, and Os. "I am leaving for a time," he said bitterly in a tone that allowed no compromise.

Lock's mouth was grim, and his eyes flashed. "Bar, I understand your need, and I will see that you get privacy, but guarded privacy," he began. Bar's eyes narrowed scornfully, and he drove his horse out into the night.

Lock searched his mind for something, anything that would stop Bar until reason returned. "Bardon, do you break you tsurtne vows so easily?" he shouted. Bar paused, remembering those vows clearly. If he lived, he would do penance for breaking them, but he would not turn back. Bar urged his horse away.

Lock cried acidly, "Do you run away *again*, my prince, as you did on the *Karras*?"

This insult was very effective, and Bar pulled his horse up so hard that the animal reared and snorted. Bar sat facing the darkness in front of him, trembling with anger and hurt from this unexpected accusation. He'd thought he could feel no more guilt than he already felt, but Lock's words proved him wrong. Lock walked to the frightened animal's head and took the reins. Looking into the stark face above him, he said coolly, "I know this pain you feel, of leading men to death and injury. They trust you, obey you, and die. I know ... and the number of my dead is much greater than yours." Bar was listening.

Lock's voice was quiet, his tone biting. He knew Bar could endure no gentleness, no kindness now, for he felt unworthy of either. "Will you add to the Bani's pain and your friends' grief by disappearing to who knows where? We have much to suffer already. Do not add to it."

Bar sighed and closed his eyes. A familiar prison closed around him. His pain shredded into grief, and his anger died, leaving regret—painful companions both. "Lock, I need—really need—to be alone for a time."

"I will make sure you get this time, but not now," Lock said. Bar knew Lock was right, but he still wanted to flee. He got off his horse, held on to his liege's promise, and buried his feelings.

———————

Three Bani warriors hid in the forest and watched the royal soldiers and merchant wagons on the royal highway. It appeared pursuit by the royal soldiers would be long in coming. The Bani guessed that the soldiers had signaled for help, perhaps by hawks, from one of the reserve camps. Even when help arrived, their first goal would be to protect the supply train and get it moving, not to pursue the insurgents. The lookouts were profoundly grateful, but they would remain to watch.

———————

When he learned of the attack, Bardock hung six men, one for each soldier he'd lost that day. He said they were spies for the Alliance, but everyone knew they were not. They were his revenge. It won him no friends among his people, but he no longer cared. He wanted the Alliance stopped. He wanted to capture his son, Dare, and the ancient swords. Then the prophecy would be utterly destroyed. The six innocent deaths had the opposite effect on Ree's citizens that Bardock had intended. Their hatred for him and his cruelty boiled over. It turned into a stubborn resistance, a slow-burning revolution that knew no fear of reprisals.

It was a turning point.

GRIEF AND JOY

BAR SLID FROM HIS HORSE SO EXHAUSTED HE could hardly stand and looked to Lock for direction. "Can you come talk with us about this day?" Lock asked.

"Aye, I can." He followed Lock to the council room, where they gave him food and drink that he did not want but knew he needed. His mentors arrived and were soon listening carefully to his detailed account of the battle and retreat. They found his thoughts concerning the hawks hopeful. After he finished talking and answering all their questions, his fatigue was apparent to all.

Lock excused himself from his companions and led Bar to his own private lodging. Fragrant flatbread and cheese lay on the table. Lock started to speak but changed his mind when he noticed Bar had turned his back to him. The young man was rigid and silent. Lock turned to go.

"Lock, wait—please." They talked for a short time. Then the Alli chief left his young charge alone. Bar released the tight controls he'd been rigidly maintaining on his emotions and allowed himself to feel. He raged and wept until there were no more tears for the two who had died, for the injured, and for his mistake and guilt. He knew soldiers had probably died also, which the Alli always tried to prevent. They were fellow citizens. Toward morning, he fell into an exhausted sleep.

When Bar woke, the warm glow of the sun lay on the hardwood floor. *I am alone. Where did Lock spend the night, I wonder?* The shadows of sorrow and grief returned. He walked quickly to the healing house. The building seemed peaceful but strangely silent. Fear caused a tingling sensation to flood from his feet to the top of his head, turning him hot and then cold. A large group of people was standing around Tier's cot. Devon's large frame was among them. Bar walked toward them and joined the group. Devon saw him and explained softly, "Tier is sinking, Bar. He cannot live the hour."

No, please, no!

"I was going to anoint him, yet …" His bright eyes searched Bar's face. "I wonder if this is not yours to do rather than mine." Amray, Tal, Lock, and Sureese nodded their approval, as did the rest of Tier's family: Calley, Kostan, and Karalise.

Bar was stunned. "Why me, Devon? You are a—"

"The scrolls say there is healing in the hands of the Maker's chosen king. You are not a king yet, but you are marked, and your commission indicates you will one day rule. I think it is time for you to do this." Bar closed his mouth and stared at Devon. He could not deny what Devon said, though he was far from possession of a throne. He could, however, deny his worthiness.

"Quickly, Bar! His breathing is so shallow," Calley said softly.

When he looked at her face, pale with grief, Bar thought his heart would break. Reluctantly, he reached for the small, round bowl and walked to Tier's side. He knew what to do; not long ago he had been the recipient of this blessing. Bar dipped his fingers into the oil and touched Tier's pale forehead, eyelids, lips, and chest with the pure olva oil. Laying his hand on the bandaged wound on Tier's chest, Bar reasoned with the one who had marked him. "Mighty Maker, we have lost two already. Do not let our enemies gloat over this death also. It is you we ask for help. We know you have the power to heal, to do all things. Heal Tier, and we will give you thanks and praise, but if not, we will follow and praise you anyway, for you are our light and our hope and your decisions are right. Be kind to us, O Maker, and heal our brother."

Under Bar's hand there was restless movement. Tier coughed softly. Color gradually flooded his pale face, and he opened his eyes. He gripped Bar's arm and said urgently, "Tell me—" Of course, no one told him anything! Stunned silence gave way to crying, laughing, and giving thanks to the Maker. Tier thought they were all acting very strangely. Even his usually levelheaded father had tears streaming down his face.

Bar was speechless. He had asked, but he had not expected to receive, especially so quickly. "The Maker be praised," he finally said, smiling shakily at Tier, who was puzzled and impatient with the uproar. Calley hugged him joyfully, bandages, blankets, and all.

Quickly, Bar went to Dare, Louke, and the other injured to anoint them also. They murmured quiet thanks, all but Louke, who seemed dazed.

In spite of their sorrow over the death of two of their best, the Bani also rejoiced that day in the fact that all the injured lived. They were especially grateful for Tier's healing, which was a gift from the Maker to their tribe. Sureese grew stern as the noise level in his quiet hall rose, and he soon ordered everyone who was not a patient outside.

At the council fire, the elders acknowledged that the Maker, in his own marvelous way, had confirmed Bar as their future ruler. He had confirmed Bar's instructions. He had confirmed the prophecy. Now, there could be no doubt in their minds. Even though kingship and victory seemed very far away, they knew that they were to keep on. Their attitude toward Bar and Dare and their own futures altered greatly.

The next day everyone was feeling a great deal better. As long as they were reasonably quiet, Sureese allowed the Pack to put their cots side by side and talk. Strangely, the reticent prince told his companions of his talk with Lock the night before. "I felt it was my fault, which Lock would not allow," he said with a slight frown. "He said that Amray and Tal did not see the danger, nor did anyone else, yet they agreed to the plan. It just happened that I led yesterday. He suggested that from now on, we work from maps and not from memory. Then such possibilities as being cut off will be easier to spot and avoid. We will have to find someone who can draw detailed maps. Because there were so many watchers yesterday, there was backup that would not normally have been there, which was a blessing."

Wassh approached them with a hesitant smile. "I may join?" he asked. They greeted him gladly and gave him space on Tier's cot to sit. He perched there cross-legged, eyes bright, listening to their conversation. Os and Chea came in, and the group was complete.

Bar continued, "I was sick, with grief and guilt. Though Lock says

Amray and Tal share the responsibility ... it is I who made the mistake. I ask your forgiveness." His voice broke. He maintained steady eye contact and went on, "I will not lead again. You must choose someone else." The faces around him reflected sympathy and compassion but not agreement with his resolve.

Chea murmured quietly, "It is the way of command. Do you think I have not done the same thing or Tal or Amray? If you lead, Bar, you make mistakes, and others sometimes suffer for them. Still, you cannot quit."

"Aye, I can, and I am."

Then Chea told them a story of his own. It involved a rogue rock bear and a good friend. "If only I had waited a little longer, but I thought the bear was dead ... that we had finally killed him. I signaled for our company to close in, and when we were almost on top of him, the cunning creature roared his fury and reared up to slash at us with his huge paws. He swatted Balth up into a tree and backhanded Crew into a boulder, where he cracked his skull. Crew died instantly; there was nothing we could do. We retreated and, later, finally killed the huge creature, but Crew was dead, and Balth was badly injured. I thought I would never lead again. I gained that day what Meggatirra calls valuable experience, and there is only one way to get it."

There was total quiet for a few minutes. Bar appreciated Chea's openness, but his resolve remained firm. Lock had told him a few sad tales of battle that were much the same but dealt with greater numbers of men. It helped, but it did not alter his decision.

To change the subject, Bar told them about the hawks and how he suspected the enemy was signaling their need for help by using the farseeing birds. They discussed this excitedly for a few minutes and decided that they must get close enough to a reserve camp to locate the hawks and capture them. Even if the soldiers were able to obtain a new pair, it would take time for them to arrive.

Louke, Tier, and Dare would be in the healing hall for a long time, but they were gaining in strength. The whole tribe and Bar attended the two Bani warriors' burials. He talked with each family; it was the hardest thing he had ever done. They were kind, which made it easier ... and harder.

During the second month of harvest, the Resistance captured all of Blalock's trained hawks. After a time, they freed them in Chi territory with the hope that they would not be recaptured and used again. The stolen birds were not replaced that year. Perhaps they were difficult to catch and train. Whatever the reason, raiding became possible again.

By the first month of winter, heavy snows covered the middle lands. As the snows grew deeper and made great drifts across the king's highway, all fighting stopped. Hostilities would have to wait for spring or a break in the weather.

During a fierce snowstorm one day in early winter, an important prisoner was released from Casterray's dungeon. He was a mere skeleton, dressed in a faded and filthy uniform that denoted high rank—at least it once had; now it was hard to tell under the dirt. He was given instructions and directions to a place that would give him shelter until he was ready for his mission. The young sergeant who patiently read the man's orders to him thought it unlikely that the prisoner heard, much less understood, any of them. *He be sick and crazy too, I'll bargain ... poor fella.*

That winter in Glimmervale the Alli enjoyed long weeks of normal activity between a few quick, sharp skirmishes with their enemies. Tipeeke and braith were released occasionally, to roam the wilderness in spite of the heavy snows, and endangered any who traveled or hunted. They did not have it all their own way, however, for the Alli tracked and killed many of them.

AWAKENING

STEAM ROSE FROM THE HOT WATER AND drifted into the black night sky above Bar. The Bani's main bathing pool had no shelter built around it but was left open to the air of all seasons, even winter. *It will snow soon,* Bar thought as he looked up. Not one star showed through the thick clouds. He leaned back, contented in the water, and let his tense muscles relax. Water flowed in one side from a hot spring and splashed over the downhill edge in a picturesque but small waterfall.

It was unusually late to be in the bathing pool. He and the Pack had worked all evening in the main hall on mapmaking. Because of the hour, he had the whole place to himself. After a long soak, during which his mind drifted and he thought about nothing important, he stepped reluctantly from the water and started to dry off with a towel. He wore short breeches in the pool, as did all the men. Women wore knee-length shifts.

He heard footsteps on the rock path and looked up. El greeted him politely. She was not dressed for bathing, and it seemed strange that she would be here so late. She said, "My father thought I would find you here. He would like to speak with you before you go to bed, if you are not too tired." At Bar's worried look, she said hurriedly, "Nothing is wrong, at least nothing he has told me." Her eyes twinkled, and she confided engagingly, "To tell you the truth, I think he is excited about something he has ... invented—I guess that would be the right term—and wants to show it to you. I'm not sure he realizes how late it is." For the first time since their miserable journey together, Bar looked, really looked, at Ellarann as a woman, not a companion or Tal's daughter.

He swallowed hard. How could he have missed it, been oblivious to the obvious? El was radiantly pretty. Her brown eyes sparkled with life in a petite oval face. Her dark hair was tied with a leather thong and cascaded down her back. She wore Bani clothing: an embroidered tunic shirt, a divided black wool skirt that fell to her ankles, black leather boots, a wide tooled belt at her waist and a thick wool shawl around her shoulders. Her small brown hands fluttered as she talked. It was hard to believe that he had ever thought her a boy; she was all female. Bar forced himself to stop staring and finished drying his back.

"This pool is much larger than most, and … the willows around it are so … beautiful …" El stuttered to a stop, and her cheeks flushed with rose color as she became aware of the intense approval in Bar's eyes and his amused smile. "We'd best go, so you can get some sleep tonight," she said tartly, strangely flustered by his interest. She reminded him of a small bird chirping on a branch; her movements were quick and full of grace, her eyes bright and alert, noting everything around her. He quickly pulled on the rest of his clothing and followed her.

Bar had known many women, both young and older, in his father's court. He had watched with great interest the romances and flirtations in which they indulged, yet he'd watched from a great distance, never permitting himself even a friendship with any of them. It had not been his desire to offer the king another weapon to use against him. Therefore, he'd cut himself off from young women his own age, just as he had from everyone else. Bar was amazed by his strong reaction to El. She was adorable, but he was determined not to act as stupidly—as foolishly!—as the young men at court. Yet there was no Bardock here. Perhaps it would be safe to get to know El better.

Excitedly, Tal showed Bar what many coats of lacidem did to enhance the strength of a shield. Since that awful battle in the autumn, when a royal soldier had smashed Bar's elong-and-wood shield in two with his sword, Tal had experimented and worked with different mediums to develop a stronger shield.

Bar hewed at the shield with all his might, but he could not break or even cut into it. He managed to dent the surface and scar it, but that was all his hacking achieved. "Tal, this is wonderful!" he exclaimed. "You've done a great thing. We must make many more like this one. Think what a difference it will make in the spring. Even now, it will help in our fight against the tipeeke and special ambush squads." Tal's angular, usually serious features lit up with enthusiasm. They began to make plans, and El watched them with amusement. They were like two excited little boys.

Later Tal asked her for some of her special tea. When she did not answer, he looked up from the notes he was writing on a thin sheet of bark. She and Bar were caught in each other's gaze and did not seem to notice the silence or time slipping away. Tal went to the fire, smiling slightly, and poured tea from the pot into round bowls for each of them. When Tal offered Bar his, he took it and thanked him distractedly, then came suddenly to himself with a flush of embarrassment. El did the same, slow color creeping into her cheeks. They both avoided each other's eyes after that. Bar left quickly after he drank his tea, angry with himself for breaking his resolve not to act like an airhead, just twenty minutes after making it.

"What has gotten into Bar?" Louke asked Dare with disgust later that week. "He's plain distracted and can't concentrate for any length of time on what he's doing. It is real aggravating, I'll tell you. Especially when we're trying to plan."

Dare agreed. "I've noticed, but I've no idea what's wrong with him. He's not finished his map. He missed the target twice at archery practice this morning. When we badgered him about it—you know he never misses, so we really gave him a hard time—he just looked at us with disgust and walked away. Can you imagine? Now that's not like him for sure." They looked at each other speculatively.

"This needs looking into, I'm thinking," Louke said with a mischievous twinkle.

"Aye, that it does," Dare agreed solemnly. They went off in high good humor to search for Bar and answers to their questions. Winter was a relatively boring time in the vale, and this mystery would liven things up a bit.

They watched Bar covertly for days but were no closer to an answer that would explain his strange abstraction than when they started. One afternoon, they found him working in the craft hall on Tal's new shields. El joined him, and the two friends saw the look that passed between her and Bar. Dare raised an eyebrow in question, and Louke nodded sagely. In agreement, they leaned against the wall to observe. Neither Bar nor El had yet admitted to themselves, much less to each other, that they found the other person wonderful. It was unfortunate that at this moment their feelings escaped the tight restraints they were both maintaining. Bar reached down to touch her small face, which was tilted up earnestly while she talked to him. El stopped speaking with a soft gasp, but fascinated, she did not move away. He traced her mouth gently with his thumb while cradling her soft cheek. A look of wonder crossed his face. El felt a tingling sensation at his touch and a warm rush of affection for this often austere, very aggravating young man who was capable of such tenderness. Their look went on for long seconds before Bar leaned down and kissed her. It was a light, short kiss; he had not planned it. El's eyes opened wide, and she said with a confiding twinkle, "So that's a kiss. I've often wondered what it would be like." Bar had to laugh at this unexpected comment, and after a moment El joined him. They both became suddenly aware that they were not the only ones laughing and that they were definitely not alone.

They whirled and saw Dare and Louke leaning against the wall grinning widely. The rogues bowed their heads in mock greeting, and Louke said with deference, "My lord, my lady, a fine afternoon, isn't it?"

Bar clenched his fists suggestively in tight anger, and his eyes narrowed dangerously. "Out of here, both of you," he ordered. "And see that you don't mention this to anyone. Is that clear?"

"Oh, aye, my lord," they agreed.

Louke added mischievously as they left, "You can count on us to be discreet. We will be telling *only* a few close friends. You can trust us." They fled laughing, not slightly intimidated by Bar's anger, though they would avoid his punishing fists until he cooled down—very impulsive, their prince. They knew their greater size would not hinder Bar slightly if he caught them.

Bar looked at El with exasperation. "I'd like to beat them both to a pulp," he muttered fiercely, his chest heaving. "But the truth is," he admitted reluctantly, "that they will just hold me down till I agree to leave them alone."

El's cheeks flushed bright red, and her eyes sparkled with anger and embarrassment. "How could they! Oh, I wish I were a man. I would …" A sudden thought interrupted her indignation. "Bar, you … you'd best talk to my father before word gets to him some way," she said. Bar had not considered this aspect of the situation, and his face turned thoughtful. The clans were nothing like his father's court in Feisan, where romance was a pastime. Here, parents and elders carefully regulated all matters of courtship.

The anxiety inside him faded a bit as he considered what to do. Then he asked El quietly, as he turned her to face him, "Just what do I tell him?" The worry in her eyes faded, but she continued to look at him with a troubled expression. "This is between you and me, Little Bird, is it not?" he asked.

She cocked her head to one side and asked with interest, "What did you call me?"

"I'll explain later," he promised with an effort. He was having trouble staying on the subject at hand. "I will truly try to shut them both up. To them it's something to tease me about … but what is it to us? I don't think we, or at least I, know yet. Let's wait and see before I talk to Tal," he suggested. There was still a frown between her beautiful eyes. Perplexed by her silence, Bar asked, "Should I apologize for kissing you?"

She smiled wryly and said with sweet candor, "No, oh no, but … Bar, I wish they had not seen the kiss. Now everyone will be talking about us!" She pressed cold hands to her hot cheeks in distress, and he knew a desire to take her in his arms and comfort her, an impulse that he quickly suppressed. The way he felt was becoming more and more clear to him, yet he knew he was impulsive. He would wait. If it was real, it would last. At least, that was what everyone said.

"Just ignore the gossip, if there is any, and act as you normally would, and I will do the same. With nothing to feed the rumors, they will soon fade away. We will make Louke and Dare look foolish," he assured her. "They know my temper, and when I do not respond to their teasing, they will assume that they are wrong about us. They will never dream I am smart or self-controlled enough to contain my anger."

She searched his face with grave trust. She had some nagging doubts about Bar's self-control but not about his wisdom. "I'm sure you are right. It is the only thing we can do," she replied with a troubled sigh. They separated, each confident that they were doing the right thing. Bar could still feel the clasp of her small hand in his. *I'm as bad as the featherheaded imbeciles at court*, he thought with disgust.

It did not take long, of course, for the two mischief-makers to tell the other hishua that Bar was in love and with whom. They all thought it a good joke, and in spite of Chea's warning, they tormented Bar unmercifully about his secret love. Unfortunately, Bar highly overrated his self-control; it lasted about half a day. He then furiously invited Louke, who was being particularly creative in his remarks, into the kuni ring with him. Louke accepted, with an overly deep and gracious bow, remarking to their friends and to Bar, "I'd be delighted, I truly would, though I have heard a man in love is a poor fighter."

Bar's eyes kindled, and he shouted, "Now, you mammoth idiot!" This remark caused a roar of laughter from the growing crowd of onlookers. Louke was two years younger but twice as heavy and much taller than Bar. Bar had years of training, though, compared to Louke's months.

No one knew how word got out that there was going to be a kuni match on the training grounds, but an amazing number of young men gathered there ahead of the two combatants. Their breath misted white in the cold winter air. Most placed their bets on Louke. Though Bar fought like a wildcat, there would be no weapons except hands and feet, and Louke was huge and unbelievably strong. Bar stared with amazement at the size of the gathering crowd. A warning bell went off somewhere in his mind that this was no way to convince people that there was nothing going on. But he was too furious with his friends—*some friends!*—to care. The quiet voice of reason told him he was going to regret this enormously when it was over. A part of him acknowledged the truth of this thought, but he was able to overcome the sensible notion.

Hot anger flowed as he stripped off his fleece vest, warm wool shirt, and leather leggings. Louke did the same, though his expression, which had been full of merriment up to now, became more thoughtful. No one doubted his love or loyalty for Bar or Bar's for him. Their relationship was almost as close as Dare and Bar's had become over the long months of hardship, hiding, and fighting. Louke was only months younger than Dare, yet he seemed to be the very big little brother of their group. The Pack was sure Dare had never been young or silly or immature. He was thoughtful, balanced, and rarely lost his temper. In spite of these excellent but nauseating qualities, they liked him enormously. He was their unofficial peacemaker as Louke was their jester.

Louke's naked, scarred torso gave Bar pause. The arrow scar on Louke's right shoulder, not two months old, glared bright purple in the sunlight. An image of his friend laughing and fighting left-handed on a plunging, injured horse flashed through his mind. It dissolved much of his heat. There were also the older purple-and-pink scars left by tipeeke and rock bear claws. A pattern of white scars on Louke's back was proof of his uncle's abuse, but only his friends knew that. Bar glared at him helplessly, knowing he could not add to the painful history written on his friend's body.

Louke looked across the ring at Bar's lithe form and frustrated expression. He acknowledged Bar's problem with a grin, for he had come to the same conclusion. He could not forget Bar somehow holding on to consciousness, in spite of terrible pain and the numbing terror caused by the selitper, while they fought the terrible thing together. He had experienced the mental attack secondhand, for Bar had saved him most of it, but that had been bad enough to give him nightmares. He remembered the hand that had steadied him while he reeled on his frightened horse. He remembered his terror when a soldier's sword had smashed Bar's shield in two flying pieces. *Rats.* It was fight him or stop teasing him, and he couldn't fight the man, so ... "All right, all right," he said softly with exasperation and disappointment. "I'll stop."

Bar's lips quivered slightly in spite of his frustration. "You," he hissed quietly, "are a colossal smart-mouth."

"Aye," Louke agreed with a thoughtful nod of his head, "that's true."

Bar gave up. It was hard to be angry with someone who admitted his fault. He grinned at Louke in spite of himself, and they shook arms laughing. There was still much to say, but later, when there were no listeners.

The Pack pounded them on the back and punched them around with relief but also some disappointment. They could not help wondering who would have won! When it became obvious to even the most hopeful warrior that there would be no fight, the usually gentle Bani were hugely disappointed and mildly angry. Bar was astounded at them, for he thought he knew their natures better.

After Louke and Bar put their clothes back on, the small but merry group turned to leave. They ran smack into authority in the form of Tal, Amray, Sureese, and Lock. The spectators scattered quickly, and sudden quiet settled over the hishua as they read the stern faces before them. They quickly dropped their heads. Covert looks passed among them as the silence lengthened uncomfortably. "Louke and Bar, would you be kind enough to come with us now, please?" Lock suggested grimly. "Would the rest of you return to your work immediately? We will talk with you later," he added quietly. The quieter and more polite Lock was, the more serious the trouble one was in and the deeper his anger. The others left quickly, realizing fully for the first time what they had done. They were all clan raised and knew better.

Bar and Louke followed their mentors to the meeting hall with trepidation, but they reminded themselves that there had been no fight. Why had it not occurred to them to have someone watch and warn them if the elders came? Why did they feel so guilty when they had done nothing? Behind their leaders' backs, they looked at each other.

Louke's eyes were full of laughter. The situation struck him as funny. It seemed to him the elders were in a difficult position: their charges had only intended harm, not actually done it. Bar glared at him in astonishment. Louke would get them both in deeper trouble with his foolish sense of humor and wicked tongue. They sat around the council fire, which a curious young apprentice had built quickly for them before leaving. The room was still cold in spite of its blaze and the warm furs on which they sat. Lock asked politely if they were comfortable.

Bad sign, very bad. "Aye, sir," they both answered hastily. It was not true, of course. Either would have gladly been anywhere else, even fighting the stinking tipeeke.

"I hope we have not disturbed your pleasant afternoon with our inquiries, but we heard some strange ... er ... rumors and would like to investigate their veracity. Perhaps you can help us?" he asked with icy civility. They both remained very still. The laughter fled from Louke's eyes, and wariness replaced it. "Could it be possible that two warriors, members of *this* band, intended to fight each other this afternoon without supervision?" he asked softly. Bar closed his eyes for a moment in dismay as he remembered this forgotten rule.

He and Louke had grown up in cities where the rule was not so strictly enforced, because there were fewer incidents. In the cities, young men were generally not trained to be warriors or soldiers but to be craftsmen of some type, as Louke was. Young men's competitiveness expressed itself in acceptable, nonviolent ways: who wove the strongest cloth, who built the sturdiest building, and so on.

If the clans had been blessed with large populations, perhaps the rules would not have been so strict, but such was not the case. Each tribe valued their warriors greatly, especially their young ones, because there were limited numbers of them and they provided valuable services to the community. As different as the clans were, their rules were remarkably alike on this matter: there was to be no fighting among clan members unless it was supervised and without any type of weaponry. Period. Before this rule, many valuable young warriors had used their skills to maim, injure, and even kill one another. This had been a true waste of manpower and a major cause of bitterness, blood feuds, and rivalry within the groups. The young were notoriously hotheaded, and this rule not only saved many lives but also preserved peace in the communities. All the populations of Ree took it very seriously, for they valued their peace and their children highly. These thoughts took only a few seconds to flash through Bar's and Louke's minds.

Lock expected an answer, but Bar couldn't find his voice or the words to explain their behavior. Louke rescued him by speaking first. "Aye, sir, we did intend to fight, but neither of us remembered that rule. I've heard of it of course, but it's not spoken of much in the city, where the idea of tribe or clan breaks down and there's less reason to fight. It was truly my fault. I provoked Bar beyond his ability to bear it."

Silence. "Why?" Lock asked finally. His chiseled, rock-hard features were faintly perplexed. The small group of six hishua, seven now with

Wassh, got along remarkably well. Oh, there were squabbles, arguments, and teasing, but nothing that must be settled in the kuni ring.

Louke's blue eyes were mild and innocent as he shook his head in bewilderment. "I don't know, sir. I have a bad, mean streak in me, they do say, for I love to tease." Amray, Sureese, and Tal suddenly looked down in an attempt to hide laughter. One had to admire Lock; his gaze never wavered, nor did he lose eye contact with the young villain. Bar stared at his friend as if he had lost his mind.

"May I ask you the subject matter of your teasing that Bar found so unbearable?" Lock asked with only a mild tremor in his voice.

Bar flushed a bright red and truly wanted to sink into the ground. For the moment, he was incapable of clear thought, much less words. Tal's presence made the situation intolerable. He tried to picture himself saying, *I have grown interested in someone ... Louke saw me kiss ... I find myself attracted to ... No! Impossible! This is no one's business but my own!*

Tal began to see the light, but Lock and the other councillors became concerned at this emotional reaction from their self-possessed, imperturbable prince. Bar did not generally lose his composure, and they had observed him in some very stressful situations. What could be going on? Louke saw them jump to the wrong conclusion and sought to reassure them, to get Bar out of this mess he had caused. Feeling guilty for the first time, Louke said in a low voice, "Lock, we did not fight. We couldn't bring ourselves to do it! We have been through too much together to be able to harm each other. He's been hurt; I've been hurt ... more than enough already. Don't ask us what it's about, for we can't tell you, and I promise that it's nothing big or important. Please." The twinkle was gone, and his face was pale, for he was in earnest.

Lock's cold stare moved to Bar. "Can't tell us or *won't*? Bar, you know I cannot let this question go unanswered."

Louke pressed his lips firmly together. He had done all that he could do. Bar must find his own answer. Louke was afraid that anything more he might say would only make matters worse.

Frustration and a strange, calm anger exploded somewhere deep in Bar, giving him strength and clarity. *Enough. Enough of this. Am I a child to be treated this way?* Bar pulled himself together and replied with cold dignity,

153

"I give you my word that it is nothing that would cause you anxiety. Because of the uproar, you will hear rumors, but I am not ready to talk about it, nor is there any reason why I should. I may choose to never talk about it! I am seventeen, I am not stupid, and I have surely earned your respect in these last months. Please trust me in this." He continued less severely, "Louke and I almost broke an important rule that I respect, but we did not break it and for the right reasons. Please consider this. Do not think I don't understand. I do. I was made to study history with my tutors, and I know what chaos there was before good king Daeron imposed and then enforced this law in all the clans and cities. More than any other law, it changed the course of our history in a positive way."

Lock and the others looked thoughtfully at the two young men before them. He nodded his head once and said abruptly, "We will do as you ask. We will trust and not insist on knowing the cause of your differences. Let us confer with each other about the intended fight. Until then, remain in your quarters. You may go." Bar and Louke bowed and left gratefully.

"Very, very impressive," Louke said in an undertone, a wicked gleam in his eye. "Such maturity. Such authority. I didn't know you had it in you."

"Neither did I," Bar answered quite seriously, his legs trembling. He leaned against a tree and closed his eyes for a few minutes until he regained his composure. Louke laughed, but very softly.

CAPTURED!

"**I**F I HAD BELIEVED, *EVEN FOR A MOMENT,* THAT the two of you would really hurt each other, I know the rule would have come to my mind," Tier said with exasperation, "but as it was ... well, it was just lighthearted fun. It never occurred to me to find a referee." The others who were clan raised agreed dejectedly. They were still waiting for the council's decision, and it was almost time to eat.

Finally, right before eve meal, Wassh brought them the news. All those who were present at the "nonfight" would be required to attend instructions the next day on the law they'd so conveniently forgotten. The two almost combatants received a stern warning and were absolved from further discipline because they had not fought, they were not of the clans, they'd very properly gone to the kuni ring, and they had not intended to use weapons. The Pack cheered. This was better than they'd hoped. Bar and Louke gave the council their promise that if they should decide to fight again, they would seek a referee. Relieved, the two friends talked amicably on their way to the fields. "I feared they would feel obligated to make an example of us whether they wanted to or not," Bar exclaimed. "Though I'm grateful, I'm not sure they were wise," he added with a troubled frown.

Louke replied with practical insight, "When they investigated, I'll bet they decided not to overreact to a really trivial incident. I'm thinking it might have done more harm than good. It's a good law but meant for serious situations. We're human! We must all let off steam somehow." Stopping on the path, Bar eyed Louke grimly. "I know someone who best not say anything more about a certain subject, or there'll be a fight, referee or no. Understood?"

Louke looked hurt. "I said I wouldn't, didn't I?" Then he grinned. Bar sighed. Perhaps he should find new friends.

Louke was never quite the same after this incident, because his fear had caused some real soul-searching. He'd found a strange emotion at the bottom of his overzealous teasing and was honest enough to admit, to himself at least, that he was jealous of Ellarann ... of a girl! He was afraid that her relationship with Bar would break up their company. This knowledge tempered his teasing somewhat; it didn't stop it, of course.

When a break came in the weather, as one usually did in the second month of winter, the elders would implement a plan they had carefully formulated on long winter evenings. Lock wanted the Bani women and children settled safely at Yad Thgil. Memories of Glidden haunted him. Because Bani lands were dangerously close to Feisan, he thought it possible, in spite of their precautions, that Glimmervale might be discovered and attacked. From the vale, the Alliance launched raids that damaged Bardock's pride and image, as well as his treasure chests. The Bani were closer and therefore more active but also more accessible than the Chi. Bardock was determined to put a stop to all insurgent activity but especially to the raids within his own province. Realistically, Lock knew he might succeed.

Snow choked the high passes and fell almost daily in the foothills and mountains. This frustrated the elder's evacuation plans, but it also made travel difficult for those who hunted them. Their piles of weaponry, including the new shields, grew as the men and women of the clans worked steadily during the long days when there was nothing else to do. Those who crafted in elong, cloth, pottery, tools, and all the other essentials of life stockpiled their goods. There was ample food on Bani tables because Amray and his council were good managers. They cleared specific meadows and fed a special herd of deer and other forest creatures to keep them from migrating to the flatlands nearer the coast, where there was little or no snow. There were fish in the mountain lakes and carefully tended sheep in protected valleys and caves. Hay, other grasses, and grain had been harvested and stored in late summer to feed the livestock during the dark, cold months. Over the years the Bani had learned to store foodstuffs in some of their caves that maintained consistent temperatures year-round.

In winter's second month, just as predicted, the break in the weather came, but it did them no good. There was simply too much snow on the ground to travel.

Lavel managed to get messages through to the vale with messenger birds and couriers, so they were informed of the king's activities and plans. The council was filled with dismay and foreboding at the sharp increase in violence, ruthlessness, and corruption that seemed to be erupting in all levels of society. It was hard to hang on to hope when all the tidings seemed so dark. Finally the days lengthened. It grew warmer, and the snow began to melt.

As soon as it was feasible, Lock sent small but well-guarded groups of warmly dressed women and children north to Yad Thgil. Tipeeke, braith, selitper, and ambush squads were a fact of everyday life, but they tended to concentrate their search near known areas of insurgent activity. To the council's knowledge, the king was not aware that the Glidden Alli occupied a new home or that its population was growing steadily. Reports indicated that the monarch believed a few dispirited survivors might still live in scattered pockets in the Bitterroots, but he thought they were few, unorganized, and no danger to him.

New groups left daily, and so far, they'd encountered no trouble they could not wait out or go around. The farther north the companies traveled, the fewer enemies they encountered, as long as they stayed in the mountains and away from the royal highway. Even on the sturdy Bani ponies and with many warriors and scouts to help them, the journey was difficult for those with children. The paths were treacherous with running snowmelt and, in places, deep mud. There was still plenty of snow to wade through, and the weather was often unpredictable. It could be overcast and damp one minute and sunny, warm, and windy the next, and then cold rain mixed with spitting snow might fall on them. Each mother carried an herb mixed with honey that would make her little one sleep in difficult situations, when absolute quiet was imperative. Even so, the warriors dreaded those nerve-racking episodes when a child's cry might betray them. There were many minor injuries but, so far, no serious ones.

———————⊰⊱———————

Bar and Dare, along with fifteen Bani, were returning to Glimmervale after turning over twenty women and eighteen children, between eight months and fourteen years of age, to Alli scouts. The scouts would guide them through the difficult region around Yad Thgil to safety. The only danger in the Bitterroots was the terrain itself. The escort party always breathed a sigh of relief at this transfer; it meant their small group of evacuees were safe. The trip home would take half as long without their charges, but it would be just as dangerous.

Bar's party moved noiselessly and with caution, watching at all times for signs of the enemy. The sky was ashen, and a cold wind whipped their fleece-lined cloaks and hair. Scouts were both before and behind them to watch for danger. The company was strung out single file as their ponies cautiously picked their way down a steep trail. The path cut deeply into a towering rock cliff. Far below, a roaring stream gushed with snowmelt. The valley this trail opened into was rugged but magnificent with ancient stands of pine and spruce. No light-loving aspen or cottonwood could survive in their shadows. Bar and Dare looked at each other with misgiving. They would be glad to be off this rough, broken trail where they were exposed and vulnerable. High overhead a goshawk hung on the currents. Could it be watching them? Their uneasiness increased, and they wished for the dusky cover of the forest. One of the forward sentries gave warning of danger with a squirrel's sharp chatter, and they dismounted to wait further information. What a miserable place to be caught! The danger could not be tipeeke; they would have heard them. That left selitper, braith, and ambush squads. Their scout appeared on the trail below them and motioned them down. Breathing hard, he gasped, "Ambush squad waiting in cover … at bottom of trail. We must go back or fight."

Then they heard chattering from the sentry behind them. They were trapped!

If they did not move quickly, either back or forward, they would have to fight on this narrow ledge of rock where they would be picked off like gourds on a fence. Dyson, their captain, chose to move forward, even though the heaviest concentration of soldiers would probably be in front of them. They were closer to this end than the other; it would take longer to turn and go back south. Dyson signaled their rear scouts to join them quickly.

The warriors followed Dyson quietly to the place where the trail opened into the valley. Industrious beavers had created ponds along the swift stream, and the trail turned sharply west into the trees in order to avoid the water. Dyson held up his hand, and they stopped. He sent the two forward sentries, who knew the soldiers' location, and six men out into the willow bushes. These tall, thick bushes covered the ground right up to the trees. He gave them instructions on how to get behind the attackers. Then the rest of the company would wait for their signal that meant they were attacking the enemy. Hopefully the soldiers would turn to fight the Alli behind them and not notice the attack of the Alli in front of them, until it was too late. Things rarely went as planned, though.

The signal came. They could hear shouting, so they galloped their ponies into the bushes and toward the trees, but an unseen royal sentry must have spotted them. He yelped a warning cry. Sudden arrows flew in their direction and bounced off their new shields. In spite of the sentry's warning, the enemy's forces were divided and caught off guard. Their response to the Alli was sporadic and lacked unity. In the confusion, the seven insurgents attacking from the front managed to reach the trees, though Cree slumped over his pony's neck with an arrow in his thigh. Once in the shelter of the pines, he broke it off and tied a scarf around his leg above the wound to slow its bleeding.

Though it was difficult to find the soldiers among the huge tree trunks, the Alli, with their speed and element of surprise, won the skirmish. They rounded up prisoners, tied them, and put them on their horses. Dare tended Cree and helped him mount. Three others were injured but none seriously. They must leave and quickly. There were soldiers behind them somewhere, probably riding down the steep trail, and they could arrive soon.

As they herded their prisoners up a gentle slope, Bar whirled at the top to look back at the site of their conflict. All seemed peaceful. No one had been left behind, and the other royal soldiers were not yet in view. As he turned to follow his companions, Bar felt a sharp prick in his neck. He tried to reach a hand up to rub the spot, but his arm would not obey him. Numbness coursed into all his limbs, and he felt himself floating down. In his mind he screamed at his companions to run, but no sound came from his lips. He plunged into roaring blackness.

Dare looked back and saw Bar tumble from his horse in a slow-motion fall that seemed limp and unnatural. Bar's head jerked back, and his arms flung out from his sides. He did not try to break his fall or make any attempt to cling to the horse. Dare was stunned. Who had done this? Where were they? The enemy's scouts must have entered the valley unseen. Who else could it be? He kicked his horse and raced back to Bar, shouting a warning to his companions. "Bar's injured! Watch for the enemy!"

Three soldiers, accompanied by two sleek braith, surged out of the deep shadows under the monstrous trees and grabbed Bar's still form. They dragged him into the forest with furtive glances at the company. Upon scenting the braith, Bar's horse turned and fled in the other direction.

Blocking Dare's path were the two menacing cats, crouched and ready to spring. They snarled fiercely and lashed their tails in time to a rhythm only they could hear. Dare's horse snorted with abject terror and reared powerfully, pawing at the air with his front hooves. In spite of the cats and his horse's attempts to flee, Dare tried to mark the spot where the three soldiers had disappeared into the trees with Bar. Unfortunately, abstraction caused him to be thrown from his plunging animal. As pain exploded behind his eyes, the air was forced out of his lungs, and he lay stunned. His frightened animal fled down the trail. Two Bani, Dyson and Twill, grabbed the young healer under the arms and dragged him to Thofeld's horse. They flung him across the man's saddle. Two were a heavy load for the horse and would slow it, but they didn't have any other options. They mounted themselves and took off down the trail faster than was safe. They prayed the braith wouldn't follow them. The braith began to pursue them, but their masters urgently called them back. With reluctance, the arrogant felines returned to the royal soldiers.

"We have won our prize, and their numbers were greater than ours!" Lieutenant Cal gloated. The young lieutenant was a practical soldier and cunning. "We must flee quickly, before they regroup to follow us. Even though we have the braith, they may try to get him back." He ripped off Bar's fleece cloak and wool shirt in order to make sure they had the right man. Aye! The mark was there, gray blue and leathery to the touch. He checked the young warrior's scabbard with trembling hands. The Gin'hana was also there. He would be richly rewarded for capturing the ancient sword as well as the prince. This sword, along with Dare's Wolf, had killed and wounded many selitper during the winter campaign, and it had driven the king and Blalock to insane fury. It would take years to rebuild large numbers of the loathsome beings. That, truth to tell, was fine with Cal. The selitper were shameful fighters. Stupid and often error-prone, they frequently injured as many comrades as enemies.

For a moment he allowed himself to revel in his prize. "Can you believe our luck? The royal cub himself!" They were very young, these three, and, until now, very insignificant. They were also ambitious. That was why they'd taken good care of the drug-tipped darts Blalock had given each member of the ambush squads. If they could return Bar to the king alive, the reward would be theirs. He was breathing, a little bruised perhaps but definitely breathing. Lieutenant Cal did not mention the sword to his companions.

⸺∘∘∘⸺

Dyson stopped the small rebel company midway through the valley. The ancient, lofty forest combined with the unrelenting gray of the skies gave the place a somber feel. They did what they could for Dare, who was still unconscious. Dyson said, "I don't know the size of the party that captured Bar, but I'm guessing it was just what we saw: the three scouts and the two braith. They must have slipped into the valley without our noticing them and decided to keep quiet, since we won the skirmish. Perhaps one of them recognized Bar, and when they got the chance to capture him, they took it. I don't know if he's alive or dead." Dyson remembered the limp body with misgiving. "But whether he is or not, we must track him. I suggest we split up. Some of us will follow Bar; the others will take Dare and our prisoners back to the vale. I don't like taking royal soldiers back, but we can't free them here. Be sure to blindfold them! When Dare is safe, Amray will have the soldiers released somewhere on the highway. It is my guess that the soldiers who have Bar will head for Feisan to collect the reward."

They argued for a time because some wanted the whole company to hunt the soldiers, braith or no, and take Bar back immediately. Dyson was torn, but he knew his first priority must be to get the marked healer to safety. That way, if this rescue attempt failed and they were captured, at least Bardock would not have both marked warriors. In the end, they agreed to his plan.

"Remember," Dyson cautioned them, "those who have Bar will spread the word to any comrades they meet that Dare is in this location. They will hunt you with everything they have. Tell Amray to have scouts search for my party. If we succeed in getting Bar back, we will need help, for the whole army will be after us. If not, we can at least tell the council where he is." When they were mounted and ready to leave, Dyson gazed at Thofeld with grief and distress. This was a black day indeed. Both marked ones were injured, and Bar had been captured—all under his command. "The Maker be with you, old friend. Guard him well," he said. Thofeld just nodded, his aging visage grim. He was a strong man, and no member of the clan knew the mountains better, but he spoke little. His graying hair, tightly woven in a single braid, was pulled back from a face as brown and seamed as a walnut. Like an old piece of elong, he was lean and tough. He and Dyson shook arms and left, each praying that the other's mission would succeed.

———⋙◈◈◈⋘———

Strange dreams intruded into Bar's drug-induced trance. Like the surf, they surged in and out of his mind whether he wanted them or no. He could neither hold nor dispel the extraordinary hallucinations. Vision and even sound were oddly distorted. Most often, he struggled through clinging fog toward a light until he gasped with exhaustion and the pounding of his heart roared in his ears. He could never quite reach the light. Nor could he wake up to the real world: to sunshine, hunger, human touch, laughter, or even pain.

In the next few days, Bar came dangerously close to death. The drug was strong, and it had entered his bloodstream very close to the brain. The prince's appearance frightened the three soldiers badly. His breathing was so slight that they could barely detect it. His skin was pale and cold as wax, and they could not rouse him at all. "I can't believe Blalock and his dangerous sleeping herbs," Harch said with feeling. "It's nearly killed him." They forced tea down Bar's throat and kept him warm, all they knew to do to keep him alive. With Bar's limp body tied to a horse, they traveled with as much speed as possible toward the royal highway and help. They did not want their prize to die.

In Bar's unconscious state, there were moments when he was faintly aware of the soldiers' presence, though he could not communicate with them in any way. Most of the time, however, he walked in dreams.

He struggled toward the light. Surely it was getting closer! Finally, the fog dissipated. He felt warm and also less anxious and confused. The light surrounded him but did not blind his vision. Searching the unusual gold of the sky, he could not find the source of the light. There was no sun or bright spot that would indicate the sun was there, perhaps hidden behind the clouds, but then, there were no clouds either. He could see radiant summer trees, verdant and green, bowing in the mild breeze. The trees were gathered beside a mountain stream that tumbled and leaped toward him over dark rocks. The smell of sweetgrasses and fragrant wildflowers rose from the meadow where he stood. Bar delighted in the peaceful beauty around him. The buzzing of bees reached his ears, as did the contented murmuring of the stream and the soft music of the wind in the pine and aspen. He walked slowly to a giant cottonwood and sat with his back resting against its deeply ridged trunk. Content, he closed his eyes. It was so good to rest. He had struggled and worked hard to get here.

Later, when he opened his eyes, he didn't know how long he'd slept or even if he'd slept at all. He saw a man of medium height, robed in cream wool, sitting near him beside the stream. The man's skin was brown, and he appeared to be very strong. Muscles rippled in his arm as he cupped water from the stream and let it fall back into the rushing torrent, over and over again. His long hair was brown with wine highlights and tied back. Bar was fascinated by the man's beautiful, strong hands. They were the hands of a workman or perhaps an artist. After a time, he asked the man, "Who are you?"

The man turned to look at him, and his face broke into a merry grin.

"You're finally awake, are you?" His voice was strong and very deep. Bar felt strangely startled and alert. The peaceful character of the valley fell away and was replaced by something more powerful and exciting. The man's features were even, but they were dominated by his deep blue eyes—eyes that were filled with vitality. Those eyes were all Bar seemed to see and, later, all he could remember.

"Aye," Bar answered from a throat dry and unused to speech. He felt something important was about to happen, but he couldn't say why. Watching the man attentively, he waited for him to speak or do something. He felt relaxed but alert and ready. Yet all the man did was gaze at Bar intently.

"Bar, remove your shirt from your right shoulder," the man said in that vibrant voice. Bar was not at all surprised that the man knew his name and knew about his mark, yet his sense of wonder grew. A sudden, vivid memory of all that had happened the day E Clue marked him flashed through his mind.

"You must go back," the man said gently as Bar untied the knots in his tunic.

Bar did not want to go back. "No," he said, "I want to stay here with you."

The man smiled a little and then assured him, "Remember, Bar, you will never be alone. I will always be with you. You are my *bar*, my deterrent to evil's plan. You stand in the king's way and block his path. But for you and the others, the whole island would be under his sway by now."

A warm glow of pleasure filled Bar at this unexpected assessment of their efforts. Sudden tears pricked his eyes. He so often felt like a failure; they all did. For every one step forward, they seemed to take two back.

"Your friend, the healer, *dares* to stand beside you and aid you. Two are usually better than one." The man looked into the distance, and his face grew grave. "If you do not go, who will I send? The king risks new depraved and base practices, even as we are speaking. He unlocks doors that were shut to protect him and all people. Each time he does, a new evil escapes to ravage my children."

His children?

Gradually, Bar witnessed the same sights the man was experiencing. Trees and buildings flew by him, until he found himself looking down on men in elong shackles who were groaning and screaming for help. They were in a low building of some kind, but he could see right through the ceiling. They were being turned into something different—something large and strong—right before his eyes. The selitper! On their necks and arms he could discern red puncture marks, and he could see writhing, perhaps venomous snakes in cages. Somehow he knew that the men had volunteered for this experiment, but now he could feel their horror at what they were becoming. He shut his eyes against the distressing sight, but in spite of all his efforts, he could still see them.

This image faded slowly away, and a new one appeared, small at first but complete with sound. It grew and grew until it was terrifyingly real. He heard the screams of villagers as the untrained men and women fought royal troops rather than hand over their young men. They were losing the fight. He felt the people's despair as they fought and the young men's terror when they were roughly bound and dragged away.

As that scene faded, a new one grew close. A soldier who refused to serve Bardock any longer was being dragged away from his weeping family. The grief-stricken man was bound and sent to Blalock to work in the mines. A mental picture of his family was ever before him as he was carried away in a wagon filled with other prisoners.

Bar gasped as a new spectacle he could not stop filled his vision. Hundreds of men were chanting in a grove filled with flickering torchlight. They seemed to be ordinary citizens for the most part, dressed according to their trades. Row upon row of Blackrobes faced this group singing loudly, and Draville, resplendent in rich red robes trimmed with white fur, led them. Guards paced the perimeter with leashed tipeeke. The men's singing and chanting pounded through Bar's body till he felt deaf to anything else. Bar's heart constricted in fear—a Mirg! *All these innocent people are listening to and even singing Draville's evil teachings! They don't understand that he wants their minds, their wills ... their very souls. Why did they all decide to come here?* He remembered Oster's close call with this kind of evil and shuddered. Oster had wanted to prove he was not afraid of anything—that his faith was strong enough to stand up to evil. He'd also been fascinated by the followers of Choack's power. Bar tried to scream out a warning, to break their focus on the influential man directing them. But the scene became smaller and smaller. They had not heard him.

A new sight drifted closer. He saw a trestle table in a small, neat cottage and a family of five enjoying their meager eve meal. One of the older children was reading from a scroll while the others ate and listened. Occasionally, they stopped to discuss some point of interest or make comments. It was a warm, peaceful sight, and Bar's heart stopped racing so hard. He was not really surprised when the door suddenly burst open and soldiers strode into the room. The family rose from their benches and joined hands in prayer. They did not seem shocked at this intrusion but acted as if they expected it. The father and oldest son were taken away to be forced into the king's service. The cracked door swung back and forth on its hinges in the cold night air. The sad scene grew smaller and then disappeared altogether.

Similar scenes from across Ree rushed by him almost too fast to comprehend, yet they all had things in common: pain, confusion, fear, and bondage. *This has to be stopped!*

Finally, the rushing visions disappeared completely. The sweet peace of wherever he was returned, yet the impact of the visions left Bar trembling and ill. He felt as if the terrible sights had been engraved upon his mind and heart. The man's eyes still beheld what Bar could no longer see. They were filled with pain, compassion, and determination. "Aye, it must be stopped," he agreed.

A growing comprehension dawned on Bar. "This is ..."

"Not exactly, just the first place," the man replied.

"You are ..."

"Aye," he said and reached his hand to Bar's mark but did not touch it. He waited patiently. Bar's eyes filled with tears. He was aware as he bowed his head in surrender that this was the same hand that had healed him from whatever the selitper had done to him. He had seen he who few men were given to see. At the Maker's touch an internal burning flared through him, suffusing his whole being. This time there was no pain but that of longing. It burned away doubt and confusion. In their place, the flame forged true acceptance and rock-hard resolve.

Bar's body spun away into nothingness. Below him he saw a scene getting closer by the second. There were three soldiers, two riding double, and two braith traveling fast down a forest path. On a third horse was a body, dressed in the black leather of an insurgent, riding not upright but thrown over the saddle like a sack of grain—his body!

Memory returned with a stab of fear. He remembered the painful prick in his neck and then … nothing. *I have been captured! They are taking me to Feisan for the reward.* With a jolt, he awoke to savage thirst and a blinding headache. He cried out, hoping his captors would release him and at least allow him to ride properly.

THE VALLEY OF SHADOW

LIEUTENANT CAL WAS FINDING IT DIFFICULT not to be overconfident. Because he knew there was still danger ahead, the young officer concentrated on staying alert. Their captive was quickly returning to health and strength. He had really frightened them for a while.

Much to Cal's delight, on the second day, a roving band of royal soldiers, Blackrobes, and tipeeke found his small party. Now they were too strong to be attacked by any but a large group of insurgents, yet he realized fully that could happen. The warriors in the prince's company would notify the Alli leaders quickly. There was no doubt that they would immediately organize a rescue for so important a figure.

Yet things are going much better than I hoped. The tipeeke give tongue if anything comes within half mile of us, which unfortunately includes every deer and leaf. What irritating animals they are to be sure! But their extreme vigilance is comforting.

The only thing to go wrong so far concerned the ancient sword, Uriisis. The shrewd Blackrobes had quickly questioned him about Bardon's famous weapon. They'd taken immediate possession of the renowned sword when he'd reluctantly shown it to them. Lying to the intolerant extremists had not crossed his mind. To conceal the sword from his fellows was one thing, but to hide it from Draville's fanatics would be insane. The Blackrobes knew how to question a man in such a way that he would tell them anything they wanted to know. *If I am not vigilant, they will kill my comrades and me so they can claim the reward for capturing the prince and the famous sword ... but not yet. We are safe for a time,* he reassured himself. *They still need my men and me, at least until we reach the road.* The company made good time; it took them only three days to reach the safety of the royal highway.

Tightly bound and with little hope of escape, Bar rode one of their horses. He pretended dazed submission and wore a beaten, defeated air in hopes that they would not drug him again. When they thought him asleep, he overheard the Blackrobes arguing about whether or not to prick him lightly with one of the remaining darts to keep him quiet and subservient. Unexpectedly, Lieutenant Cal advised the dark-robed vultures against it. He explained that the potent drug he'd used to capture Bar had come close to killing him. He did not want to chance using it again unless it was absolutely necessary. For now at least, he persuaded them to leave their prisoner alone. Bar intended to keep it that way.

Some chance of escape might come, and he wanted to be awake and alert if it did. He realized the Alli would be following him, but the large pack of hunting tipeeke would keep Dyson, or whomever, from getting close. It would take time, too much time, for the warriors in the escort squad to return to the vale and organize a rescue party, yet an Alli hunting or raiding party might be in this area.

If only he could slow the company somehow. But he would have to do so soon! It was definitely possible that more soldiers could join them once they reached the highway. He could only think of one thing he could try. It would be dangerous, and he would have to convince Cal that he was really sick, or the lieutenant would use a drug-tipped dart. His hands were bound with some play in the elong rope, so that he could hold the reins. Also a tether line around his waist was firmly held by Cal, his constant companion. He couldn't get away, but perhaps he could slow the company, for a time at least.

Bar started moaning and moving his head from side to side, as if it hurt him. He slumped in the saddle and let his body slip back and forth as if he were going to fall off his horse. Of course the ever-vigilant Cal noticed. He jerked the tether line and shouted at Bar, "Stop that, or I'll use a dart on you!" Bar ignored him and started slipping sideways until he fell to the ground. He faked unconsciousness and let his body go limp. The whole troop came to a halt.

Cal quickly got off his horse and knelt down by his hostage to examine him. He was sure Bar was faking. However, Bar was deathly pale and really did look sick. Cal agonized over what to do. Should he use a dart again? What if this was just an act? What if it wasn't and the dart made Bar worse? He remembered well how long it had taken Bar to wake up after the first dart. The reward was for a living prince, not a dead one! The Blackrobes came running. They were terrified that their prize was dead. After a long, contentious argument, they decided to make camp and rest until their prisoner woke up. Bar thanked the Maker that his plan had worked. It would take them one day longer to get to Feisan—one day longer for the Alli to plan a rescue.

From a distance, eight hidden Bani warriors scrutinized the combined company. They could conceive of no plan to free Bar or even to get closer, because of the thirty or more tipeeke. If they tried to pick off the tipeeke one by one, some of the Blackrobes, with the mangy animals' aid, would hunt them unmercifully, and the Alli were few. Frustrated and angry, they simply tracked Bar and waited.

When Lieutenant Cal and company reached the king's highway, they were joined by a troop of weary soldiers whose duty it was to guard the royal road. The soldiers were overjoyed when they discovered the identity of Cal's prisoner. The young lieutenant flushed with pleasure at their cheering and praise. He told them the story of Bar's capture, only slightly embellished, that night around the campfire. The three young soldiers enjoyed the admiration of their fellows immensely, but they were made uneasy by the Blackrobes' furtive conversations and sneering glances.

Bar suffered harassment all day from the soldiers, who made the most of their opportunity to even the scales a bit. Royal troops had endured humiliation at insurgent hands since the beginning of the conflict. They looked like fools because, even with their superior weaponry, numbers, and training, they could not defeat a few hill tribes. One could not blame them, but the Blackrobes and Cal kept the abuse at a verbal level. They did not want Bar damaged before they delivered him to the king.

At first, the vicious baiting provoked Bar to fury, which revealed itself clearly in his flushed cheeks and angry expression, but he kept his mouth tightly closed. After a time, he was able to shut out most of it. He was filled with an inner quiet in spite of his capture. Bar's experience with the man in his dream or vision or whatever it was had changed him. He found that he trusted the Maker's plan and the prophecy and the promises E Clue had given him. He would wait for the plan to unfold. There was nothing he could do just now anyway, except be ready when the time came to act.

———————

Fifteen days later, Bar saw the turreted granite buildings of Ree's capital sprawling in the distance. Beyond the great city, the sea glittered in the sun. *We are nearing Feisan. This is perhaps the twenty-first day since my capture ... or maybe longer ... not much time for Dare or members of the escort squad to return to the vale and launch a rescue. If the Blackrobes drug me for causing trouble now, it no longer matters. Soon I will be beyond my friends' help.* He felt the familiar weight of despair that always crushed him at the sight of Feisan. What had this city ever been to him but pain and darkness! Because of Cal's diligence, no opportunity to escape came Bar's way. He was confident Dyson or someone was watching his progress right now, yet what could the Alli do? Because Cal continually threatened him with the drug-tipped darts, Bar feared angering him in any way. Drugged and unconscious, he would be no help to anyone who might try to rescue him. Cal was a most vigilant guard.

Like the rest of the troop, Bar shivered in the raw wind. He had not been truly warm since his capture, an unfortunate effect of being bound night and day in cold temperatures. He really felt weak and sick—it was no act. Snow showers blew over them occasionally, but so far there was no real buildup on the dirt road. The first month of planting season was always unpredictable.

Fearing he would lose his lucrative prisoner, Cal had tied the other end of the tether line around his own waist so there would be no way Bar or anyone else could jerk it out of his grasp. This arrangement was extremely inconvenient for both warrior and soldier but much safer. Cal eyed Bar suspiciously, as if he sensed his thoughts, and suddenly, he gave the tether a hard jerk. Bar gasped and fought to regain his balance. "What was that for?"

171

"I know what you're thinking, my friend. I've seen it in your eyes all day. If they don't free you soon, it will be too late. Well, let me warn you that I'm more than ready for anything you or they might try ... so don't make a move, or you'll regret it." He held up a dart and then shoved it back in its case. Bar was astonished at the man's skillful perception. Surely he was not that easy to read! He had spent most of his first sixteen years, seventeen now, hiding his true feelings, and he knew he was good at it. His shock was apparent, and the lieutenant laughed harshly. The warning was humbling and left Bar feeling angry with himself.

As Cal watched the road and the rolling meadows surrounding it with fierce concentration, his nervous tension was obvious in his quick movements and irritability. He was expecting trouble. Strangely, Bar did not dislike the man. He was greedy and very ambitious but not truly wicked, not yet anyway.

Traffic picked up steadily as they turned east toward the royal city. It slowed their progress somewhat, but true to their imperious reputation, the king's troops ruthlessly cleared the way. They ordered wagons, people, horses, and pack ponies off the road and into the ditch. Snow started to fall thickly by midafternoon, and travel became more difficult.

Somewhere on the road in front of them, a terrific uproar started. Bar could not see what was happening through the blinding snow, but their progress slowed and then stopped. He carefully hid his alert response to this possible opportunity by slumping dejectedly in the saddle. He hoped he looked the picture of soggy, cold misery; it took little acting. Cal's irritability was at the breaking point. This delay would give whoever might be watching a perfect opportunity to attempt a rescue. Their horses pawed the snow and shook their heads impatiently. They were cold and wanted to get to the end of the day, when there would be bags of tasty oats, rest out of the wind, and warm blankets. Bar shivered and blinked wet flakes out of his eyes in an effort to see, but everything was a white blur, even Lieutenant Cal, who was right next to him. The tipeeke that were prowling the meadows around them howled in nervous frustration. They could smell trouble but could not find it in the fog of white flakes. The cold stuff frustrated their noses as well as their keen vision. Cal's agitation increased as his eyes darted here and there in an attempt to pierce the smothering whiteness. Chaos took place up and down the royal road as merchants', farmers', travelers', and soldiers' tempers grew short in the freezing wind and blinding, wet snow. The royal troop tried to push the company's way through, but they could not untangle the milling horses, carts, and people in front of them.

Suddenly, Cal could bear the tension no longer, and he took swift action. Bar was working circulation into his stiff hands and fingers under cover of his hunched posture when pain exploded at the back of his head. He found himself falling forward into darkness. The lieutenant rammed his sword back into its scabbard and looked quickly around. *Good. No one noticed.* He dismounted, grabbed his now unconscious prisoner by the neck of his cloak, and pulled him off his trembling animal. Then Cal heaved Bar across his own saddle, like a sack of grain. He mounted again, and with the prince's limp weight in front of him, he urged his horse and Bar's off the road. He rode forward toward the still-audible commotion ahead of them. He and Bar were a strange sight, but who could see them in this blinding storm? He kept a tight hold on Bar's horse. If he escaped with the prince, they would need the animal; he did not want to slow his own horse by making it bear two any longer than necessary. He guided his steed mostly by the sounds of animals and people on the road to his right. He knew his choice was dangerous. There were good reasons for staying on the highway. However, he could not have remained where he was and waited for insurgent warriors to find him for one more minute. He felt sure they were searching this long line of traffic for their marked prince. They had probably caused the delay in the first place with a fake accident of some kind. He would do his best to make sure they did not find the king's treacherous son.

Cal's astute deduction was quite right. Lavel, his spies and some warvers were the ones who had executed the delay. Glimmervale had sent Lavel, who had become the head of their spy network, what information their warriors and scouts had gathered about Bar's captors and location. The information had arrived just this morning! He gathered those he could find quickly and they hurried to execute their simple plan. They blocking the royal road with a large cart of chickens that they over-turned quickly in the middle of the road. In the blinding snow, no one on the road realized they had done it on purpose. It stopped traffic in both directions. The cart and the wildly squawking, and now free fowls created a tangle of people, horses, carts and soldiers that grew more chaotic by the minute.

The blinding snowstorm, which was part of no one's plan, worried Lavel. He feared he and his men might easily miss Bardon under its thick cover. The small Alli party, that had faithfully followed Bar, were far behind Lavel and his group, and they were also watching for Bar. They took advantage of the snowstorm, which hid them from their enemies' eyes and searched the stopped traffic. The Alli were only seconds behind Cal, yet those seconds were enough to frustrate their purpose. In spite of all their careful searching, they did not find the prince. Soldiers finally righted the chicken cart, untangled foot, horse and cart traffic, and all travelors on the royal road were able to move again. Even the heavily falling snow was dwindling to a few flakes and people could see once more. Sick with disappointment, the Alli knew they would not get another chance to find their prince. They fled back into the foothills before they were discovered. Blackrobes were furious when they discovered Cal's disappearance with *their* captive, as were Lieutenant Cal's irate comrades.

Meanwhile, Cal was fast approaching Feisan towing Bar's horse, which now carried the young warrior slung across its back. The desperate soldier had lightly pricked Bar on his hand with one of the drug-tipped darts when he'd started to wake up. Cal hoped for the best. The young lieutenant wanted no interference, no outcry, and no struggle from his foolhardy young captive as he worked his way through the capital's busy lanes and byways toward Casterray.

It was long after dark when Cal finally approached the first gate of the ancient keep. The massive stone structure seemed to brood in the darkness, and the young lieutenant shivered unconsciously. He shook himself, muttered, "Fool!" and rode into the dark mouth of the entrance.

Because of the lieutenant's uniform and fierce manner, the guard took him seriously and called for the captain. Privately, though, he thought it unlikely that one young soldier could bring in such a prize. The officer was surly and sarcastic until he saw Bar's Bani clothing, his familiar face, and then ... the mark!

Cal and Bar were hurried through gate after gate. Ahead of them in the velvet darkness, broken only by row upon row of torches to mark the way,

Cal suddenly saw lights appear in the castle windows. The royal apartments were ablaze. Curious voices shouted across the ebony spaces at the sides of the road. Cal rounded a bend and found a huge contingent of retainers and soldiers gathered on the steps of the castle. The twenty-foot-tall doors were flung open, and the king himself appeared on the steps. Cal swallowed with difficulty and tried to still his hammering heart. Could this really be happening, or would he wake up and find it to all be a dream?

The king walked slowly down the steps, his long fur cloak whipping out behind him. His fierce gaze never left the still form tied across the horse, whose reins Cal still clasped tightly. The king's face was gaunt and lined, and his eyes glittered darkly in the flickering torchlight. Cal found himself fighting a desire to back up, to flee in panic. The man radiated power, a quality that the lieutenant greatly admired and desired to have for himself. However, this power was of such a cruel and violent nature that he quailed in terror before it.

"Cut him down!" the king cried in a harsh voice, but no one on the steps moved. Cal came out of his frozen state with a frightened jerk. The king meant him! He dismounted quickly and cut Bar's bonds with shaking hands. He gently lifted the prince off his horse and held him in his arms, unsure what to do next. Surely he couldn't lay Bar's unconscious body on the newly wet steps. He remembered the stories of the king's rages if anyone so much as touched Bar's royal person in anger. The snowstorm that had enveloped Cal on the road now swept over the castle and fell on the watching crowd. Flakes fell thickly all around them. The king gazed with bitter satisfaction at the still, pale features of his son glowing in the torchlight.

It's a proud face, even in rest, but he's so young, Cal thought in unexpected sympathy for Bar's plight. In a flash of memory, the lieutenant heard the prince's raw voice pleading with him. Bar had tried to explain to Cal what awaited him at Draville's and Bardock's hands. Cal knew better than to listen to such stuff or anything else the young man had to say. It was probably lies anyway. It was important to keep his resolve firm. Cal had backhanded the earnest young warrior hard anytime he'd tried to speak of his future treatment. Fearfully, he searched Bar's face, hoping the blows didn't show. *Now, whyever did I hit him?* he wondered anxiously. If the king asked about the bruises on his son, what could Cal say? He thought it unlikely that he—or anyone—could lie to the man, no matter how much he might want to. He felt sick with anxiety.

The king climbed up the steps to the castle and motioned Cal to follow him. With soldiers and servants watching silently, Cal did so and felt the great keep close around him like a fist. All that was happening had a nightmare-like, slow-motion quality to it.

By the time he reached the richly appointed study the king led him to, he was trembling with fatigue and out of breath. Bar's limp form was heavy. A strange little man in an ornate red robe waited there and turned eagerly when they entered the room. "Is it true?" he asked with suppressed excitement.

"Aye," Bardock answered carelessly. "Undeniably true." He threw his elegant cloak on a chair and strode to the huge fireplace to warm his hands. "It's beginning to snow," he said absently.

After the long day, Cal felt he could not carry Bar another minute, so with or without permission, he had to put Bar down. He laid Bar on a fur-covered bench and arranged his limbs carefully. Cal stumbled over a bear rug and fell to one knee. He had trouble getting to his feet. He was weak from hunger, thirst, exhaustion, and something else … fear.

The king poured red wine into a cup and drained it quickly. He offered Draville some, and the little priest graciously accepted it. They both pondered the body with a detachment that denied the youth's humanity. Cal shivered at their cold unconcern. To them Bar seemed to be a thing to be used. Evidently the prince had told him the truth about Bardock and Draville's intentions. The lieutenant knew a moment's regret.

Cal was both thirsty and hungry. He felt a spurt of anger that even a king would be so rude to offer him no refreshment. The man had not yet looked into his face, not even once, or, for that matter, acknowledged his existence.

As if reading his thoughts, the king turned and asked softly, "Why does my son sleep?" Now that Cal had Bardock's attention, irrationally, he didn't want it. His sovereign's large, dark eyes were hypnotic and full of menace. Cal explained quickly, in a voice jerky with tension, that because he had brought Bardon in alone, he had decided he must drug him. Awake, the prince might have given him a lot of trouble or even managed to escape. Bardock nodded in agreement, and Cal was greatly relieved.

Between the prelate and monarch, every bit of information about the prince's capture was sifted from Cal's memory. He was still standing and growing faint in the hot room. "May I have a drink, sire?" he asked suddenly without intending to do so. He knew he was at the end of his resources; soon he would keel over.

Shocked at such impertinence, the king frowned for a moment, but then, for the first time, he seemed to notice the young lieutenant's physical state. "Certainly," he replied quickly and poured out a cup of wine. "Sit down. You look like you're about to fall. Tell me, Lieutenant, where are you from?"

The questions went on into the late hours of the night. Cal wondered why he had ever wanted these two men to notice him. To his great relief, Bar slept deeply because of the drug. Cal could see the gentle rise and fall of the prince's chest and did not fear for his life. The king and his major advisor's interest in such a lowly person as himself was very flattering, but he felt uneasy in their presence. He felt like an insect caught in the complex web of two very large spiders. Was he entangled, or would he be allowed to walk away?

The lieutenant had indeed come to the attention of powerful people. For the moment, they were delighted and intrigued by him. He had done what no one else could. They admired his intelligence, determination, and ability to think on his feet and take chances, but mostly they admired his *success*. Such a man was very valuable to them, as long as he kept succeeding.

A moan came from the low bench where Bar lay. The lieutenant was amazed. The last time it had taken days for Bardon to come around. It had only been hours this time. Yet Cal had intentionally tried to make the dose small, and it evidently had been. Hoping Bardock and Draville would not think him impertinent, he suggested tactfully, "It would be a good idea, sire, to get Bardon warm as quickly as possible. He has been cold and motionless for a long time, which can make a man very sick." He regretted his presumption immediately yet wondered why these two cunning men seemed unconcerned with the prince's health. To his surprise, they agreed with him; however, their response was strangely hollow. Draville called a servant to escort Cal to a warm bed. After a short struggle with himself, he decided not to mention the reward and left gratefully.

————◦◦◦◦————

Later, in Bar's own room, servants soaked him in a tub full of warm water, dried his unconscious body, and then lifted him to his bed. Bar's father stood looking at his son's naked chest. For the first time, King Bardock touched the triangular mark on Bardon's left shoulder—the mark he had heard so much about but never seen. It was undeniably real. Until this moment, he'd harbored a hope that the mark was a ruse, something clever that would fool the peasants but not an educated man. The hope died within him, and a sharp fear intruded itself into his stubborn mind unbidden. *This part of the prophecy is fulfilled. Could not the other part succeed also?* He clenched and unclenched his fists. *Fool! What is there to fear? You have him in your power now, to use however you wish.*

He looked around quickly, afraid that Draville might have seen his apprehension. The man was uncanny. He frequently knew what his king was thinking—or at least he seemed to.

Bar groaned and rolled his head from side to side as if it hurt him. The king's own healer had treated the wound caused by Cal's blow to the back of Bar's head. The healer said it was too soon to know, but he doubted it would be serious, which was good news. Draville and Bardock had plans for Bar. The king smiled slightly and left the room.

————◦◦◦◦————

The next day, Bar woke in his own room with an aching head. He thought for a time that he was his younger self, before he had left Casterray. Then memories of the last two years returned in a confusing torrent, and he frantically tried to piece together how he'd come to be here, in his own room. His heart raced with sudden fear as he realized the significance of the guards at the door and windows, the elong ropes that bound him to his bed, and the ominous Blackrobes at his side. He strained at the bonds in sudden terror, but the ropes held him tightly. He sought to calm himself, to control the fear overwhelming his senses. Tal's instructions for difficult circumstances came back to him. *"Quickly size up the situation."* Situation! He was bound and guarded by five soldiers and two Blackrobes. He was in Casterray, and the back of his head ached. Somehow, Cal had brought him here, but he remembered nothing after the uproar on the road and waiting in the cold, wet snow. *I hope he enjoys his reward,* he thought bitterly. *What is Tal's next instruction in the drill? "What is the enemy's probable next move?" Aye ... what next? It will be coercion or torture to force me to cooperate with the king, to follow Choack ... to renounce the Alliance. Then they will give me re-al, to make me reveal the names and hiding places of the Alli. Maker, no! No!* At this point, rational thought deserted Bar. He gave in to blind panic and the images his imagination created. After a time, he forced himself back to calmness, to logical reasoning. One name especially he forced out of his mind; one sweet face he chased away each time it crossed his vision. To betray his love for El would place her in terrible danger. Amray, Lock, and Meggatirra—they all knew, had always known his capture was a possibility. They would be ready.

Bar had just recovered from one drug and a blow to the head. As he turned the facts over in his mind, he decided they would give him the other drug next, to get the information they wanted, and after that would come imprisonment, which would surely involve coercion—coercion that might include captured insurgent prisoners. Eyes closed tightly against the sight, he prayed for control and for peace. Slowly, peace came.

He must have dozed. For how long, he had no idea, but sudden pain brought him awake. Someone was slapping his face. The slaps did not really hurt, but they made his injured head ache. He recognized the hand, the face—Draville! This was, perhaps, the only man in the kingdom who could safely strike him, unless the king had changed dramatically.

The time was here. He recognized the vial the wretched prelate held. With no water or food in his system for hours, the re-al would take effect quickly. Desperate, the child in him cried out for his father to save him ... to help. But even as he searched the room frantically, he reminded himself that there would be no help from that quarter. He did not know why he continued to hope.

Suddenly, Bardock was there with a compassionate smile lighting his face. "There is no need for this, my son," he assured Bar gently, and Bar wanted to believe. "Give us the information we need. We are going to get it anyway. Why go through the pain? Join us! You will rule by my side, and with Choack's help, we will make Ree more prosperous than it has ever been. You can save your friends from sure and painful death. Remember, in a few minutes, after the re-al, we will know where they are and have your best advice on how to capture them." In spite of his rigid self-control, Bar strained frantically against his bonds, to no avail. Chest heaving, he lay still with his eyes closed, but he could not shut out sound. His father continued reasonably, "If you join us, the fighting and the bloodshed will stop. Blalock will stop creating the selitper; we will have no need for them. Join us and save your people. We are going to win the battle anyway ... with or without you. Why not be on our side?" Bar almost believed him, but he knew the truth. Bardock no longer knew what the word *truth* meant. Though it seemed worse than useless, though Bar could not stop them, he would not help them.

He gazed at his father. He had to try. "It's not too late to turn back, Father. Leave Choack and this evil man. There is no pleasure, no real reward in serving darkness." His words felt wooden, stupid, and, worse, impotent. For just a second, the king paused. His eyes registered shock, but then his face turned bright red with anger, and he shouted, "Stop this! Who do you think you are! Answer me. Will you join us or not?"

"I will not," Bar said firmly. His heart ached, for himself but also for this proud man who was as much a prisoner as he.

There was no logic in fighting them, but he did. They poured the drug down his throat. His last rational thoughts were desperate, earnest prayer. Many of Bar's words were audible, and Draville laughed softly at such nonsense. The Maker, if he existed, was building elsewhere in his vast universe. He obviously no longer cared about little Ree, or he would have interfered with Choack long ago.

Dark vapor rolled over Bar like billowing black smoke from a forest fire. He choked and coughed and then lost his sense of self in a tangle of insistent, pounding voices that asked question after question. He didn't want to answer them. He wouldn't answer them! But then he forgot why. There was something he needed to remember, but he couldn't remember what it was.

"Majesty, you must let his body rest and recover. Even if you no longer care what happens to his mind, this will kill him," Bar heard an insistent voice say. He ached from head to toe and couldn't seem to move anything very well. His body lay on something dark and cold and scratchy.

Suddenly, a physical need reached his conscious mind; it was imperative and urgent in its demand. *Water. Thirsty … so thirsty.* All attempts at reasoning stopped, and he whispered eagerly, "Water, please." The voices stopped their discussion, and a cup was held to his lips. He drank gratefully, but then the cup was knocked away. "No! More please." Since none came, he asked again; it was very difficult. "More water, please!"

"Silence!" an angry voice roared. It was a familiar voice, but Bar couldn't remember whose. Surely they did not understand, whoever they were, how important it was for him to have water. He had to make them understand.

He opened his mouth again, but before he could utter a sound, someone hissed, "Quiet, Bar. Not now!" He obeyed reluctantly. The voice was not unkind.

After a time, he tried to make sense of the conversation somewhere above him. "Majesty, hear me. Of what use are all your plans if he dies too soon? You wish to humiliate him and show your victory over the prophecy, to demonstrate Choack's dominance over the Maker. His body must have rest before you do this to him. Let him eat, drink, and sleep for a few days and get the re-al out of his system. You need time to make your preparations anyway. The plan will work, but you will have a living prince, instead of a dead one." The mists cleared a little, and Bar could see a glowing torch, guards, the king talking to a familiar-looking man, and a dungeon cell, small and dark. He fought terror to the back corner of his mind, where it lurked, ever ready to pounce again. He watched and waited while these two decided what to do with him.

With his mighty right arm, the king slammed the captain to the damp rock wall. "Care for him, then, but in two days I expect you to put my orders into effect. Is that clear?"

"Aye, sire," the soldier answered with a tremor in his voice. The king glared into Bar's aware gaze. He raised an eyebrow and nodded in surprise to acknowledge Bar's consciousness and then whirled and left. A tiny spark of hope within Bar died again. It hurt again.

Bar would have been surprised to see the king halt in the dark passageway outside the cell. Memories flashed through Bardock's mind: his son on a horse for the first time, the child's delighted smile when given a bow, his eagerness to learn to throw his first knife, happy laughter when he tricked Tal Qua ... He almost weakened. Willing the flood of memories to stop, he hurried down the corridor.

The captain's hands still gripped the wall as he stared after his sovereign. He laid his head back against the rough stone and closed his eyes for a few moments. Bar cleared his throat hopefully. The man turned. It was Captain Ganshof! He gave Bar water until he could hold no more. "Alati, thank you," Bar gasped with gratitude. Eyes closed, Bar held on to the captain's hand, the one that held the cup, for a long time, as if it were an anchor in a troubled sea. Ganshof watched the pale, gaunt face with pity. Bar had deep circles under his eyes and was drug dazed, yet the captain sensed a detachment, a peace in him. He had seen the prince's stillness when the king looked at him—a stillness that was hope without hope. As he thought of his own family, he wondered how the man could turn away from his son without a word or touch.

Working in the dungeon was definitely a demotion, though his rank was still the same. This position was Bardock's punishment for Ganshof's failure to bring Bar back by the specified time. Compared to the other things the king had threatened, this punishment was definitely a mild one. Ganshof felt sure his sovereign was secretly pleased that he had brought his son back at all but felt he had to give him a token slap on the wrist. This post, for which Ganshof was overqualified, kept him out of the king's notice, and he did not have to obey the king's orders that went against his conscience, until now anyway. For over a year, he had been left in peace to run the dungeon as he wished. He should have known that couldn't last. At least he could see that Bardon got good treatment for these next few days. It was unlikely that anyone else would have advised the king to let Bar rest and heal. That much he'd accomplished for Bardon, who had once saved his life. It helped diminish the terrible guilt of his other deeds, a little. When the time came, he would refuse to be a part of Draville's vile plan. He and his family would die, most unpleasantly, but no matter the price, he was through obeying Draville's and Bardock's orders. He was not brave; he was just no longer able.

FRIENDS IN NEED

IN THE LAST PLACE BAR EXPECTED TO DISCOVER comfort, he found a friend. Ganshof stayed with him during the long hours of the night. The captain wrapped him in a blanket and sat next to his pallet of straw. The constant cold of the ride to Feisan and now the damp cold of the dungeon had made Bar sick. The re-al also had contributed to his weakness.

The guards that paced the dreary halls looked in Bar's cell with astonishment. When the prince woke from terrible nightmares or in pain, Ganshof gave him hot drinks of a meat broth laced with otet and sought to distract him from the gnawing fear. Bar was at first baffled and then concerned by the man's total lack of discretion. The guards could get the captain into a great deal of trouble. Bar frowned over Ganshof's strange behavior. *I must stop this for his sake ... The king will take terrible revenge. Why is he openly aiding me?* There was only one reason Bar could think of for the captain's reckless behavior. He decided to find out if his guess was right.

In the dark hour before dawn, Ganshof was overcome by fatigue, but he could not doze off. His back ached, and he was stiff and uncomfortable. Bar was awake also; he was too anxious and sick to sleep. Gradually, the futility of resisting Bardock's might became plain to Ganshof. *What is the use? I cannot bear to think of this young man, only a few years younger than my daughter, suffering anymore ... or dying.* "Bar, pretend to cooperate! Live any way you can. We need you alive. While you and Dare live, there is hope!"

"They intend to ... kill me, then?" Bar managed to reply. He was stunned.

Death, so soon, was unexpected. In some distant future, he'd thought the king might resort to execution, if he couldn't break Bar's resolve. But he'd expected his father to try again. Never had he suspected that Bardock would plan his death in a few days' time. Unexpected, uninvited grief squeezed his heart. He did not fear death. Being with the Maker would be joy itself, but he really hadn't thought his father would take his life. Torment him and use him? Aye, he would do that. But kill him?

"Aye, they do," Ganshof answered grimly. *And that is not all.*

Gloom surrounded Bar in the small, dark cell and pressed him down with shocking force. He repeated to himself over and over, *Remain loyal and speak the truth.*

Voices whispered in his mind, *If you pretend to cooperate, then your father will love you. He will be proud of you.* Bar gasped at the powerful emotional reaction this suggestion evoked. *Why do I still care? Will I ever stop caring?*

Again voices whispered and then thundered at him. *You could pretend to cooperate. You could lie to them. Then, when the opportunity comes, you could escape! Why suffer? Why die for nothing? Who will know or care that you refused to help them? You have told them most of what you know anyway. Think! They will capture the Alli! Dare will be captured, as will many others. What if they capture Ellarann? What if ...*

Bar had not allowed himself to even think El's name or picture her face in this corrupt place. He prayed he had not spoken of her under the influence of re-al, and he hoped he would not whisper her name even in his dreams. The sweet image he tried so desperately to erase from his memory appeared to him in soft, beautiful clarity. Reluctantly, he pushed it away.

He recognized Choack's attack for what it was. The mind and the imagination were corruption's favorite targets, but he had no energy to defend himself. The images continued to flood his mind, draining him of the will to resist and filling him with darkness.

He implored the Maker for aid, and words from a scroll Devon had read to him came back ... something about a shepherd? *Even if I walk through a dark valley ... I don't need to be afraid, because you are there with me. That's it! This valley is really dark, Maker, but I trust you are here with me, even though I can't see you ... I trust you.* He grasped at another tiny, bright thought. *What is the promise?* Bar struggled to remember the phrase E Clue had made him memorize so long ago: *"If he remains loyal and speaks the truth, the crown he will surely win."* What his friend Ganshof and the voices were suggesting was not loyalty to the Maker, nor was it in any way the truth. "No," he breathed. He would trust the Maker and the promise.

"Ganshof, help me! Please don't side with them," he cried in distress.

Ganshof stared at him a moment and then agreed harshly, "So be it."

After a few minutes, the captain suddenly knocked his head back against the wall. "What is wrong with me? Forgive me, Bar. I don't know what I was thinking," he confessed, perplexed.

"I do," Bar replied brokenly. "Choack always attacks when we are weakest and where we are most vulnerable."

"Choack?" Ganshof whispered, eyes wide and puzzled.

"Choack is pure evil. Look at the terrible things his worshippers do. The Maker says that good trees produce good fruit and bad trees produce bad fruit. A bad tree cannot produce good fruit or a good tree bad. The Maker is pure goodness. No matter the circumstances you or your loved ones are in, he will give you peace. Call on the Maker and he will guide and help you, and one day when you die, you will be with him in his wonderful home."

In his time with Ganshof, Bar shared all Devon had taught him about the Maker. The prince knew that the Creator, the Maker, and the Spirit were one, but many of the scrolls about them had been lost in the persecutions. His knowledge was limited, but he knew enough to help Ganshof find the Maker. In helping Ganshof, he helped himself. His spirit lifted, and peace returned; Bar reminded himself that the Maker was in charge … not the King, not Draville and certainly not Choack.

Bar received another ten-day reprieve, as the king's plans were taking more time than his staff had anticipated. No one told Bar what caused the reprieve, nor did he ask. He would know soon enough. As he thought about it, he realized that Lavel was at work. Though he was afraid to believe the situation could last, Bar took encouragement from the fact that so far there were no other insurgent prisoners in Bardock's dungeon.

He thought back to the day Draville had poured re-al down his throat. It was his hope that he had not mentioned Yad Thgil or the Bitterroot Range while under the drug's influence. Usually, a drugged prisoner did not speak about topics not mentioned. People given re-al spoke of subjects that their interrogators suggested repeatedly, and even then, their minds could wander away from the topic. To Bar's knowledge, the king and his advisors did not know about Yad Thgil, so they could not ask him to divulge its location.

But there was so much they could know! They knew the Bani had a hidden home base. They knew there were hiding places all over Ree, and they knew there was a network of spies that crossed the country. They knew the Chi existed and were hidden in the mountains somewhere. It was possible Bar's knowledge about these subjects was now in the king's and Draville's hands. When the Bani, the Chi, and Lavel's spies heard of Bar's capture, their only option would be to flee and hide themselves someplace new.

Unbeknownst to Bar, they were doing just the opposite. The prince's capture had ignited the slow-burning fire of a hidden resistance into the flames of organized revolution. It was time. Almost all of Ree's people now remembered the prophecy and were watching it unfold before their eyes. They'd heard the wonderful stories about the marked prince and his marked companion and their ancient swords. They secretly cheered them on and began to hope. Clans that had been thought long dead had reappeared and were not just protecting the pair but also helping them fight the king, Draville, and his soldiers. And they were winning!

The leaders of the clans and of Ree's citizens were getting together and planning. What had begun as an underground resistance had turned into the Alli, an alliance of Ree's clans, known and unknown, and its citizens.

The imprisoned prince and his jailers knew none of this. Neither did the king or those who supported him. Bar thought that the Bani warriors and any folk left would escape from Glimmervale to Yad Thgil, where most of the women and children were already located. The spies in the city, like Lavel, would bolt to prearranged hiding places. And the Chi would close their mountains' hidden passages and doors, retreat to their valleys, and disappear again. The O'Hatch were safe as long as he had not spoken of them, but if he had, there was no place for them to run ... unless they, too, could retreat to Yad Thgil.

There was no one to tell Bar that his companions were planning a rescue ... of him and the people of Ree!

He prayed his friends were safely hidden somewhere. He missed them. This was the first fight he had faced alone in a long time. *No, no, not alone,* he reminded himself.

A strong voice echoed in his mind, *"Remember, Bar, you will never be alone. I will always be with you. You are my bar, my deterrent to evil's plan. You stand in the king's way and block his path. But for you and the others, the whole island would be under his sway by now."*

Bar thought, *I am afraid and confused, but I will remain loyal and speak the truth. I don't know how I can inherit a throne if they kill me, but I will trust.*

He lay down on the fragrant, clean straw, Ganshof's doing, and rested, confident only that the Maker was with him and that his promises were true. They seemed completely impossible now. How would the powerful Bardock and Draville be defeated and he, a sick prisoner, come to rule? Because of his circumstances, he smiled at the thought, even though he believed he would indeed come to rule, as prophesied. Peace flooded his whole being and he was able to sleep the whole night through.

A guard woke Bar when he entered the cell the next morning with his morn meal on a tray. For the next ten days, he laughed weakly with his jailers and complied with their requests to tell stories about the Alli. When he was able, he shared his and the Alli's adventures, but he was often too weak to utter a word. Much to his surprise, the soldiers were very interested in him and Dare and especially in their blessed swords, Uriisis and Wolf. They listened intently to his tales of his and his comrades' battles. They also wanted to know more about the Maker. It seemed Bar's ancient God had great power. He had saved Bar's, Dare's, and the Alli's lives over and over again. The rebels had fought the king's soldiers and won. They had stopped the merchants' wagon caravans, no matter how well guarded. Surely their God was with them! Bar was amazed that the Maker could use a prisoner in a dark dungeon, a prisoner about to die, to tell the soldiers stories about the wonderful things the Maker had done for the Alli.

Bar found his guess concerning the captain's motives to be fact. Ganshof was making no attempt to keep his actions secret because he no longer cared if the king retaliated. Now he, too, followed the Maker. If possible, he would have disappeared long ago with his family and hidden himself in one of the island's big cities, but his oldest daughter was married to a government official. She would not leave her husband, nor would her husband flee with her, so they all stayed. Bar extracted a promise from the captain that he would wait for the king's wrath and not seek it. There was a chance Ganshof's aid to a disgraced prisoner would be overlooked in the larger picture.

On the tenth day, they came for him. Draville and three Blackrobes, whose faces Bar couldn't see, marched him out of the dungeon and up into the castle. He thought he was too weak and sick to feel terror; he was wrong. After walking only a few hundred feet, he fainted, and they had to carry him. Bar woke in his own rooms, where servants bathed and dressed him in royal robes that were not his own, as he had grown in the last two years. Because he was very weak, they were forced to help him with the simplest tasks. Every time he moved, he became dizzy and breathless, his hands trembled, and his head ached. He found infirmity depressing. The servants were completely silent during all their attention to his person. He had never felt so alone.

Puzzled, Bar wondered why an elong rope hung over his closet door and was anchored to his heavy bed. His heart beat faster with apprehension as a possible reason occurred to him, but why? Then Draville motioned the Blackrobes to suspend Bar just enough off his richly carpeted floor to cause queal. He stared at the prelate, perplexed, but he was too weak to put up even token resistance. Triumphant malice gleamed in the man's black eyes, but he said nothing. They carefully protected Bar's finery with a sheet before they left him.

There were guards in the room who would witness his progressive reaction to the strange sickness that was queal. How he wished they would allow him to endure this humiliating ordeal alone. The guards held a basin for him when the first unstoppable effect had its way. *Why? Why this?* The consequences of queal came more swiftly than ever before because of Bar's weakened condition. As his limbs went numb, doubt and fear attacked viciously. The mental battering was worse than the physical paralysis. *Why would the Maker save me? Surely I imagined all of this. What are they going to do to me next? I've held out this long; surely this is long enough. He will forgive me … He is so kind.* Bar felt his resolve failing and cried out loud for the Maker, no longer caring in his distress what the soldiers thought of him.

His cry startled and frightened the guards. They gazed at each other in dismay, uncertain what their short-tempered sovereign expected of them. No one had prepared them for this. In whispered conversation, they expressed the hope that the ailing prince didn't die from his queal. He had been so sickly when the Blackrobes had brought him here. Surely Bardock would have them punished if his son died before the big event this afternoon. They discussed offering him water but decided against it and waited nervously.

When Bar's vision shattered like pieces of a puzzle scattered on the floor, he groaned in misery. Suddenly, all his faith breaking, all his pettiness, temper, arrogance, failures, and weaknesses poured into his mind until he was filled with despair. Accusation and condemnation whispered repeatedly. *Why would the Maker save you? You caused the death of two of your companions. What have you ever done to deserve his championship? You hate, and that's against his law, isn't it? Right now you would like to break Draville, that cockroach, in two, wouldn't you! Aye! Aye, see, you would. You are unworthy, unworthy, unworthy …* Broken, weak, and helpless, Bar cried for mercy … and mercy came! The horrible voices faded. He remembered Devon reading from one of his scrolls that there was no condemnation for those who followed the Maker. When they confessed their faith breaking, the Maker forgave them and forgot about it.

The next hours were the darkest Bar had ever known, yet he had never felt the Maker's presence more strongly. No part of his body functioned properly except for his hearing and thinking, and he wasn't too sure about his thinking. He was cold, thirsty, and in pain from protesting muscles and nerves. He tried to imagine where all this was leading and could not.

When the guards released him, he was intensely grateful, though he realized they did it for no good reason. The tight band of pain around his chest, caused by the rope, lessened and made breathing easier. When they laid him on the floor, he passed out.

Bar fainting terrified Choack's servants, who thought him dead. They were sure the king would have them killed. His fury had grown over the last two days to a volcanic state. Each delay enraged him more, and there had been many. Being in his presence was dangerous to life and limb. Not even Draville's oily smoothness could soothe his raving.

The irascible prelate rushed into the room and demanded to know what was keeping them. They backed away from him without a word and gestured to the still form sprawled on the floor. Draville gasped in horror and knelt quickly at Bar's side. He sought the prince's pulse, his soft, white fingers pressed to the royal neck. The pulse was weak and erratic but there. "Quick, you fools, he lives. Give me some tea or wine." They hurried to do his bidding.

Meanwhile, Draville slapped and shook Bar until he groaned and opened his eyes. "Swallow this," Draville commanded, holding a cup of tepid wine to Bar's lips. Bar did and felt a little stronger. Some part of him was amused at their frantic, terrified expressions. *It wouldn't do for me to die too soon!*

They arranged him gracefully in an ornate chair on a platform with carrying poles attached to its sides. After tying his paralyzed limbs in place, they covered the rope with a rich green cloak. Many Blackrobes filed in and lifted the platform, chair and all, and carried Bar out of his room and down to the huge audience chamber. It took him much time and effort to organize what his fractured sight was observing. He was exhausted and having trouble holding up his head by the time his bearers put the platform down.

There appeared to be hundreds of people present. They were lavishly dressed in brilliant colors, but he wasn't sure of their numbers. What seemed a huge throng to him might only be a group of a hundred or so. He did know that the boisterous crowd *sounded* immense and intoxicated. They gradually became silent; Bar assumed it was because of him. Even the beautiful music stopped. He thought one of his colorful splinters of sight contained Lavel's face, but he chalked that up to wishful thinking. The smell of food and the sour odor of wine reached his nose and made him queasy. Because he knew what the elegant audience chamber looked like, he could be fairly sure that the dais was in front of him.

The king's throne was on the raised dais. Behind the throne was the castle's western wall. In the now hushed audience chamber Bar could hear the sea pounding against the rampart outside. Huge windows covered with a multicolored, transparent substance called mirsma filled the western wall. Even with his splintered sight, the array of colors was beautiful. The brightly colored sunlight landed on the dais and made it radiant. The effect was very dramatic, but Bar saw it clearly only in memory.

The king of Ree stood and walked to the edge of the platform. An undercurrent of whispering rippled through the hall as both wellborn and common citizens recognized the chair's occupant. They were delighted that one of the marked was captured and a prisoner. It served him right! This would stop the rebels! The invited citizens' profits had been greatly reduced by the insurgents' attacks on their wagon caravans. Obviously, these citizens had been carefully selected.

To prove his fairness, Bardock offered, in a commanding voice that reached the farthest corners of the hall, to forgive his son's treason. All Bar needed to do was repudiate the insurgent cause and pledge allegiance to his true sovereign anew. It was, after all, a simple, very reasonable request. An expectant hush spread over the crowd as they waited to see what Bardon would do. They did not know that he could neither move nor speak. He understood now why they had incapacitated him for this spectacle. He could do nothing at all!

When the great throng realized that the king's ungrateful, treasonous son had no intention of even responding to his father's magnanimous offer, angry shouts of "Traitor! Murderer! Thief!" broke out here and there among the crowd. An angry murmur grew and swelled until it finally became a deafening roar. "Kill the traitor!"

Of course, this mass of humanity had been carefully picked and then invited to a special audience with their king. Also, wine from the king's cellar flowed freely. His servants moved quietly among the crowd and kept their pottery cups well filled. Draville scattered his own men throughout the throng to start the people shouting the proper insults and slander.

As the tumult and shouts of "Kill him!" burgeoned, authority in the form of the king, Draville, and other high-ranking officers remained silent. They made no effort to contain or dissipate the dangerously explosive atmosphere. Pent-up anger at losses caused by the rebels, real or imaginary, ignited into violence. Carefully chosen men in the crowd broke furniture to make clubs, tore down ancient hangings, and threw their heavy pottery cups at the arrogant young traitor. Soon other folk in the crowd joined them. Their aim was faulty, perhaps because they still knew some restraint in the form of fear. When no one stopped them, they threw in earnest with every intention of harming the prince.

Bar listened with dismay to the growing riot of sound and screams of "Kill the traitor!" and "Down with the rebels!"

So this is how I am to die!

Chaos filled the huge chamber. He heard things being broken and smashed. Someone shouted, "Choack, Choack!" and the chant was picked up by voices from every corner of the great hall. The king's intent became clear to Bar, and he tried to prepare himself for what must come. A longing to die on his feet and fighting swept over him. He forced himself to ignore this impossible dream and to trust the Maker's promise. He countered their chant with one of his own that no one could hear. *I trust you, Maker.*

When the first shard of pottery smashed into his cheek and cut it, he knew he had little time left. A great peace filled him. Other cups, broken and whole, battered his body. Suddenly, someone threw his body across Bar's to protect him, but the crazed mob tried to drag the huge man off. *Who in this mad rabble would try to help me?* Bar wondered in confusion. Then he recognized the man who had come to his aid. *It is Lavel!* Bar could not imagine how his friend had come to be here. Lavel clung tightly to the chair and was quickly joined by others. Somehow he and the Alli had infiltrated the audience chamber. Lavel let out grunts of pain interspersed with shouts to his men.

Then Bar saw familiar faces. The Pack was here! They had surrounded him. Dare was on his right, and Louke was on his left. Louke shouted over the noise, "It's one thing after another with you, my prince. We just keep havin' to get you out of trouble. Now look what you've gotten us into!"

Dare added, "Youth fighting the king of Ree and his select soldiers! No problem! Just another day in the life of the Pack."

Bar felt his bonds release as a knife sliced through them. He managed to remain upright for only a few seconds, and then he slumped down in the chair. Someone carefully lifted him out of the broken chair. Dare held him in his arms, and the Pack surrounded them. The king's soldiers would have to get through the Pack to harm Bar or take him back.

All was noise and confusion to Bar. He desperately tried to understand what was happening around him. Even with his broken vision, he saw more and more familiar faces. The Bani war chant broke out in ever-louder cries across the audience chamber until it thundered and shook the room. Some were also beating on their shields with their swords, adding to the uproar.

Dare shouted over the noise so Bar could hear him, "A hundred Alli fighters are pouring into this room and the king's other strongholds across Ree. Today we take back our island! The Chi, the Bani, the Basca', even the O'Hatch are fighting. It's hard to believe, but many of the soldiers and common people have joined us. They hate what Bardock and Draville have done to Ree and its people ... to them!"

Fighting? The revolution had begun! Without conscious thought, Bar's eyes frantically sought his father. One shattered fragment of vision contained Bardock's face. The king was watching the mob scene with a gloating expression and high color on his cheeks. The expression on Bardock's face suddenly changed to horror as he realized that somehow, someway, chanting Alli warriors had taken over his entire throne room. They had his son and were protecting him from his soldiers. He screamed at his soldiers to get Bar back.

It was too late. The Alli were slowly battling and pushing his elite royal troop back against the walls.

The Alli had used the lungala to secretly usher hundreds of warriors into the city. Some had fought their way into the palace, and some had used secret entrances. Lavel and his rebels had been planning this invasion for a long time. They'd known the time had come to carry out their plans when Bar had entered Casterray as a prisoner and fallen into the king's hands. Under the influence of re-al, he would tell them much in spite of not wanting to. They'd quickly gone into action. Their surprise attack completely overwhelmed the few royal soldiers in the castle on guard duty.

The streets of Feisan were also filled with Alli fighters from every trade. The citizens were stunned at first and then cheered them on. Most of the king's elite soldiers were out in the countryside seeking the rebels. It made taking over the city easier. None of Bardock's advisors had warned him not to leave Feisan or the palace so lightly guarded. They'd believed they had the rebels on the run. Plus, it would be insane to attack the royal city! After all, they had captured the king's son and put him in the dungeon, and they'd thought Bar would soon die. None of them knew how the Alli had gotten into the city or into the palace.

Because of Bardon's capture, this day ... this battle had come much sooner than they'd expected, and yet their plan was working well.

The Alli in the throne room were now forcing the crazed crowd and the king's royal guards back against the wall. The Alli ordered them to drop their weapons, broken pottery, and pieces of furniture and also ordered them to be silent. The stunned mob and guards quickly obeyed. Surely this was not part of the king's plan!

Bar was also stunned. And filled with joy! Before he could take it all in, something else caught his attention. *What is that?*

Behind his father, through the colored windows, Bar saw something through his splintered vision. A gigantic dark shadow was moving toward them! A low rumbling noise became an earthquake of thundering sound and violent shaking.

The wall at the far end of the chamber shook and then shattered with a deafening explosion into flying boulders and stones. People screamed in abject terror at just the sound and were reduced to hysteria by the sight that met their eyes. Huge talons struck a terrible blow again, sending debris flying in all directions. An immense, magnificent being entered the castle through the enlarged opening.

People ran in terror for the doors, which were blocked, and pushed on them uselessly. They couldn't get out. Others stood in frozen immobility as the enormous being, described only in ancient legend, stepped into the towering audience chamber. He dominated the whole chaotic scene with his size and majesty. "A Uriisis!" men screamed in alarm and some in awe.

Silence quickly blanketed the chamber when E Clue gazed at the sight before him in blazing, heart-stopping anger. He moved one giant horned foot forward onto the dais, and the stunned king fled in terror behind his throne. Draville stared up at the creature out of legend in undisguised horror. He slowly backed off the dais and disappeared into the crowd. The Uriisis threw back his head and gave a furious cry that shook the palace to its foundations and brought down weakened timbers from the ceiling.

E Clue lowered his great horned head and folded his enormous blue-black wings. He stepped with confidence into the clouds of rock dust and disorder, moving toward Bardon. Lavel gazed up at the mighty creature with awe, then bowed his head in respect.

"Are you well, Listener?" E Clue asked gently. The Urissis considered Lavel's position as the head of the underground's spy network a work of listening.

Lavel heard this question in his mind. "Well enough," he replied out loud with a shaky grin, "though I'll be sore from their battering for many days."

"Battering" was a mild word for the beating Lavel and his men had received until the Pack had surrounded Bar and protected him. Of course Lavel and his men had not let the Pack go in first; they did not want Ree's future leaders wounded or dead. Once the Pack had arrived, Lavel and the Alli had quickly joined the battle for control of the audience chamber. E Clue nodded his head with grave understanding. *"I got here in time because of your efforts. Many tried to stop me, oh, many! But I won through with my brother's aid. I thank you,"* E Clue responded.

The Uriisis turned to the conscious but battered young man in Dare's arms. *"Maker's Bar, can you hear me?"* E Clue called softly.

"Aye, great friend. You ... were wonderful! He has saved me against all hope ..." Bar whispered weakly, and then his voice trailed off. Pain and weakness took away his strength to speak. Dare gratefully lifted Bar to E Clue. He knew the Uriisis was here to help Bar. The Uriisis took Bar gently in his great scaly claw. Bar groaned and passed into oblivion.

Lavel whispered, "Alati, mighty one."

E Clue turned and flew out over the shining sea with the small, sick human in his grasp. His giant wings were a blur as he sped toward a speck in the swelling waves that grew ever larger.

Lavel and his men began the enormous task of securing the castle and imprisoning its ruler. Captain Ganshof and many of his soldiers were delighted to help them. Draville was nowhere to be found.

HEALING

E CLUE LANDED ON AN ANCIENT SEAWALL THAT sparkled with foam from the ever-crashing waves. "Lark," he called urgently. "Come quickly! One is badly injured."

"I come, ancient king," a deep voice answered. A tall man strode into view. He had the superb, muscled body of an athlete. His limbs were strong and his skin brown. He wore a short green robe belted at the waist. His jet hair was parted in the middle and flowed to his waist; it was straight and bound with a thong at shoulder length. He bowed respectfully and deeply to the majestic creature that towered over him. "I will take him, Great One." He held out his arms for the prince who was a far-too-light burden for a young man his size. Bar was bruised and barely breathing. E Clue laid him gently in Lark's arms with a sorrowful look. He fluttered his great wings in distress, causing a minor windstorm in the stone courtyard.

"Lark, I will speak to the Maker on his behalf. Give my greetings to your mistress. Fare thee well," the Uriisis said as he unfurled his great wings and splashed into the waves. E Clue paddled through the water with his webbed, clawed feet until his wings gathered enough air and he was able to mount high into the sky with powerful strokes. Over a certain portion of the ocean that looked like any other on the surface, he dived from a vast height, like a hawk after prey. But unlike a hawk, E Clue disappeared into the sea and did not emerge again.

Lark, whistling softly like his namesake, took Bar into the great, rambling building that covered the southern fourth of the island. His white-haired mistress, Ecalos, nursed the young prince carefully and brought him back from the edge of death.

Bar woke from strange dreams to an aching body that was restless with fever. Memory returned slowly, memory of that terrible afternoon in Casterray's audience chamber. His heart pounded again as he heard the people screaming "Traitor!" He flinched and groaned at the graphic flashback. More memories returned. Lavel and a large force of Alli had come to his rescue, and the Pack had been with them. He had seen them all and many other familiar faces. They'd taken over the whole audience chamber. However, the biggest shock had been the arrival of E Clue. Bar whispered with wonder and a heart overflowing with gratitude, "I am alive! Maker, you saved my life! I thank you, great friend. Blessed be your mighty name!"

The doors of his room were open wide. Beyond them, he could see a large stone porch that faced the ocean. Bright with sunshine, the sea glittered a deep blue green. Waves rolled in and broke upon jagged rock, and white gulls screamed as they circled overhead. In spite of the brilliant sunshine, the air was cool, but he was warmly covered in blankets.

Someone with a soft step entered the room, and Bar turned his aching head carefully to see who it might be. The green-robed woman who entered was tall and slender. Some terrible accident had twisted her upper body and scarred her face. Her beautiful snow-white hair was a braided crown on top of her head. Her large blue eyes were undamaged and twinkled softly, but her mouth was so disfigured that he could not tell its expression. While he stared at her, she waited patiently for him to speak.

"Where am I, Lady? Is this … the great kingdom?" he asked hesitantly, for he had visited it once before and this place had the same peaceful feel.

"You are on Epoh, a small island close to your own great one of Ree. E Clue brought you here two weeks ago. You were very close to death, and you are still sick and weak," she answered slowly. Speech was difficult for her because of her deformed mouth, and she spoke slowly so that he might understand her.

"E Clue brought me here to heal," he mused to himself, gazing at the blankets that covered him.

"Indeed," she responded.

He looked up with the difficult question in his mind written on his face.

Her eyes were sad and filled with understanding. He took a number of deep breaths to steady his voice before he asked, "How did my body survive the beating it took?"

"We don't know yet," she said truthfully. "Your recovery will be slow and painful, Bar. You have much in your favor. Your spine and trunk, where your vital organs are located, are undamaged, probably because you were sitting and they aimed their missiles at your profile. The chair protected you from many of the blows. If you had been standing ..." She shook her head in dismay. "After a few minutes, Lavel and the Pack were able to reach you, and they protected you, but your arms and legs were already badly battered. Only time will tell how much use you will regain of them." Bar closed his eyes against the image these words conjured, and he tried to remain calm. *A cripple!* He was quiet for many minutes.

"You have nursed me all this time?" he asked her finally, his mind still numb.

"Aye, Lark and I have cared for you. He is out fishing for our dinner now, but he will return soon."

"What ... must I do, Lady?" he asked hesitantly, a tremor in his voice and confusion as well.

"Just what you have been doing. Rest, eat, sleep, and trust," she replied with certainty.

"Aye." He nodded wearily as drowsiness stole over him, but even in rest, his heart ached at her unwelcome tidings. *A crippled king!* He moaned as he drifted off to sleep.

It took Bar three long months to slowly heal. It was not just what he had suffered in the audience chamber that had made him ill. He had not been in good shape when the Blackrobes had taken him there. The long, cold journey in Lieutenant Cal's hands and Draville and the king's use of re-al on him had weakened him. Then the many days in the cold, damp dungeon, in spite of Ganshof's help, had continued to make him weak and sick.

With Lark and Ecalos's constant encouragement and aid, he was able to regain the use of his limbs. The island had the same sweet peace that he'd experienced in his vision of the Maker, yet there was no peace inside him.

Bar was a terrible patient. During the tedious, miserable process of relearning things he had conquered as a child, he raged, despaired, wept, and grumbled. In his terrible weakness and subsequent depression, he depended hourly on his two helpers. Each time he failed or fell, they encouraged him to try again. He grew angry and pled with them to leave him alone. Yet they persisted, with great patience, insisting that he continue to try.

Bar was proud, sometimes arrogant, and capable of enormous stubbornness. However, Ecalos and Lark were old hands at their task; they could not be forced or fooled into aiding him more than necessary. Disability brought out the worst in their patient, yet they remained calm and pleasant.

Feeling exhausted and very sorry for himself, Bar refused to try again after an attempt to walk to his bedroom had ended in a stumbling, humiliating fall. It had been a long and difficult day. His muscles ached, his limbs were trembling, and he felt queasy. "Enough! Please, help me," he demanded, longing for his bed.

They both refused and urged him to get up. "You can make it."

Bar couldn't believe what to him was their lack of compassion. All that he had endured for the last few weeks poured through his mind in a painful, humbling litany. "Go, then, and leave me alone. I don't need you, either of you! Leave me alone. Leave!" They left.

After a long, miserable time on the floor, he realized they weren't coming back. The oil lamp flickered and then went out, and he lay in darkness. The cold from the tile floor seeped into his muscles, and they cramped. Hurting and bitter, he managed to crawl to a chair and, with its help, rise. It took him a long, painful time to walk across the sitting room. Then his right leg betrayed him again, and he stumbled to one knee. Pain shot through his aching joints and tore a stifled cry from his throat. Utterly spent, he crawled to his bed, dragging his traitorous right leg.

Resentful tears slid down his cheeks as he lay in the dark fighting for control. Warriors did not crawl or limp or fall or acknowledge pain. They were not awkward but skilled and swift. His harsh laugh broke the silence. *Swift!* It had taken him long minutes to walk—no, to *limp*—across a room. Shame and humiliation sank their claws into him and made him writhe mentally. His misery deepened until he cried out in his mind, *You have saved me. Now heal me or let me die. I cannot—will not—be a king like, like … this! What respect will my subjects have for me … a crippled king? King Bardon, the Cripple! No ... a thousand times no. Maker, hear me—I can't do this!* But no response came. The silence was deafening. No lightning descended from the heavens to heal his damaged limbs or to take his miserable life. Either one would be good, but not *this* ... this brokenness. His friends, his people would pity him! Bar tried to keep his anger alive, but it died and left him in despair and fully aware of his physical pain. As he quieted, he realized that there would be no massage, no hot bath, and no comforting ointment to ease his suffering. He lay awake and wretched in the dark.

At first, he railed against his helpers' hard hearts, but an innate honesty forced him to admit the facts. For all his protesting that he couldn't, he *had* made it to his room by himself. For weeks, he had treated his kind helpers to the temper and self-pity of a child. They'd endured his childish resentment and passions patiently and with humor, but now they had borne enough. Bar knew guilt as he looked back at his behavior over the last four weeks, and color flooded his pale cheeks. He struggled with himself for a long time. He knew what he needed to do; he had known it for weeks. He remembered Brother Devon's teachings, "*Be obedient. Be loyal. Speak the truth.*"

Bar's "I cannot—will not—be a king like, like ... this!" came back to him, loud and clear.

He groaned aloud as he remembered the scenes the Maker had engraved on his mind of the suffering of Ree's people ... now his people. He remembered the compassionate, pain-filled eyes that had asked *his* permission to send him back to Ree to help them.

Bar felt suspended in time, as if the earth itself waited for him to speak. His small rebellion crumbled under the might of heaven, and he found words one by one. *You have not healed me, yet I am alive for your purpose. You sent Lavel, his men, the Pack, and E Clue to save me. You are faithful and true.* Bar closed his eyes and added brokenly, *I am alive at your intervention, and I will ... follow you ... crippled or whole. Maker, forgive me. The truth is I am a coward—afraid of ridicule, afraid the people will not accept me this way, afraid I will see pity in my friends' eyes ... in her eyes. Help me! Be my courage, Lord, less I fail you, for it seems I have none of my own.* Acceptance of the Maker's plan, even if it meant infirmity, brought peace. Still praying, Bar fell into an exhausted sleep.

The smell of food and the sound of splashing water woke him. It was later than usual; the sun was high in the sky. Ecalos held a tray, and Lark was filling his sunken bathing pool. Bar swallowed a lump in his throat and asked them both to come to his bedside. Painfully, he pulled himself to a sitting position. Their faces were calm and displayed no anger. He was grateful.

"I have been a difficult patient," he said with a rueful smile.

"Aye," they both agreed. After looking at Ecalos, Lark added, "Though not our worst."

"But close?" Bar asked.

"Somewhere in the middle, perhaps. Many of our patients are injured much worse than you," Lark said.

"Maker help them! Last night and for the last few weeks, I have been rude, demanding, and childish. But last night was the worst. Forgive me for my temper and for my lack of gratitude. I do appreciate all you have done, though I haven't acted much like it."

They both replied, "Forgiven," with twinkling eyes and went on with their tasks. There were no lectures, no recriminations.

Slowly, Bar managed to become a more positive patient. He even came to the point where he could laugh and joke about his failures and make fun of his awkwardness. From that time on, Ecalos and Lark knew he would make it, no matter how far his physical recovery progressed.

Bar knew a three-inch cut scarred his right cheek because it was sore and he could feel it with his fingertips, but there was no polished mica or still ponds on Epoh, so he could not see his face. It was the least of his concerns.

There was no one in the large, rambling house but the three of them. Bardon wondered at this but did not ask. There was a mystery here, but he was content to leave it so.

For four months after the first three, he exercised and sought to regain his former strength and agility, but he knew in his heart that no matter how hard he worked, he would never be the same. He swam in the pounding surf with Lark for a companion and fought the sea's ebb and flow. They ran in the sand and practiced with weapons of all kinds. Sometimes they fished and brought white brin home to Ecalos for dinner. After they ate each night, she made Bar work with his damaged right hand. When it cramped and hurt beyond bearing, she would massage a herbal balm into the muscles that took away most of the pain.

He could grip a sword, for a time, with his old strength, but his agility with the bow and arrow was much diminished, as was his ability to throw knives. The injured fingers of his right hand had lost their dexterity. He was learning to use his left hand, but skill came slowly, and he felt unbearably awkward. His right leg below the knee was undependable and ached after he had been on his feet for only a few minutes. It slowed his stride and caused him to limp.

One look at Ecalos's scarred face and twisted back caused any desire to complain to melt like snow on a hot day. She bore her disability with patience, almost with pride; laughed at herself; and rarely complained or spoke of it. Unconsciously at first but later quite intentionally, he imitated her attitude toward suffering and impairment. She focused on her gifts and abilities; she bore the pain and disabilities with patience.

He respected her deeply and learned how to read her expressive blue eyes very well, for she spoke more eloquently with them than with words. He felt encouragement in their approval, comfort at their understanding, and amusement in their teasing. She was warmly human and wise.

Lark, on the other hand, was far too perfect to be mortal. He always seemed to be listening to voices that Bardon could not hear. Though Bar held all of Lark's attention when they talked, Lark was still somewhere else as well. It was disconcerting. Yet it was Lark who addressed Bar's very human anxiety about his impaired warrior skills. Could he be king with weakened muscles, fragile endurance, and less-than-average fighting abilities? The lowliest foot soldier could outfight him now.

"Warriors will fight for you. A king does not have to be the best warrior. What is important, it seems to me, is who rules the ruler or, put another way, who leads the leader," Lark said.

"The Maker has many followers who believe in his law and are committed to him. They are whole and strong," Bar said.

"Yet he chose you. Do you think he is unaware of your physical problems?"

"No!" Bar protested. "It is plain he sent E Clue to help rescue me and then instructed him to bring me here to you and Ecalos to be healed. I have felt his presence … every day, his encouragement …" Bar trailed off. He was still distressed … dissatisfied.

"Perhaps your pride is hurt? You who were faster and better with weapons than anyone else, even those twice your age, you will need help to do certain things, simple things like tie knots. And you will certainly limp to the end of your days."

Bar winced at Lark's stark portrait of this reality. *Yet it is the truth.* "The Maker could heal me completely if he wished. Why hasn't he?"

"Bar, would you rather have a king who could empathize with your pain and struggles or one who has never known want or suffering? Would you want a king who couldn't possibly know what it's like to be an ordinary man or woman—to be lonely, to be afraid, to be ridiculed, miserable, anxious, hungry, or hurt?"

Unconvinced, Bar shook his head and looked at the ground. After a few minutes of silence, Lark added softly, "It is wise to trust his decisions, even when we do not understand them, because he knows all things. He is love, and love motivates him to desire the best for each of his children. Also, he knows—oh, how well he knows—man's heart. Even I must trust, and I know more than a man."

Bar gazed at him a moment and said, "You guard her—Ecalos, I mean—and me also, do you not?"

Lark nodded. "I do."

"You are not alone in your mission, I think," Bar said.

Lark smiled at his acuteness. "No, there are many of us. Blalock and Draville are not imprisoned as the king is, so, you see, he whom you call Choack still has human servants as well as spirit ones. At Blalock's direction, they seek you, but we have protected you."

"Alati," Bar said with a slow grin, "for the protection and for your wisdom as well. I find it hard to be … weak."

"Aye." Lark nodded wisely. "Most humans do." He grinned back.

Bar felt a sudden swirling windstorm and then heard a voice that was familiar to him. E Clue said, *"Child, come to me. It is time for you to leave this place. Your subjects await you."* Bar's heart pounded with excitement, nervousness, and fear. It had been so long. He missed his friends, he missed Ree, but most of all he missed a slip of a girl named Ellarann.

"I'm coming, E Clue," he answered quickly. He and Lark dashed around the house to the seawall and found Ecalos had arrived there before them.

"He has no proper clothes," she fussed at the giant creature as if he were responsible. He fluttered his massive wings gently, a sign of distress, and dead leaves swirled wildly around the courtyard. "E Clue! Please don't," Ecalos said as she held down her billowing green skirt.

"I am sorry, Lady, but the messenger gave me no instructions concerning clothes. I must take him now."

She sighed and walked up to Bar. "I lose all my wounded friends eventually. I will miss you, Bar. Do not be afraid. You are ready." Her eyes misted with tears.

Bar hugged her tightly. "Thank you, Ecalos ... for the nursing and for your instruction." Her eyes widened in question. "You know what I mean," he said with a grin. She nodded assent. There was a reason the Maker sent her the badly injured. He shook Lark's arm and said, "I thank you for the same and for your protection as well."

Lark nodded and advised, "Trust him."

"I will," Bar promised.

He stepped onto E Clue's claw. He was dressed in a short green robe and leather sandals that didn't even belong to him. They belonged to Lark. His hair was seven months longer and tied back with a leather thong. He waved at Ecalos's and Lark's diminishing shapes as E Clue circled up into the blue sky. Soon he sat down in his unusual cage in order to rest his leg, and then he lay down and soon fell asleep. Ecalos's description of Epoh as near Ree was an understatement. It would take an hour to return to Feisan.

"Awake, Bar. We are almost there," E Clue said softly. Bar stretched and saw the coastline of Ree approaching quickly. It was the second month of harvest season, and the coastlands blazed with the color of changing leaves. He was enthralled with Ree's beauty as he viewed the island from great height. Immense snow-covered mountains and peaks that glowed with red fire or breathed dark smoke, speared the misty clouds that hung over them. Lush green forests robed the slopes that flowed downward in graceful folds to the rolling plains that were a patchwork quilt of farms and grazing land. Along the rugged coast, cities rose here and there near the towering cliffs

of dark basalt and granite. Tiny ships bravely rode on the glittering sea or rested in quiet bays. His heart ached with love for his country.

He wondered how the citizens of Ree had reacted after the Alli fighters had taken over the castle and imprisoned the king and perhaps much of the ruling class. With Bardon possibly dead and certainly gone, where had the government turned for leadership? He looked toward Feisan. He would find the answers there.

In the seven months since Bardon's fantastic flight with E Clue, the Alliance and citizens of Ree had come together, at first very informally and later in organized meetings, to discuss their country's future. Meggatirra of the Chi, Tal qua of the Basca', Lock of Glidden Mountain, and Amray of the Bani rode with their warriors into the royal capital. It had been two weeks since the Alliance takeover of Casterray and Bardon's mysterious flight somewhere with E Clue. The clan leaders had sent emissaries ahead of them so that their appearance wouldn't frighten the citizens of Feisan. However, there was no way to prepare the citizens of the province of Possan for an army that numbered in the hundreds and was composed of people who were thought to no longer exist. Their passage caused an uproar, and the people talked of nothing else for months. The Chi's brilliant, colorful eyes, white hair, and tan skin tones astonished the population, who remembered this people only from legend. However, it was Wassh of the O'Hatch who drew the most attention. The diminutive O'Hatch smiled benignly on the people from his pony. He awed them, for he was not a part of even their most ancient tradition.

Emissaries, sent by Lock, requested that leaders from all the provinces come to the royal city. The Alliance wanted to make sure all the structures of government and the army stayed in place until they could be reformed. The large army was ordered to preserve order until they knew whether Bardon lived. Specially placed warriors made sure that the soldiers did as they were told.

Tar Andrew was well known and respected by all the merchants of Feisan, as Morin was respected on the waterfront. Lavel asked these two men to call all the guilds together. He asked Ganshof to bring representatives of the palace guard and soldiers who were stationed in the capital to the same assembly. At the meeting, which was held in a huge warehouse on the waterfront, hundreds of men and women milled around waiting for Tar Andrew to call them to order.

Lavel was shocked and then amused, though he hid it well, by the large group of uninvited visitors with defiant attitudes who filed in silently. Morin, who recognized them, immediately went to greet the hidden and unofficial head of the wharvers' quarter and his company. This highly irregular body was a well-known secret.

What a diverse bunch they all were: wharvers, farmers, merchants, fishermen, warehouse workers, soldiers, guards, warriors, and spies, all gathered together in the same huge room. Tar Andrew called them to order and spoke for a few minutes. Then he turned the gathering over to Lock. They hammered out their plans and secured the royal city until their prince returned. The very sudden change of leadership was still new to the citizens of Ree and their leaders, and so far there had been little disagreement. This couldn't last of course, but for now, most were simply overjoyed that the king and his friends were in Casterray's dungeon.

Bardon's council, made up of leaders and friends, clung to the prophecy and the hope that he lived.

CORONATION

STARFIRE AND HER PUPS CAUSED QUITE A STIR as they trotted down the royal highway beside Karalise. Karalise rode her favorite pony, a sturdy mare called Nateea. In spite of the gangly pups, they were making good time. Everyone left them strictly alone. Karalise smiled to herself. She had anticipated trouble on the road, but the people of Possan were growing accustomed to the extraordinary. To see the Bani's special wolf pacing beside a young maiden, with three warriors for her protection, on the road to Feisan was unusual, but they were not afraid. Merchants, travelers, and farmers speculated what this new wonder might mean.

"Is it much farther, Bani daughter?" Starfire asked.

"I have not been this way before, but I think we will arrive before nightfall," Karalise assured her. She was enjoying the trip. Amray's daughter was a self-reliant young woman, and she was delighted to be traveling for the first time in her short life. Starfire loped off the road and lay down to rest under an old cottonwood. She allowed her puppies to nurse and let them nap before they started again. The passing populace stared in amazement at girl, warriors, and wolves. Karalise and one of the warriors carried the two puppies for the rest of the trip. Because the young ones were exhausted, they were content to ride rather than run and play by their mother's side.

———✦———

Many months later, E Clue, mildly anxious, circled the city of Feisan many times so that his presence might be noticed by as many of the citizens as possible. No need to worry; they noticed! The damage to the Chamber of Colors or the audience chamber, as it was commonly called, was still fresh in the people's minds. Many hid in terror in their homes or businesses. Others watched E Clue with awe and gladness, confident that he meant them no harm.

Bar's council of four—Lavel, Devon, Tar Andrew, and Lock—were in the keep talking with some tribal leaders when they heard a great commotion outside. They rushed to the balcony to see what was causing so much excitement and craned their necks to watch E Clue's fantastic, graceful flight. Finally, the massive Uriisis landed near Casterray on the seawall. They hurried down to greet him with hopeful hearts. They were sure he had news of Bar.

"Welcome, Great One," Lock exclaimed. "What news?"

"*Your prince lives, Duke! Prepare to welcome him three weeks from today. The coronation must be on the same day that he arrives. Invite all the leaders from all the provinces, for they must swear allegiance quickly that day or die. Is this sufficiently plain?*" he asked cordially.

Plain, very plain! Lock's voice was suspended as gratitude and joy clogged his throat with emotion. He was finally able to whisper, "Aye, E Clue, I ... we understand."

E Clue's jet eyes searched the small group and quickly found the one he was seeking. "*Lavel, you will stay a moment. I have instructions for you. The rest of you may go about your preparations. I am to stay here for two days, so do not be disturbed by my presence. It is as the Maker orders,*" the Uriisis said. It was a dismissal, polite but firm. All, except Lavel, bowed and left him.

A huge crowd had gathered behind them as they'd talked to the great creature. The council of four minus one made their way through the excited, curious throng, shaking arms and sharing E Clue's message with the people. The city took on a festive air as citizens left their work to spread the shocking news that Bardon lived and would soon be crowned. E Clue's presence was proof to the doubtful that momentous things were happening. The people hung out windows and sailed close to the wall in boats to get a good look at the Uriisis. A crowd stood in awe as they watched him preen himself. The bright sunshine made his scales glitter like polished mica. As the afternoon progressed, the crowd grew and grew until every street with a view of E Clue was packed with the curious. Never had so many wonderful beings come to their great city! They talked of nothing else.

As the sun sank into the sea, a small figure escaped his frantic tutor and threaded confidently through the massive crowd in front of the Uriisis. The child was as much a wonder as the creature from the sea. "It is the Chi king's child! Look how white his hair is. Why does he visit the Uriisis?" people murmured as he passed. They reached out carefully to touch his soft, snowy hair and unusual tan skin.

Rafiel gazed at them seriously from luminous gray eyes and answered their questions politely, but he was a man on a mission and did not slow his pace. There would be only so much time before his tutor or guards caught him and made him return to the safety of the castle. He sighed. It was very hard to always be so closely watched and confined.

"Greetings, Chi heir," E Clue said in response to the child's low bow. His powerful wings expanded slightly and quivered, causing a minor windstorm. Those in the crowd closest to him grabbed for their hats before they blew away. A Urissis has huge powerful hind feet and smaller front feet that he can use as people use their hands. The huge creature reached out one of his powerful front feet and opened his talons. The throng gasped fearfully, yet Rafiel climbed with assurance onto the giant creature's claw. E Clue raised Rafiel up to his great, bright eyes. Exclamations of alarm came from the crowd, yet the child was clearly unafraid. They marveled at his courage and quieted, waiting anxiously to see what would happen next. The tiny boy and the great creature just gazed at each other. They seemed to be talking, yet no one could hear a sound. It was an amazing scene, and the people drank in this new spectacle with delight.

Suddenly, there was uproar near the castle. People shouted, and a powerful, pleading voice shouted back, "Please! Let me through!" Meggatirra, by this time a frantic father, was trying to push through the crowd and get to his son. When they realized who he was, the people of Feisan parted respectfully before him.

The Chi king strode purposefully toward the giant apparition on the seawall. The creature held his only son in his grasp. Meggatirra strove to maintain a royal bearing and not show his fear or anger. As he approached E Clue, he was as astonished as any peasant. *The size of the creature! Great*

Creator, protect my son! Meggatirra bowed respectfully and tried to think of what to say. However, before he could say anything, a gentle voice came into his mind.

"*Do not punish him, Chi king, I pray. He will ask permission before he comes to see me again. I apologize for any anxiety we may have caused you.*" E Clue's gentle courtesy and Rafiel's obvious well-being dissipated much of Meggatirra's anger. His generally obedient six-year-old sometimes shocked and confused both his parents greatly. He was a very unusual child whom they loved with all their hearts.

E Clue gazed at Rafiel tenderly for a few moments and then gently set him down next to his shaken sire. Rafiel, prompted by the Uriisis, was properly penitent and apologized, but Meggatirra knew the boy thought his adventure well worth any punishment his father might impose. The king realized Rafiel was often puzzled by what seemed to him unnecessary anxiety on his parents' part. Meggatirra sighed and ran his fingers through his thick hair with exasperation. He lifted Rafiel into his arms and strode through the crowd to the castle, where Rafiel's anxious mother waited.

The council of tribal leaders and Bar's council met to plan a coronation, but the meeting turned into a celebration as the members' hearts overflowed with gratitude to the Maker, who had remembered his promise and kept it. No work was done that day. The prophecy had been fulfilled! Soon Ree would have a new king.

The preparations went forward throughout the kingdom like a fresh breeze. The people's anticipation and enthusiasm blew away the dark, evil fogs and mists Bardock had loosed on his people. Some of Choack's creatures fled before the light, but many simply hid themselves away to wait for another, more auspicious day, a day when things were difficult again and they could whisper temptation into ears more receptive to their message. They would begin again. After all, they still had many loyal servants in the land.

E Clue continued to draw enormous crowds who watched his every activity with awe. He was moved with pity and affection for the people.

Creatures of the land were so small, so vulnerable, so weak, like the many schools of fish he tended.

On his last day, just before it was time for him to leave, a slight man in the plain clothes of a farmer left the buzzing throng and approached him. E Clue sensed the man's trembling and fear yet recognized immediately that these emotions had nothing to do with the Uriisis's great size. *Ah, this must be the one!* E Clue looked the man over carefully. He was young, but his face was strained and lined, as if he had been through much suffering and anxiety. The clothes did not fit his carriage—this was no hardworking farmer. He walked as straight and tall as a ... a soldier perhaps, with unconscious dignity and pride but no trace of arrogance. In spite of his fear, the man lifted his head to look up into E Clue's face. Muscles jumped in a twitch under his right eye, but his gaze held. The Uriisis was startled by his resemblance to Bardon. They could be brothers!

Testing him, E Clue reached down one of his great front feet and laid it palm up on the paving stones. He opened his gleaming talons and waited for the man to come ... without one word of instruction or encouragement. The man's eyes widened in shock, and he hesitated. E Clue saw his shaking and thought the creature might faint, yet the Uriisis remained silent. The man looked up at E Clue in terror but stepped up onto the proffered claw. The hushed crowd strained to hear his words, but they could not.

"Great One, I was instructed to come to you. I seek ... healing," he said unsteadily and collapsed on the warm, tough flesh.

"*Healing shall be yours!*" E Clue responded with joy. He threw back his great head and sang a triumphant song of praise.

The sound of an Uriisis singing was a wonderful thing but alarming if you had never heard it before. Pandemonium broke out among Ree's citizens. E Clue had been careful never to do anything that would frighten the excitable human creatures, but his "song" terrified them. Many in the crowd screamed and tried to flee. Others felt a wonderful joy and waited eagerly to see what would happen next. The sea behind the Uriisis responded to its master's pleasure, and waves rose up, swirling and dancing in exultation. Using the great height of the seawall, E Clue spread his magnificent wings and leaped into the air. He sailed out over the ocean and then began to stroke powerfully upward.

As the ocean raced beneath him, Tori sat hunched in a tight knot. He reflected on the strange events that had brought him to this moment. Upon his release from Casterray's dungeon, he'd fled from the keep and its master without strategy or plan. Thin, weak, and ill, he'd simply run until he could run no more, desiring to put as much distance between Ree's fiendish king and himself as possible. His body and emotions were wiser than his mind. He disobeyed all the careful instructions they had given him without a thought for the repercussions. It didn't matter what the consequences were; he wanted no part of Bardock or Draville or Choack ever again. Eventually Tori realized he was on a familiar highway headed for a small farm that seemed to beckon him. He suffered along the way, for people feared him. His eyes were wild and strained because of the terrible things he had experienced in his small cell. Those ghosts still haunted his sleep and made him cry out in the dark. He was pale and thin. He wore a tattered uniform and had the look of a madman. No wonder decent folk and thieves alike avoided him. Like a lost dog, he scavenged for food, drank at streams, and slept beneath bushes, but he kept going.

He promised himself that he wouldn't stay long or talk to the farmer and his daughter. He would just look and make sure they were well. No one knew better than he what terrible danger they would be in if he allowed them to shelter him. Yet, in his weakness, he fell asleep beneath the tree he had climbed to watch them, to see them one more time.

Their curious dog found him and set up an excited howl. Master and mistress came quickly to see what their watchdog had found. They revived Tori and carried him between them back to the farmhouse. He protested bitterly and then fainted from hunger and weakness. They bathed him with dismay. Never had they seen such deeply ingrained filth! It was as if he had not bathed for months, yet surely that was impossible. He was a high-ranking officer in the king's army, wasn't he? When Tori revived, he was too weak to speak, and tears of frustration flooded his eyes. They put him in a clean bed, and he fell into a deep, peaceful sleep for the first time in months. When he finally woke up, they fed him, and he slept again. This pattern repeated itself for two weeks. Finally one day, he woke in his right mind and with enough strength to insist that they listen to him.

He explained to Liras and Euras in painful detail who he was and what he had done. He was astonished at the shame that flooded his thin cheeks with color. It made him look away from their shocked, sorrowful faces. *Never did I feel shame before—well, at least not enough to stop. Why now?* He told them that sooner or later someone would start a search for him. He told them everything in the hope that they would throw him out. He did not have the physical strength to leave them on his own. They did not force him to leave or even hate him but instead tried to nurse him back to health. In their presence, the terror that gripped his mind fled ... but not far. Following the Maker and their foolish creed of love could get the farmer and his daughter killed.

His love for Euras and Liras led him to the Maker, which led to a command and then to this magnificent but terrifying creature! A tiny seed of hope, carefully planted by his new friends, struggled to live in his heart. He despised himself for fleeing to them; he despised himself even more for staying. But he didn't leave their refuge until a messenger came with the order to go to Feisan and find E Clue. The great Uriisis would take him to a place where they could heal his damaged body, mind, and spirit. The messenger was Lavel. He admitted to Tori that he obeyed E Clue reluctantly and with distaste. Tori knew the sight of his wild eyes; thin, white face; and sick, trembling body had softened Lavel's anger. It had taken all the courage Tori possessed to return to Feisan with Lavel. If not for Lavel's constant encouragement, he would have turned back many times. *Now I am on my way who knows where in the clutches of a creature I didn't know existed.* Exhausted, he lay down on the great claw that held him safe. After a time, he slept.

———◆◇◆———

During a large meeting in a waterfront warehouse, the only place big enough to hold them, the insurgents and guilds hammered out plans for feeding and housing the huge crowds that would come to the coronation. Lavel saw Karalise and quickly walked through the great throng to talk to her. He was amazed at her and Starfire's surprising arrival. Others in the crowd were also amazed and kept their distance from the wolf.

Lavel and Karalise had been friends for a long time. As he looked down into her strong, determined, and very precious face, he felt his sureness that he would never fall in love melt away into nothingness. Shaken by the thought, he lost the thread of their conversation and flushed. *I am too old for her! I will be gone too often to have a family. I am not the marrying kind.*

She gazed at him in stricken silence. *I am not like other women. I will always craft in elong, and I hate to keep house. I am not the marrying kind!*

He kissed her in the middle of the chattering crowd, which swirled around them unnoticed. The people smiled indulgently at the oblivious couple and continued with their business, all but two of them. Devon stared in amazement, and Amray watched with resignation. Karalise and Lavel broke apart with wonder and embarrassed smiles. They walked hand in hand toward Amray. The chief of the Bani sighed.

On the same evening, Dare sat in a corner of Tar Andrew's unusual home talking to the merchant's only grandchild. The marked healer and Tantisangel talked for hours, each thinking the other wonderful. He called her Angel.

Resplendent in new clothes, the Pack and council waited for E Clue at the front of a merry crowd of Ree's citizens. *Crowd* didn't do the mass of people justice! Countless people crammed the royal city and the meadows surrounding it. All the streets were jammed with folk dressed in their best. They all waited for the giant Uriisis's arrival. The day E Clue appointed had finally arrived, bright with sun and warm harvest temperatures. There were, of course, those who had made huge profits under Bardock's rule and were not happy about this event, but they pretended for their own safety to be pleased.

Wings stroking leisurely, the graceful Uriisis flew into view. A great cry rose from the multitude as he descended into the city square, which had been prepared for this moment. That cry was the first sound Bardon heard on his journey, and for a moment, he couldn't identify its source. When he realized what it was, he was astounded at the vast numbers of people jamming the royal city. E Clue trumpeted impressively, and the crowd cheered in appreciation.

"Very nice," Bar said with an amused but nervous grin.

"Thank you," E Clue answered smugly. He landed with a flourish of his wings that caused widespread amazement and admiration for his might.

Bar's grin widened. "E Clue, you show-off!"

"Only when the situation demands it."

Bar stepped onto the platform, acutely aware of his scarred body, his limp, and simple clothes. No one seemed to notice. The crowd went wild! Dare climbed the steps alone and approached his old friend amid the tumult. His heart ached at what he saw, and tears filled his eyes. The short, sleeveless robe hid nothing of Bar's battered limbs. Dare turned to the massive gathering and in a loud voice identified Bardon as the marked one in the prophecy. He ripped the simple robe off his friend's right shoulder and showed the crowd the mark. Then Dare unfastened his own tunic and displayed his mark. Most of the people could not actually hear one word he said above the cheering, but they understood the meaning of his actions. The uproar increased in volume and E Clue added his resonant bugle to the tumult. Dare knelt on one knee and offered Bar his sword. "We cannot find Uriisis," he explained. "Take Wolf. You will need a sword this day." Bar accepted the sword and raised it for the crowd to see. The roar of the people became even louder.

The Pack joined Bar and Dare on the platform, and the citizens of Ree roared their approval for long minutes. They loved the stories of these young men's exploits and knew each of them by name. Lavel and his trusted underground had made sure the people near and far heard the daring feats of the Pack. These young men had helped the Alli to defeat an evil regime and change the history of Ree.

Dare took off Bar's green tunic and then dressed the prince in front of the people for his crowning. The crowd was suddenly very solemn. Silence spread from those closest to those filling the streets and buildings of Feisan to those in the fields. Many had suffered to bring about this coronation. Bar's scars were a constant reminder of what he, the Alliance, and the people had been through under Bardock's arrogant, cruel, and finally evil reign.

The council, led by Devon, who still wore his simple brown wool robe, climbed up the steps. Devon raised his voice and recited ancient words handed down from generation to generation. There were men placed strategically in the crowd all the way back to the fields around the city, and they repeated the words for the folk around them. A solemn spirit spread through the throngs of people.

These words had not been spoken at Bardock's coronation because it had been his desire, even then, to rule his way. He'd felt he needed no help, no person, and certainly not a worn-out God who appealed to only the ignorant and poor.

Bar knelt before Devon, and the monk poured oil out of an ancient vessel on Bar's head. He spoke the sacred words that anointed a king and dedicated Bar to the Maker. These words had not been heard on Ree for generations. The humble monk raised the crown high for all to see and placed the circle of gleaming gold on Bar's head. E Clue had brought the crown with him. There was no metal on Ree; lacidem proved to be a good substitute. Devon raised Bar and turned him to face the crowd. "I present you with your king, chosen and marked by the Maker. Do you accept him and give him your loyalty?" The response was deafening and went on and on. The citizens of Ree were overjoyed.

Bar marveled at the change with grim inner humor. Just seven months ago a crowd had wanted to kill him. Of course, that crowd had been chosen by the king and Draville. Still, he knew how quickly the people's loyalties could change. But for now, all seemed well.

His council led him to a white horse held by Tal qua and his daughter. Bar's heart stopped at her mischievous smile. Forgetting decorum, Bar took her in his arms and kissed her. Again the crowd went wild and shouted their approval. Ellarann blushed but smiled at Bar. He mounted with help from his former weapon's master. Tal pressed Bar's battered, twisted right hand to his forehead and lips and murmured an emotional greeting before he turned to lead the horse. They walked leisurely to the castle amid the cheering crowds that lined the streets. Soldiers loyal to the Alli kept the people from pressing too closely on Bar and his companions. The council, Bar's companions, and the tribal, clan, and provincial leaders followed behind him in a colorful parade.

When they arrived at Casterray, Bar mounted the steps on Lock's and Morin's arms. The crowd thought it protocol, but those close to him knew it was sheer necessity. In spite of all his conditioning and exercise, he was tiring. Bar held Wolf in his left hand, point resting on the flat stones of the high porch, and gave his right to those pledging fealty. Many were deeply touched by his warm smile, his youth, and the obvious suffering he had undergone to reach this day.

He stood for long hours and named all the kingdom's leaders as they passed. They knelt before him one by one and spoke the requisite words out of sincerity and love or out of necessity and fear. No one who pressed that broken hand to his forehead and lips was untouched. Some wondered if Bar could still fight; most did not care. He was the Maker's anointed.

It had not been necessary to kill anyone for refusing to swear allegiance to Bar ... so far. Who would dare or be so foolish? E Clue watched the proceedings from one of the towers, to ensure that the leaders understood that he'd meant what he had spoken. This was to be a peaceful day and a peaceful transition. Any who refused to swear fealty to Bar would die.

The last in the long line were very familiar and important to Bar: Dare, Louke, Tier ray, Oster, Chea lar, and Wassh. They were all grave and earnest, even Louke. Ram's horns were blown to signal the end of the ceremony, and the crowds were dismissed to a great feast. The king's coffers had been raided to pay for the celebration. After the solemn proceedings, the crowd was more subdued than before the ceremony. Most of the people had a deep confidence that things would be different from now on.

Bar turned to enter Casterray as its master, not as a bound prisoner to be locked in its dungeon. He murmured a word of praise to the Maker for this change. The Pack led him, laughing and talking, to Bardock's rooms, now refurbished, and allowed him to relax before a small fire. Later, he would attend an extravagant feast with all of Ree's leaders, both old and new.

As Bar collapsed gratefully into a chair, he groaned. His right leg ached, his right hand ached, and his head ached, but he was content. Thanks to his loyal friends, this day had gone well ... very well.

Something cold nudged Bar's right hand, and he jumped. Two gangly wolf cubs sat on their haunches, tails thumping wildly, and watched him with bright gray eyes. Behind them was Starfire, also sitting on her haunches, with Dare at her side. Dare grinned at Bar's startled, questioning gaze. "It seems the Maker has a special gift for each of us. Starfire will say no more than that, except that their names are Trofmoc and Dia." He pointed to each pup as he named them.

Bar said thoughtfully, "Bani for 'comfort' and 'help.'" He leaned down to look at the fluffy, healthy creatures. "Whose is whose?" he asked in wonder. Trofmoc rose and came toward his proffered hand with hesitation. The Pack stopped their boisterous conversation and watched with interest. Bar fondled the soft, furry head and stiff ears and then carefully lifted the cub into his lap. She placed her paws on his chest and sniffed him curiously, then licked his face. Trofmoc lay down in his lap and watched the amazed group from her perch, as if she knew she belonged there. Laughter filled the room at her smug expression.

Dare replied, "Well, I guess that answers that question!" He crouched down and petted Dia, who responded enthusiastically and climbed into his lap. Sometime that day—no one noticed when—Starfire disappeared.

After an hour, Lock and Shonar firmly ushered the boisterous Pack out the door. The hishua protested noisily, but they went. Shonar ordered, "Now, my lord, a bath and rest, or you'll not get through this long evening." The "my lord" sounded strange to Bar; it would take some getting used to.

"But what if I don't want a bath and rest?" Bar said, challenging the healer with bright eyes.

"That will be enough of that," Shonar replied tartly as he began to strip Bar's clothes off. "You just do as I say, Your Majesty," he added sternly.

Bar laughed. "I am so glad nothing has changed even though you say I am a king!"

Lock grinned at him. The bath and massage that followed eased his many aches, and he fell asleep instantly when they laid him on the bed. Trofmoc stretched out beside Ree's king and growled fiercely when Shonar ordered her down. The healer frowned, then smiled at the small creature and decided to leave her where she was. "What other wonders will this day hold?" he inquired of his amused son.

The feast was merry and tense by turns. Bar would be heartily glad when it was over. Down the long table, Ellarann and he secretly exchanged quick glances of amusement at someone's jest or of longing for a moment alone. He watched her leave on Tal's arm, her long claret gown trailing behind her. The color brought out the beauty of her jet hair, warm red lips, flushed cheeks, and sparkling dark eyes. Bar was not the only one who watched her with approval. When the last guest departed, he and his friends went up to his apartments and stayed up talking until the wee hours. He caught up on all that had happened while he'd been recuperating on Epoh. One by one his companions fell asleep, sprawled wherever they lay or sat, until the large room was silent.

Bar could hear only the crackling of the dying fire and a soft wind rattling the windows. He bowed his head over his cup. An enormous, very complicated task was before them, but they were not alone. Bar heard a soft growl and lifted Trofmoc into his lap. He thanked the Maker with a full heart for all he had done. Bar had gone from a relentlessly pursued, friendless fugitive to an honored king! He was content and filled with gratitude and peace.

Not the End!

To the reader of
The Battle for the Isle of Ree ...

I take no credit for creating this story; I simply typed it. The Maker is Jesus, God's holy son. Jesus' Father is Almighty God and is called the Creator in the book. The spirit in the book is the Holy Spirit.

Who is this Jesus? God's son came to earth as a man and shared the good news that God loves all of us and he has a plan for our salvation. Jesus suffered and died on a cross, which paid the penalty for everyone's sins. On the third day after His death, He rose from the dead and ascended into heaven.

His suffering and death are a payment for my sins and yours if we ask Him to forgive us. He is my Savior and will be your Savior, your friend and your God who you can talk to at any time. If you pray the following prayer, you will become a follower of Jesus and go to Heaven when you die.

Jesus, please forgive me for my sins and be my Savior. Thank you for suffering and dying on the cross to pay for my sins. I want to be your son/ daughter here on earth and live with you forever in Heaven, your eternal home, when I die. Thank you for saving me and being my Lord and friend.